Stardust Dads
The Afterlife Connection

11/17/08

To Zach, my good friend + colleague. Thanks for Everything!

David R. Long

Enjoy the Read - Again!
Josephine C. George

Stardust Dads
The Afterlife Connection

A Novel

DAVID R. GEORGE
JOSEPHINE C. GEORGE

iUniverse, Inc.
New York   Bloomington

Stardust Dads
The Afterlife Connection

Copyright © 2008 by David R. George and Josephine C. George

All rights reserved. No part of this book may be used or reproduced by any means, graphic, electronic, or mechanical, including photocopying, recording, taping or by any information storage retrieval system without the written permission of the publisher except in the case of brief quotations embodied in critical articles and reviews.

This is a work of fiction. All of the characters, names, incidents, organizations, and dialogue in this novel are either the products of the author's imagination or are used fictitiously.

iUniverse books may be ordered through booksellers or by contacting:

iUniverse
1663 Liberty Drive
Bloomington, IN 47403
www.iuniverse.com
1-800-Authors (1-800-288-4677)

Because of the dynamic nature of the Internet, any Web addresses or links contained in this book may have changed since publication and may no longer be valid. The views expressed in this work are solely those of the author and do not necessarily reflect the views of the publisher, and the publisher hereby disclaims any responsibility for them.

ISBN: 978-0-595-51236-2 (pbk)
ISBN: 978-0-595-50459-6 (cloth)
ISBN: 978-0-595-61815-6 (ebk)

Printed in the United States of America

*In memory of our fathers,
David R. George, Sr. and Michael C. Chiarella;
Bratly, our beloved calico;
and all the others whom we have loved and lost.
Until we meet again ...*

Strange, is it not? that of the Myriads who
Before us pass'd the door of Darkness through,
Not one returns to tell us of the Road,
Which to discover we must travel too.
The Rubaiyat of Omar Khayyam

ACKNOWLEDGMENTS

We wish to thank the following people for their generous time and helpful feedback: Barbara George Hagan, Vickie Erickson, Heather Cherry, Kathleen Ruthkowski, Trish Elder, Geraldine Baxter, Zach Brockhouse, Sandy Brodsky, Gary and Jean Friedrich, Ryan Trahan and Leslie Ray.

We also are grateful to John A. "Jack" Vikara, Kym Osborne, Ruth Chalupka, Brooke Bertuzzi, JoAnn Maldonado, Billy "Pops" Aguilera, Brian DeVaynes, Beth Hiner, Billy DeVaynes, Michael DeVaynes and Janelle Kibbel, without whose valued support and encouragement—and that of so many other family members, friends and coworkers—this book might not have made it into print.

Chapter One
The final days

Mickey Parks woke up feeling scared.

The sense that something bad was about to happen stayed with him as he showered and dressed for work. He tried to suppress the anxiety he felt during breakfast, avoiding direct eye contact with his daughter Allison.

"Are you having any more of those pains?" she asked between bites of an English muffin.

"No, I feel fine," Mickey lied, not wanting to worry her. The hurt in his side never really eased up completely. There were times, such as now, when the pain stayed subtle, a dull ache in the left side near his stomach. And then there were other times when the pain felt like an invisible ice pick being jabbed into his gut.

Mickey knew something was wrong, but he put off seeking medical help for fear that a doctor's diagnosis might lead to a death sentence as it had with his dad and brother. So he dealt with the pain by walking around, day after day, rubbing his side and chewing on antacid tablets as if they were candy.

"Why don't you let me drop you off at the store today?"

"I'm okay with the subway. It's only three stops." Mickey hoped she wouldn't hear the anxiety in his voice.

"Whatever you like, Dad, but it's really no trouble. Like I told you last night, I've got to go into the office for a couple of hours and pick the photos for the Williamson layout."

Despite her elaboration, Allison knew her dad had made up his mind. She wished she knew how to share with him the solitary crying episodes she'd had over the past few months. How to tell him she had seen herself standing over his casket, grieving over losing him. How she had not only dreamed the nightmare again and again, but also experienced the vision day and night, at home, at work, even while shopping.

"I'm off," she said, getting up from the table, knowing she still couldn't bring herself to share such horrible thoughts with her father. She put her dishes in the sink, then came back and kissed Mickey on the cheek.

"Have a good day. I'll see you tonight," she said.

"You, too, honey." Mickey was sure she could hear the pounding of his heart.

"I love you, Dad," she called back as she headed for the door.

"I love you, too, sweetheart."

Mickey poured himself another cup of coffee and stirred in the milk that made the dark liquid turn beige. *Where the hell has my life gone? One day I'm young and healthy, the next I'm pushing sixty and feeling twenty years older'n that. And the goddamn pain.* Mickey's self-pity quickly turned to anger, then back to fear. He finished his coffee and left the apartment a few minutes later. The scared feeling stayed with him as he rode the subway downtown. Mickey felt as if the dread would consume him, even as he approached the refuge of his antique store.

The jingling of the entry bell and the chiming of a grandfather's clock greeted Mickey the moment he opened the door. He inhaled the familiar smells of old wood and musty books as he made his way through the maze of long-forgotten library tables, discarded Victorian rockers and once-prized music cabinets.

Mickey considered the store his sanctuary, his retreat, a place where he felt safe and secure. The solid oak roll-top desks, the walnut barrister bookcases and the mahogany china cabinets all stood in quiet repose, resplendent in their exquisite craftsmanship. The cherry colonial table, the cedar chest, the oak spinning wheel—each spoke silently of history, of another time, a time of slower pace and workmen who took pride in their craft. Over the years, the antiques had become his friends, his companions—adding joy to his otherwise mundane existence.

But despite the usually comforting surroundings, Mickey felt as if he were suffocating from the fear that continued to grip his entire being. He laughed nervously to himself, trying to shake it off.

Keep busy, he decided. *This will pass.*

Knowing that Saturday meant there would be more visitors to the store than usual, Mickey turned off the alarm and walked straight to the back room where he repaired and refinished old pieces of furniture.

He yanked on the silver-balled chain to the overhead light and studied the top of the end table he had sanded and stained the night before. Although the faint fumes of the varnish still lingered, the first coat had dried sufficiently for Mickey to apply the second coat. He decided he still had time to do this before opening for business.

He tossed his jacket onto a nearby chair, rolled up his sleeves and flipped the switch on the exhaust fan from low to high. When he turned the radio on, the sentimental strains of his favorite song, "Stardust," filled the room.

As Mickey listened to the music, moving the brush back and forth in smooth, even strokes, he fought the urge to pick up his guitar and strum along to the melody. He thought about his daughter Allison, missing her presence at the store, helping him with customers, redecorating and switching around the lamps and chinaware to enhance the layout of the antique furniture, talking to him, laughing. He remembered how her smile had always brightened the otherwise dimly lit store.

But he realized Allison's career in publishing overshadowed his need for her to help him move antiques around, and so he had protested only mildly when she announced her intention to rent her own Manhattan apartment. And after his wife Margaret had walked out on him, it didn't take much convincing by Allison for him to move in with her.

"C'mon, Dad," she had coaxed. "It'll save us both money, and we'll be together. And I'd feel better knowing you were getting some home-cooked meals once in a while."

Mickey's thoughts were interrupted as the sudden stabbing pain doubled him over.

He dropped the brush and clutched the area just under his heart, as if his hand could somehow stop the spasms of sharp pain. It felt much worse this time and Mickey knew he had to get help. He stumbled to the phone and called Allison at work.

"Honey, I think—" He passed out and fell to the floor in mid-sentence.

"Dad … Dad!" Allison cried. The silence on the other end of the line terrified her. Seconds passed before she hung up and dialed nine-one-one, carefully reciting the address of her dad's antique store to the operator.

Minutes later, an ambulance raced down Madison Avenue, siren screaming its urgency.

Danny Wallace looked up as the ambulance blurred by him, then snatched an anxious peek at his watch as he hurried toward the restaurant. He knew his dad would already be there, waiting for him. Lloyd Wallace considered punctuality a virtue. He never showed up late for an appointment. Never. And he expected everyone else to be just as punctual, including Danny, who by this time had managed to reach the front door of the restaurant eighteen minutes past the agreed-upon hour.

He plunged through the door and practically knocked the hostess down.

"Do you have a reservation, sir?" she challenged Danny.

"Yes, uh, Lloyd Wallace's table."

"Right this way, sir."

Danny followed her, making a quick study of her ample posterior as it undulated beneath the clinging black skirt. *A five or a six*, Danny decided. *Nothing to get too excited about.*

"Daniel," Lloyd Wallace addressed his son loudly above the clattering din of dishes, silverware and chattering patrons. "Over here!" He half stood, waving his napkin.

"Sorry I'm late, Dad."

"That's okay. I'm just glad you could make it. Y'know, it's been a while."

Danny studied his father's beaming face and smiled. Handsome, with thinning gray hair combed straight back, his father was, as usual, carefully groomed. He wore an expensive suit tailored just right, a white shirt and maroon silk tie.

"That's hardly my fault, Dad. You're always so … um … busy."

"I know, Danny. I'll try to do better. Say, why don't we order? I'm famished."

Danny pretended to study the menu, not really caring about the food. He knew his dad meant well, but he also knew his father's job—and the women—came first. Despite that bit of painful insight, he decided the important thing was that his father had made time for him today and he should seize the moment.

Danny ordered a vodka martini, straight up with an olive. He carefully avoided asking for the drink on the rocks. He wanted that glow as fast as he could get it, and he didn't need ice getting in the way and diluting the alcohol. Lloyd already had a diet cola in front of him and told the waiter he was okay with what he had.

The waiter returned with Danny's drink and they both ordered.

"I'll have the trout almandine," Danny said. Lloyd ordered a chef's salad.

By the time the waiter came back with a basket of warm rolls and a small dish holding pats of butter, Danny had finished his drink. "I'd like another one of these."

"You belted that one down pretty quick," Lloyd said. "Maybe you ought to slow up."

"I'm a big boy, Dad." Lloyd's parental advice annoyed Danny. He had already gotten past the denial stage of alcoholism and had admitted to himself that he had a drinking problem. He just wasn't ready to go to the next step and actually do something about it. And he resented anyone else telling him he had a problem, least of all his father.

"I've been there, Danny. I just don't want you to go through the pain I've had."

"Listen, I know you're in AA and all that, but I can take care of myself." Danny tried hard not to sound arrogant or testy. He respected his dad too much, loved him too much to hurt his feelings. "I'm working on cuttin' down."

"All right. I'm sorry. I know I hit a nerve." Lloyd recalled his own sensitivity when anyone admonished him for drinking too much.

The food had arrived by then and there was no more discussion regarding alcohol. The craving for a third martini nearly overpowered Danny, but he somehow managed to keep the urge in check.

After finishing lunch, they ordered coffee and discussed the news of the day. Lloyd asked his son about his personal life, if he had been seeing anyone in particular. Danny mentioned one or two women he'd been dating but assured his dad there was no one significant.

"I have cancer, Danny." Lloyd blurted the non sequitur matter-of-factly, as if he were telling Danny about an ingrown toenail.

Danny was stunned. He felt a rush of adrenalin and a lump in his throat.

"What ... where?"

"It's my prostate. They're going to operate next week ... Tuesday. Hopefully, they'll get it all." Lloyd went on to explain some of the details concerning the operation, but Danny barely heard him. The thought of his dad possibly dying frightened him.

Outside the restaurant, they said their goodbyes, with Lloyd promising to call right after the operation, or as soon as he was able to.

Danny hugged his dad, not really wanting to let him go.

Lloyd could feel his son trembling and he felt sorrier for him than for himself.

"Goddamn it ... just a few days left now," Mickey Parks said aloud, staring at the ceiling from his hospital bed. Allison, who had just walked back into the room, clearly overheard the remark but decided not to ask him what he meant. Subconsciously, she knew.

The last three months had been a blur of fear and anxiety. The diagnosis of cancer. The surgery. The doctor's apology that the tumor had metastasized and spread rapidly to his liver and lungs, and even to a part of his brain that rendered his left arm paralyzed.

Mickey's eyes glazed over as he watched his daughter move closer to the bed.

"You're back," he said softly, ignoring the possibility that she had overheard him. "My watch ... can you tell me what time it is?" he asked for the third time that evening. Allison knew exactly what he wanted. She pushed the long, dark brown hair from her eyes and carefully raised his left arm so he could see that he still wore the wristwatch she had given him a few months earlier.

Allison smiled warmly. "Dad, I spoke to the head nurse and she gave me permission to stay for as long as I'd like. Is there anything else I can get for you?"

"Well … my guitar, but I can't play it in this condition."

"Maybe later," she fibbed, "when you're better." Allison's face flushed. She never felt comfortable lying, even when it was an attempt to keep from sounding negative to a dying father. *Still … there was always hope.*

"Yeah … maybe later. You know, I feel better when you're near …" Mickey's voice trailed off and he closed his eyes, drifting into sleep.

Allison waited another hour, thinking about the times they had shared together, good and bad. She thought about her mother and how she had constantly harangued her father over his opening the antique store. She had badgered him relentlessly, needling him about how well other husbands in the neighborhood were doing at their jobs.

"You're not a businessman," Margaret had bitterly accused him. "You'll never make a go of this. There's nothing like bringing a paycheck home every week. Why don't you get a job like everyone else?"

Allison bit her lip when she remembered how her mother had nagged her father night after night. *What a cruel, selfish woman,* she thought. She had conflicting emotions, feeling both sad and relieved when Margaret had announced she was leaving Mickey and getting a divorce. *Maybe now Dad can get something more out of life,* she had convinced herself in an attempt to ease the pain she felt over her parents splitting up.

Allison finally went home later that evening, confident that her dad was sleeping comfortably.

Sometime during the night, however, Mickey Parks slipped into a coma.

Allison arrived at the hospital early the following morning and stayed at his bedside until the doctor pronounced his passing the next day. It was June 15, 1973, and Mickey Parks began a journey he could never have even imagined.

Three years later.

"Much obliged," Lloyd Wallace said into the phone, his deep, pleasant voice only hinting at the trace of a Midwestern twang. He put the phone back on its cradle and called to his secretary through the open door.

"Beverly, would you please come in here a minute."

A buxom blonde with a body that oozed sexuality, Beverly swung her hips suggestively as she sashayed into Lloyd's office.

"Listen, I've got to go back into the hospital for a few weeks. I'll fill Harvey in on what's pending, but I need you to help me collate things." He tried not to stare at the blonde's abundant chest. The newspaper's personnel office had sent her over to Lloyd as a replacement for Harriet, who had recently retired. Unfortunately, due to his first prostate surgery he'd had three years ago, Lloyd's woman-chasing days were virtually over.

"Is it serious?" Beverly asked with genuine concern, moving in close to Lloyd.

"Just routine," Lloyd lied, looking down and memorizing her melon-sized breasts that threatened to spill out over the top of her low-cut blouse.

Lloyd worked through the rest of the day, making phone calls, proofing ad copy, rewriting press releases. As director of promotion and public relations for the *Long Island Herald*, his workdays seemed endless.

Not that his illness hadn't taken its toll. He had lost a lot of weight and he found that he tired easily. But being a workaholic by nature, he just increased his consumption of coffee and caffeine-loaded Cokes.

The pain in his groin would often stab at him, and sometimes it lingered for far too long. But the pain pills helped get him through the day, and allowed him to sleep at night, though fitfully.

Finally, long after the rest of the staff had left for their commute home, Lloyd decided he had done as much as he could. He had worked hard to leave things in the best possible shape. The surgery tomorrow would be his third and, he hoped, his last. He thought about his son Danny and for a brief moment considered calling him to tell him of his impending surgery. But because Danny had a tendency to overreact emotionally, he decided he would call him *after* the fact.

As Lloyd drove home to his townhouse about a half-hour away, the song "Stardust" played on the car's radio. It had always been one of his favorites, but for some inexplicable reason, Lloyd felt an odd, almost eerie sensation come over him as he listened to the familiar tune.

Susan, his live-in girlfriend, stood waiting in the open doorway.

"Hi, stranger," she said in her usual seductive tone. Susan certainly knew all about Lloyd's medical condition and his upcoming surgery in the morning, but she preferred to act as though they had just begun their affair. It always evoked a smile from Lloyd, and that was all Susan needed. She deeply loved the man, adored him actually, and was determined that both of them enjoyed every minute of their relationship.

"I didn't eat," she said. "I wanted to have dinner together. I can heat it up and—"

"I'm sorry," he interrupted, "I'm really not hungry. You go ahead if you like."

"Well, phooey. I'm not all that hungry, either. What do you want to do?"

"I think I want to play some," he said, sitting down at the baby grand piano.

Lloyd began to play, pounding down hard on the keys the way he always did. Susan immediately recognized Lloyd's jazzed-up version of "Stardust." She didn't know why but she felt a peculiar sensation as he played.

Later, in bed, Lloyd held Susan tightly, as if he would lose her if he didn't keep her close.

"Did you call Danny and tell him?" she whispered.

"No. I'll call him after the surgery."

"Your son has a right to know."

"No need to stress *him* out, too."

In the morning, Susan drove Lloyd to the hospital. She stayed with him every minute until they wheeled him away into surgery, holding his hand tightly until an attendant physically forced her to let go. Somehow, she knew it would be the last time she saw him alive.

Lloyd Wallace, age sixty-three, expired on the operating table at Mineola Hospital on Wednesday, August 3, 1976, at 7:58 AM.

And so began Lloyd's new journey, a journey in which he would reconcile his relationship with his son Danny. A journey that would soon connect him with Allison's father, Mickey Parks—at an extraordinary place called Midway Manor.

Chapter Two
Welcome to Midway Manor

Mickey Parks sat alone in a far corner of the Renaissance Room at Midway Manor, brooding over his death at the early age of fifty-eight. He thought back to the exact moment his heart had suddenly stopped beating.

He recalled his initial shock, and then the acute awareness of the peaceful silence within him. There also had been a feeling of powerlessness. And loss. Mickey remembered the inexorable heartache of knowing he could never cross back again.

"Allison!" he had cried out.

The echo of his daughter's name had soared skyward like a runaway helium balloon. His eyes had followed in pursuit, a pursuit that left him momentarily blinded and confused as countless light paths appeared before him.

In a split second, however, he had been overcome with an unwavering willingness to watch the light show. To accept the transition as it continued to take place. To wait as each light began to mysteriously fade away, leaving just one brilliant beam—a single stream of light that beckoned the way to Midway Manor, his first destination in the afterworld.

Mickey leaned forward, stretching his arms out across the leather-top table, and then focused on the wristwatch that always brought back the tender memory of his beloved daughter Allison. She was the reason he had been drawn to Midway in the first place.

Mickey had been overwhelmed with appreciation when the director of the Manor, Joseph Patrick, provided him with a timepiece that looked exactly like the one his daughter had given him a few months before his passing. This gesture was typical of the Manor, just one more example of its accommodations, amenities and kindnesses.

But the amenity that truly attracted residents to the Manor was the well-noted Data Room and its banks of vast, liberally imparted information regarding those who were left behind. The facts and particulars—via the written word—provided a link with loved ones that would comfort and encourage the residents to eventually continue on with their journey in the afterworld.

Three years had gone by since Mickey's arrival in 1973. During that period, he remained content to simply observe as hundreds of residents availed themselves of the Data Room to monitor loved ones and then moved on to other destinations. However, Mickey, unlike these other guests, chose not to utilize the Data Room with all its records readily available to him, and in particular, the events pertaining to his daughter. He just couldn't seem to come to grips with the idea of actually witnessing how Allison handled all that life had to dish out without his being there to help.

Maybe tomorrow, he decided. *Maybe tomorrow I'll just go up there and see what's going on with my baby girl.* And this carried Mickey day after day, knowing a daily account of Allison's life was as near as a staircase away and that he would probably go up there tomorrow. It made him feel closer to his daughter.

But when Mickey touched the glass cover on his watch, fond thoughts once again turned to sadness and despair.

"Damn it!" he swore under his breath. Frustrated by conflicting feelings, Mickey reached for his guitar, seeking the familiar, unfailing consolation of music. He had no idea how swiftly and dramatically his uncompromising routine was about to change.

On that day Lloyd Wallace, who responded to the same beacon of light, arrived at Midway Manor. The distinguished, silver-haired gentleman, dressed in an expensive, hand-tailored suit and silk tie, stood before a stiffly postured attendant at the front desk.

"Welcome to Midway Manor," the aide said softly, laying a feather-tipped pen across the opened page of an oversized leather-bound register book. "Please sign here." And Lloyd complied, signing his name with a flourish.

"Very good, Mr. Wallace. Now, let me show you to your room."

When they passed by the Renaissance Room, however, Lloyd heard Mickey Parks picking a tune on his guitar. The melody flaunted an earthly familiarity, and Lloyd was drawn to the doorway. He paused for a moment and looked around the room.

A slight, autumn-like breeze wafted through the wall-to-wall windows, causing the intermittent sheer white drapes to billow down from the high ceiling to the finely polished wooden floors. In the center of the room stood a glossy black piano.

The sound of Mickey's music and the sight of the Steinway distracted Lloyd from thoughts of his arrival and the attendant he had been following. The attendant, keenly attuned to Lloyd's every action, moved to one side and lowered his head. That's when Lloyd undid the top button of his shirt and loosened the knot in his tie as he headed toward the center of the room.

After standing just briefly in front of the piano, Lloyd sat down, laid both hands over the ivory keys and began to accompany Mickey, who continued strumming on the strings of his guitar. Together, the melancholy chords of "Stardust" echoed an ironic joviality. Minutes later, they ended in unison. The few residents in the room stopped what they were doing to applaud them.

Mickey lowered his guitar and held it by the neck, extending his right hand to Lloyd. "Welcome to Midway. I'm Mickey Parks," he said with a friendly smile, delighted to meet the talented stranger.

Accepting the handshake, Lloyd returned the greeting, "Lloyd Wallace. What a fine song. One of my favorites. I was heading toward my room when I heard you playing. Are you new here, too?"

"Nah, I've been around a while, quite a while," Mickey answered in a barely audible tone, preferring to focus on their spur-of-the-moment, short-lived jam session. His voice lifted then. "When they delivered the piano this morning ... well, obviously it was for you."

Lloyd laughed, "For me? You've gotta be kidding."

"No, I'm not kidding," Mickey said. "This guitar was waiting for me in my room when I arrived. Obviously your room isn't quite large enough to accommodate a piano, so they put it out here. I think they want to keep us happy while we're at Midway."

"So who's running this place anyway?" Lloyd asked, as though he had just arrived at a vacation resort. "And what can you tell me about the so-called Data Room?" not waiting for Mickey to answer the first question.

Mickey, though he had instantly felt a bond with the handsome newcomer, deliberately avoided both questions by asking, "Hey, isn't that your attendant?"

Lloyd became aware again of the aide patiently waiting and felt obliged to back away from Mickey. "Yes, it is. I guess I'll see you later."

As Lloyd entered his room for the first time, he saw a lavishly furnished private space that he could have easily been comfortable with back on Earth. Earth. Home. Struck with the realization of what had happened to him, where he was, and heartbroken that he would never see his only son again, his face paled at the thought. Lloyd brought his hand to his chest.

"Mr. Wallace, why don't you sit down for a moment," the attendant said, intruding with concern. Lloyd headed toward the leather recliner on the right side of the room. "May I get you a glass of water?" the aide offered.

Lloyd sat down, still feeling somewhat traumatized. He shook his head, summoning up that other time and place when feelings this intense would certainly have called for a few rounds of Canadian Club and soda.

"No thanks," Lloyd said soberly. "Paul, isn't it?"

"Yes, Paul."

"Well, Paul, it's certainly been one hell of a day for me. What can *you* tell me about the Data Room?"

Paul hesitated for a brief moment before responding with an air of discretion. "Mr. Wallace, I'm really not at liberty to discuss any details about the Data Room, but what I can tell you is that tomorrow you will personally be given the grand tour of the Manor." Paul remained detached without elaborating any further. And when Lloyd said there was nothing else he needed, the attendant left the room.

Alone and weary, Lloyd leaned back in the recliner and looked over his new surroundings. The walls were painted in a semi-gloss ivory with extraordinary hues of gold. An antique oak dresser stood on one side, and above it hung a matching mirror with a hand-carved frame. A light brown comforter and matching pillow shams covered the king-size bed. A night table at the side of the bed supported a brass-based hurricane lamp with a green-glass shade. Just past the door, which he assumed was the entrance to his own private bath, he noted a fine-looking old mahogany secretary and right next to it a built-in bookcase.

The books on the shelves piqued Lloyd's curiosity, but at that moment a warm, subtle breeze blew in through the open window and the scent of lilacs filled the air. He closed his eyes and inhaled the familiar bouquet, and didn't open them again until the following morning.

Lloyd slept through that first night on the recliner, awakening to a sunlit room. He became keenly aware that the constant pain he had lived with during the last few years of his life had completely disappeared. And so had the scars from his surgeries. He showered and dressed and headed off to find the dining room for breakfast.

Lloyd followed the smell of freshly brewed coffee down the hall to the dining room, which was actually located near the Renaissance Room, where he had met Mickey Parks the day before. The designated area appeared to be grand enough to accommodate several hundred residents, but he saw only about a dozen or so having breakfast. Mickey, seated at a table facing the doorway, waved his hand and called for Lloyd to join him.

"Good morning," Lloyd said cheerfully, pleased to see a familiar face. He noticed the second place setting at Mickey's table and sat down.

Mickey began with small talk as he poured coffee into Lloyd's porcelain cup, asking him if he had slept well on his first evening at the Manor.

"Well, Mickey, I'd have to say I was so damn tired that I fell asleep on the recliner and never made it to bed."

Mickey couldn't help but laugh at Lloyd's declaration. He put down his own coffee cup and leaned over the table to whisper, "Go ahead and tell me that you didn't remember a thing right after you smelled those damn lilacs."

"What are you telling me, Mick?" Lloyd said, surprised by his remark.

"Oh, there are a lot of unusual things that go on here, but none of it is anything to worry about. Just like those damn flowers. They put me to sleep, too, but not before I sneeze about a dozen times."

Mickey continued, "Even when I was alive I used to sneeze a lot. And my daughter Allison, bless her sweet heart, she used to get all upset when I couldn't stop. Let me just say that the Manor is a great place. A really great place. But hey, I'm rambling on. Why don't you go over to the buffet and grab yourself something. The food here is really excellent."

Lloyd decided to follow his suggestion and walked over to the tantalizing lineup of food choices. He actually wanted a moment to compose himself. Perhaps Mickey was just pulling his leg about the lilacs, he thought, but his gut told him his new friend was on the level.

The buffet had an array of items, including bagels and lox, which Lloyd used to enjoy on Sunday mornings with his girlfriend Susan. He filled his plate and went back to Mickey's table. "So," Lloyd said, selecting his words carefully, "you have a daughter?"

Mickey smiled shyly, "I do. She was the light of my life." His eyes glazed over and he refrained from saying more. "And you?"

"A son. He's an adult now, of course, and real smart," Lloyd answered with apparent pride. "Never married though. I guess you could say he favored the women too much to settle down with just one."

The statement was truthful enough, but Lloyd had neglected to add that his own abbreviated relationship with his son Danny had been for the same reason. His chasing women, coupled with his demanding job, had simply left no time for him to spend with his son.

"And your daughter? Is she married?" Lloyd asked.

"No, she's not married, either. Well, I guess I should rephrase that and say she wasn't married when I left." Then in light of what he said, and hoping that Lloyd would not ask him how long he had been a resident at the Manor, Mickey looked down at his plate, picked up a strawberry and exaggerated his efforts to pull out the green stem.

Lloyd immediately recognized the change in Mickey's body language and, realizing he may have touched on a delicate subject, decided not to pursue it. As for the lilac mystery, he figured his tour of the facilities might explain that as well as some of the other enigmas of the Manor that Mickey spoke of so casually. As he finished his second cup of coffee, a maître d' approached their table and asked Lloyd if he would mind accompanying him to the administrator's office.

Chapter Three
Danny gets the news

Lloyd's son Danny sat in a bar downing his first drink in four months. The whiskey burned momentarily as he swallowed. But then the familiar warmth of the alcohol taking effect began to anesthetize him. He heard the words of his father's buddy at the newspaper telling him not more than an hour ago of his dad's death. "Yeah," he heard the hardened newsman say over the phone, "he did it. He's gone."

Danny Wallace remembered his own stunned reaction. His father had been in and out of hospitals for nearly three years, and the last time he had visited him, his dad had looked gaunt and tired and pale. In fact, his dad's appearance and the knowledge that he had cancer had left him with the fear that he might actually lose his father. But despite all of this, the news of his father's passing still came as a shock.

Danny motioned to the bartender for a refill, visualizing his dad from earlier years. He pictured his dad's James Mason eyes, his quick, friendly smile and affable manner. He remembered his father's charismatic ways, his hail-fellow-well-met demeanor. It wasn't hard to understand why his dad's newspaper career had finally led to one of considerable success in public relations.

The memory of his father, and the alcohol, began to take over. Tears welled up in his eyes, dripping to the mahogany bar and blending with the spilled droplets of whiskey.

Danny tried to focus his thoughts as his mind raced through the tableau of his life. The pain in his heart, in his gut, grew severe. *What the hell is this life all about anyway? Death, I guess. My father's gone for good. Mom's still here, but Granddad, Grandma and Uncle Edward are gone, and Aunt Louise died two years ago. Which pretty much leaves me on my own.*

Danny clearly felt sorry for himself, but the pain was real and he continued to drink at it until the numbness set in.

Danny awoke the next morning with the worst hangover of his life. He vaguely remembered how he had lurched off the barstool and stumbled out into the warm Manhattan night to hail a taxi. The night air had momentarily sobered him enough to slur an address to the cab driver. He didn't remember anything after that.

"Shit, Bratly, it's Thursday and I'm late for work," Danny said to the calico cat rubbing up against his leg. He reached for the phone and dialed the number. "Did you hear me, Bratly, I'm late for work and Walter's gonna have my ass in a sling."

He found himself counting the rings as he thought about Brightside Publications, a small publishing company that produced a number of monthly men's adventure magazines. Danny winced at Jeanie Switchboard's familiar high-pitched, singsong phone greeting, "Good morning, Brightside Publications. Look at the bright side."

"Hi, Jeanie," Danny rasped into the phone with difficulty. "I'm running late this morning. Would you please tell Harold to cover for me until I get in."

"Will do, Dan," Jeanie said. Danny thought he detected a knowing smile on Jeanie's face, as if she knew he'd tied one on the night before.

Danny was the managing editor of three of Brightside's men's magazines: *Macho, For Guys Only* and *Adventurer's World*. The first two were published monthly, and *Adventurer's World* came out every other month. *Macho* was already behind schedule and he knew Walter Ashburn, the publisher, would be on his case.

When Danny arrived at the office two hours late, Jeanie gave him a knowing wink, unable to suppress the wide grin on her face. "The phone's been ringing off the hook for you," she said, "and Mr. Ashburn's looking for you."

Danny hurried down the long, narrow, carpeted hallway, attaché case in one hand and a small paper bag holding the still-hot container of coffee he'd bought downstairs in the other. He passed one of the bullpen areas housing five of the associate editors and one editorial assistant. The familiar clackity-clack of multiple typewriters in action made him feel less noticeable. He tried not to look at the faces through the large interior glass windows facing the hallway as he moved on down the corridor.

Following his usual morning ritual when he came to work, he slid his attaché case onto the table behind his desk, carefully extracted the container of hot coffee from the now-wet paper bag, smoothed out the bag and placed the coffee on top. He carefully lifted the lid off and nearly burned his lips with the first sip. He took another sip and shuddered, trying to shake off the pounding in his head.

As he placed his blazer on the hanger behind the door, he noticed the stack of familiar pink while-you-were-out slips on his desk. Sure enough, there were three calls from Walter Ashburn and one from Ralph Corona, the editorial director. Ralph wasn't anything for Danny to worry about. He didn't do too much directing as an editor. Matter of fact, Danny doubted if Ralph had any editorial ability. In Danny's mind, Ralph was a dilettante editor. Mostly, Ralph concentrated on his own Brooks Brothers sartorial splendor, went on long, so-called business lunches, and kissed Walter Ashburn's ass on a regular basis.

Danny sat down and dialed Ralph's office. Anna, Ralph's secretary, answered and put him right through.

"Danny, for chrissakes, where the hell've you been?" Ralph asked rhetorically. "Walter's on the warpath. We're really late with *Macho*, and you're not even in the goddamn building."

Danny spoke softly, trying to calm Ralph down. "We're waiting on one story from Peterson, which I believe we'll get right after lunch. I'll edit the fucker myself and we'll put this puppy to bed before your first martini of the evening."

Danny thought about his father then, and considered telling Ralph. But he rejected the idea and decided it was too personal, too heartfelt to share with such a jerk.

"All right," Ralph responded. "Let me know what Walter says."

"Don't worry, Ralph," Danny said. "I'll keep you in the loop." He could hear Ralph's long, frustrated sigh as he hung up.

Danny knew he had to call Peterson about the story and get the writer's ass in gear, but first things first. He had to deal with Walter and resolve the lateness issue. He picked up the coffee container and realized his hand was shaking. *Is that because of Walter,* he wondered, *or is it alcohol withdrawal?* He took another sip of coffee, put the cup down and hurried off to Walter's large corner office.

"Danny!" Walter shouted across the room from behind his enormous walnut-grained desk. "What the hell is going on with you? Don't we pay attention to schedules anymore?"

Danny tried to smile and dismiss the issue with a confident wave. "Everything's cool, Walter," Danny said. "I'm on top of it."

"Bullshit, Danny!" Walter snapped. "One of your books is gonna be so late one of these days, we're gonna have a hundred fifty thousand copies sitting in a boxcar on a siding somewhere, waiting for the distributor to fit us into the schedule again. You know what that'll cost me?"

Danny looked down at the plush carpeting, his shoulders sagging. "My dad died yesterday, Walter," he said almost in a whisper.

Walter was silent for a moment. The cacophony of typewriters and phones ringing down the hallway seemed louder then.

"Oh," Walter said finally. "I'm sorry, Danny."

Danny fought back the tears. He thought about Charlie's, the bar around the corner from the office, and how good a stiff drink would be right then.

"Why don't you take the rest of the day off," Walter suggested. "Go home. I'll get Ralph to handle things."

It was all Danny could do to keep from screaming. *Ralph handle things?* he thought. *Ralph could barely handle his own dick.*

Danny thanked Walter, relieved that his publisher had mellowed back to a rational level. He left Walter's office and returned to his desk, his mind racing. *That's all I ever do. Please people. Appease people. Calm people down. I guess that's my full-time job. But women especially. The problem is, I never seem to be able to get it right with women. All my life, I've been trying to figure them out. If Freud couldn't figure it out, how can I?*

Danny called Peterson and told him if he didn't get the story in by 4:00 PM, he would personally send someone over to cram all his fingers into the garbage disposal and turn it on. Bill Peterson knew Danny wasn't a violent man. The guy even owned a cat, for crying out loud. But this time Peterson also knew that Danny wouldn't go for any more delays.

After Peterson assured Danny he would have the story in on time, Danny called his associate editors in and brought them up-to-date. He also had Nancy, the young editorial assistant, join them. Her presence wasn't necessary but he enjoyed looking at her long blond hair, her generous breasts straining to burst free from the restrictive fabric of her blouse, and her cute little buttocks bouncing under her tight, clinging skirt when she walked through the door.

Danny thought about asking Nancy out, but he knew getting intimate with the staff invited trouble. Still, he needed a distraction from the job, and from the devastating news of his father's death. That's when he decided Charlie's Bar, or "The Clubhouse" as the Brightside staff referred to it, would be his destination right after work.

He didn't know it then, but destiny awaited him at Charlie's. That destiny was Mickey Parks' daughter, Allison.

Chapter Four
Lloyd takes the tour

The brilliant beam that led to Midway Manor differed from the other lights because of its streaks of pale crimson and indigo. The light ended its journey in a valley of lush green grassland reaching as far as the eye could see. And in the distance stood the mystical grand manor of Midway.

The manor house, a three-story flagstone building engulfed by exquisite colorful blooms and fragrances, welcomed its new residents at the reception desk near the main entrance. The director's office was located directly behind the reception area.

"Welcome to Midway Manor, Mr. Wallace," the tall, lean administrator said to Lloyd when he entered his office. "Please take a seat. I'm Joseph Patrick, the director. I hope your transition here was satisfactory."

He continued without expecting Lloyd to say that it wasn't. "There is actually no physical need for any of the amenities here, including clothing, food or sleep. There isn't even any need for your physical appearance. We are all essentially spiritual in nature. But the number one rule is to make our guests as comfortable as possible. So we make sure that you retain the physical appearance you had on Earth, and hold on to the familiar routines and material niceties that kept you happy there. There'll be plenty of time for the spiritual side later on in your journey through the afterworld."

Mr. Patrick smiled. "We also smooth out a wrinkle or two and alleviate a few of the earthly encumbrances such as the need for insulin for former diabetics, or for eyeglasses or hearing aids or walking canes, or even for ill-fitting dentures."

The director glanced momentarily at a document on his desk, and then continued. "I understand you were originally from Springtown, Illinois. You were sixty-three years old at the time of your arrival at Midway, divorced, a published writer of one novel and seven hundred-plus detective stories, worked in public relations and had a stretch with cancer for the past three years. And let's see, you've chosen our establishment because there's some business to complete regarding your adult son Danny. Is this all correct?"

"Yes. Yes, it is," Lloyd said somberly, uneasy over hearing Mr. Patrick refer to his life in the past tense.

The director got up from his seat and walked around to the front of his desk. "Well then, follow me and let me show you around."

Walking down the lengthy hall on the main floor, as he had done the day before with the attendant who had shown him to his private room, Lloyd saw dozens of rooms restricted by closed doors. Lloyd continued to follow the director to a curved staircase that would take them to the second floor, but their climb continued to the third level and the Data Room library.

At first look, Lloyd could see endless rows of bookshelves that loomed to the ceiling. But the sight of the shelves baffled him—the unusual condensed height with each and every one crammed neatly with small, identical white-covered journals. With intense curiosity he moved closer to the first row. His confusion cleared when he saw printed on the spine of each journal, distinguishing one from the other, a person's name in diminutive gold lettering followed by numbers that obviously signified a *single* day, month and year.

Lloyd's inquisitiveness intensified, realizing the daily diaries were filed not only in chronological order but, more importantly, sorted alphabetically by last name. He began to briskly pass row after row of the journals, deliberately looking for the W's. But to his dismay, when he finally reached the section that should have held records in his son's name, there was absolutely nothing there.

"My son Danny ... Daniel Wallace? There's nothing here," Lloyd said in anguish, a sinking feeling in his stomach.

Mr. Patrick, who had now caught up to Lloyd, responded apologetically.

"No. That's right, Mr. Wallace, but you don't understand. There are no journals in your son's name because none has been printed out yet. I'm so sorry that you presumed there would be. I just wanted you to see the extent of the library section of our Data Room. Let's go back to the second floor and I'll show you how to turn out a journal."

Lloyd followed the director as he retraced their steps back to the Data Room on the second floor. They walked across the corridor to a set of double doors. The director opened them simultaneously, as though the view beyond them would be extraordinary. Lloyd initially noticed nothing but another lengthy hall and doors that appeared to be quite similar to the layout on the main floor, but many of the doors on this level were slightly ajar. Mr. Patrick turned to his right, opened one of the doors all the way and invited Lloyd to enter.

The room, though surprisingly small, contained a computer unit on a desk, one material-covered swivel chair half-tucked under the desk, and a second office chair positioned just a few feet away. On the wall directly in front of the computer hung an unusual-looking movie screen, rectangular in length. And at first glance there appeared to be two screens side-by-side, because a thin black line ran right down the middle of it.

"Here, you sit at the computer," the director told Lloyd as he pulled the other chair closer. But Lloyd couldn't keep from staring at the domed ceiling that crowned the room. He found the architecture both unexpected and most impressive.

Mr. Patrick cleared his throat and said, "Okay, now. As you can see, the letters of the alphabet on this keyboard are positioned exactly the same as on a typewriter, which I know you're quite familiar with. But first you have to turn the computer on and the switch is right here."

Lloyd flipped the switch and the monitor screen just behind the keyboard lit up with the words: *ENTRY ONE. Please type in your full name. Hit Enter.* "Go ahead," the director said enthusiastically, and Lloyd typed in his name, keeping his focus on the screen at the same time. As soon as he typed in his full name and hit the enter key, the words *ENTRY TWO* appeared, requesting a second name.

"Now wait," Mr. Patrick interrupted, "here's where you'd type in your son's name. But for privacy, type in your name again." Lloyd did so without hesitation and *ENTRY THREE* appeared with the command to type in a single day, month and year. The director instructed him to type the date of his arrival at the Manor, which resulted in a synopsis of Lloyd's final hours on Earth projected on the side-by-side wall screen. The image looked exactly like an open book.

"Okay, now," Mr. Patrick said, seeking Lloyd's attention. "If you take a look back at the computer screen, the program offers you three options: to print the journal that appears on the wall, to type in an alternate day to read, or to just end the session entirely." The director then pointed to the thin slot in the base of the computer showing him where a journal would print out, if that's what he selected to do.

"And that's it," he said cheerfully. "Do you have any questions about what I've just shown you?"

Lloyd acknowledged that the director's instructions were quite simple to follow. He also knew that earthbound computers and their components during the 1970s had been limited to a few.

"This is one hell of a gizmo. A computer like this would surely revolutionize the publishing world back on Earth," he said, obviously in awe of the machine.

Mr. Patrick explained that a few years up the road there would be computers quite similar to the one he was now using. He said there would be computers that would make problem-solving and countless answers to questions readily available, and both businesses and individuals would be communicating with each other all over the world in a vast network called the World Wide Web.

When the director finished his basic scenario on computers of the future, Lloyd had some other questions. He was pleased to find out that the residents were at liberty to take printed journals back to their rooms to read leisurely and in private. His son Danny, who had recently celebrated his thirty-sixth birthday, lived most of his life away from his father, and consequently Lloyd reasoned there would be a vast amount of reading in order for him to catch up.

"Is there any way I could go directly to specific topics rather than typing in a single date?" he asked.

Mr. Patrick was delighted with Lloyd's question. Their computer program had in fact numerous options, but few residents required more than the first series of instructions. Pointing to the keyboard, the director explained:

"All you have to do after you've entered your name and son's name is type in the word 'query' instead of the date. The list of topics regarding your son will be quite extensive, and in alphabetical order. Just follow the commands on the computer screen until the information for that particular journal is projected on the wall screen.

"If you're seeking general information that doesn't directly concern a loved one, just type NA when the computer asks for a family member's name," Mr. Patrick added.

Lloyd found the instructions to be very straightforward once again. The director answered several other questions, and then reiterated to Lloyd that he should not hesitate to seek out his attendant, Paul, or himself if he had additional questions or if there was anything else he needed during his stay at the Manor.

Lloyd considered asking the director if it were possible to get hold of a photo of both himself and his son taken a few years back. Before he could ask, however, Mr. Patrick told him an exact copy of that photo was being held for him at the reception desk on the main floor.

Once again, the Manor staff's precognitive abilities amazed Lloyd. Though anxious to pick up the photo, he decided to stay in the Data Room for a while longer. When Mr. Patrick left, Lloyd sat in silence for several minutes before he typed in his son's name and the day of his arrival at Midway Manor.

Lloyd began to read the projection on the wall, "... *Danny sat in a bar downing his first drink in four months.... But the news of his father's passing still came as a shock.... The pain in his heart, in his gut, grew severe ...*"

"No," Lloyd cried aloud. "What have I done?" His vision blurred with tears. He tried to wipe them away, but his hand trembled and he knew he couldn't read any further. Not another word. He attempted to dry his eyes again, looking directly at the computer screen, aching to shut down the session. And finally he did.

By the time he reached the main level, all sorts of thoughts raced through his mind. He deliberately stopped by the reception desk to pick up the photo of himself and his son, and then headed toward his room. Holding the photo with both hands, he fought to clear his mind.

My son cannot waste his time grieving over me. Not even for a single day, Lloyd thought with heartfelt determination. *He's got to get on with his life, and I have to find some way to make that happen.* Suddenly, Lloyd stopped, realizing he was next to the Renaissance Room.

Just like the day before when Lloyd first arrived, Mickey sat inside the room, yet this time unaccompanied. His strumming on the guitar was barely audible. Lloyd entered and walked over to the far corner. Mickey, instinctively sensing something was wrong, covered the guitar strings with his fingers to stop the hum. He knew his new friend needed undivided attention.

"You've been to the Data Room, haven't you?" he asked in a passive yet friendly voice.

Lloyd took a seat on the opposite side of the small leather-top table. And although they had only met the day before, he handed Mickey the photo of himself and his son Danny.

"Yes, I was in the Data Room," Lloyd said softly, "and I just don't understand why my son would be taking the news of my death so badly." Then, in a singularly higher-pitched voice, he said, "He knew I had cancer and that it was only a matter of time. And truthfully, Mick, we'd each lived our lives separately, because I was too damn busy living mine. Too damn busy to be a father."

Mickey listened sympathetically as Lloyd continued.

"What's so bizarre is that in less than a split second after I crossed over, I knew that I had to come here to make things right. But there has to be more than my printing some journals and reading about what I didn't do for him. Do you know what I mean?"

When Lloyd refrained from saying anything more, Mickey realized he had expected him to answer his own hypothetical question.

"What can you do?" Mickey asked. "Look, I wish I had an answer for you, but I've never gone back to the Data Room since they gave me the tour. And to tell you the truth, that was three years ago. Not three years like you knew three years back on Earth, because here you're literally unaware of the passage of time. Your reason, if I heard you right, is that you don't want to read about what you didn't do for your son. My reason is the opposite of yours. I don't want to read about what my daughter's now doing on her own, knowing that I can't be there. All her life, I was always there for her."

Stardust Dads

"Opposite reasons, yes," Lloyd said, "but we're both on the same page about the Data Room." He paused for a moment. "I've got a few ideas," he said, his thoughts running wildly. "I know it's been a while for you, but can you think back to when you took the tour or maybe there's someone you've met during your stay here who knows what else the computers in the Data Room can do. Like today, for instance, the director told me you can ask the computer about different subjects. Did you know about this?" he asked, hoping Mickey would offer something more.

Mickey admitted he actually had no knowledge at all about the computers at the Manor. He even mentioned his daughter, Allison, having worked quite a few years at a publishing company and how she'd never used anything but a typewriter. "The first and last time I ever touched the contraption in the Data Room was the day after I arrived at the Manor," he said without any misgivings.

As for the residents Mickey had met during his stay, there wasn't anything that he could contribute. Lloyd was not at all discouraged by his admission.

"What's this about your daughter? She's in publishing?"

"What does that have to do with anything?" Mickey asked, wondering why his friend had changed the subject.

Lloyd then touched briefly on his own lifelong career, including his writing hundreds of stories for detective magazines.

"And my son's in publishing, too," he said. "Lives and works right in the heart of Manhattan."

"Manhattan?" Mickey repeated, his bond with Lloyd growing stronger. "Wow. That's where my daughter was three years ago. I wonder … if she's still there."

"If she is … maybe Danny and Allison know each other. Wouldn't that be something?" Lloyd said with a smile, figuring that if he and Mickey were so in sync with one another, why not their adult children. The fact that there were no fewer than eight million souls living in New York City, and the odds of two of those specific people meeting each other overwhelmingly remote, never entered his mind. Then, almost in a whisper, he said, "Danny really needs someone to help him get through his grief right now. Your daughter went through it three years ago. Maybe there's a chance she could help him—"

But Mickey interrupted defensively, "I don't know. I told you I haven't been to the Data Room in all this time. I have no idea what she's doing now." His eyes watered and he ran a hand through his closely cropped dark hair. He stayed silent for a moment and then looked up at Lloyd. "It's time, isn't it? It's time for me to know."

Lloyd touched Mickey's arm to console him. "It's okay, Mick. Come on, my friend. Let's go to the Data Room. We'll make things right, I promise."

It was then that Lloyd realized they were both at Midway Manor for a reason, on a mission that would forever alter the lives of their adult children before propelling Mickey and him on to the next level in their spiritual fulfillment.

Chapter Five
Allison Parks is still grieving

Mickey Parks' daughter Allison slipped a blank cassette into her tape recorder. It was early evening and she had just arrived at her quaint Victorian-decorated apartment to find it haunting her once again with an unbearable emptiness. It was three years since her dad's passing and she fervently missed their talks. She reached for her cigarette lighter and used it to light a large white candle that accompanied an old gold-framed photo of the two of them together. Then she hit the button on her tape player to begin recording.

"Dad? Are you there?" Allison called out to him, as though he were at the other end of a telephone call. She hesitated a moment to watch the flame on the candle flicker. Though she had always wondered whether it was the breath from her spoken words that caused the miniature blaze to waver, she regarded it as her cue to continue. "Hey," she said, her voice now sounding younger than her twenty-eight years. "I need to talk with you about something."

Allison continued. "I went to see Aunt Terry this past weekend." Then, effortlessly selecting her words with care, she admitted, "I'm so sorry, Dad, but when the conversation got around to our losing you, I'd confessed to her that I was still crying. 'Allison. No!' Aunt Terry had yelled. 'My God, it's been three years. You can't do that. You have to let your father go or he'll never rest in peace.' I had no idea she'd get so upset over my grieving for you."

Allison paused again and then said defensively, "She may be your sister and I don't mean to be disrespectful, but truthfully, Dad, I'd expected some sympathy. Aunt Terry's reaction threw me off guard. And this overpowering gut feeling I've always had that you're grieving, too, well, I decided it was better to keep it to myself. But is she right? Am

I hurting you?" she asked her father, knowing full well there'd be no verbal reply.

The thought of Allison preventing her father's soul from resting in peace brought her to tears. "Oh, Dad, if I'm hurting you, I'm so sorry. Please forgive me. Please. My tears just won't stop and I need you to give me just a little more time." And as though he had indeed accepted her plea, the flame on the candle flickered once again. Allison sobbed, "I love you, Dad …" This time the lights dimmed and the snapping sound of electricity charged through the air.

Momentarily startled and unable to stem the flow of tears that now blushed her cheeks, she hit the stop-recording button on the tape player.

Odd, perhaps, that Allison used a blank cassette to tape her talks to her father. But it was for therapeutic and not psychic reasons that she did it. She had been professionally advised to record a final farewell to her dad. To replay the tape whenever she felt depressed and reinforce her acceptance of his death. To let go. To focus on her life and a promising future. The advice, she supposed, might have worked for others, but she couldn't do it. The hundreds of cassettes that had accumulated over the months were casehardened proof of that.

Allison reached for a handful of tissues to dry her eyes. She kept a small, decorative box of tissues in every room. It was just another ritual she had refused to let go from the time when her dad had been living with her. Because of his allergies, the boxes were placed strategically throughout the apartment. It was the best she could do for his uncontrollable sneezing binges.

Her dad's allergies, she reasoned now, were insignificant compared to his having cancer and how that silent killer took him from her in less than four months. "Enough," Allison said to herself, turning on the radio. She desperately needed the distraction and a chance for some more positive thoughts to emerge. However, a chill went through her when one of her dad's favorite songs, "Stardust," began playing. It was a version she hadn't heard before, one that consisted of a guitar and a piano. Her dad had played the guitar. She cried again, softly, remembering how deftly her father's fingers would move as he sang the words.

When the song ended, Allison headed off to the kitchen to prepare some dinner. It had been an extremely demanding day at work for her and she had skipped lunch, as usual.

Allison remembered how she'd loved to cook for her father. "The lucky guy you end up marrying better appreciate your cooking or he'll be answering to me," her dad would pledge, trying to compliment her but only managing to maintain his role as the overprotective father.

But marriage was no longer on Allison's agenda, even though there had been plenty of opportunities. "I'm so sorry, but I can't see you anymore," she remembered telling one good-looking Italian guy, Tony, after being honest with herself that his all-consuming love was strictly one-sided. She hated to hurt his feelings, and she felt guilty about it for weeks, but she knew she had to stop the relationship before it snowballed out of control.

And then there was Johnny, a guitar-player like her dad. She certainly felt attracted to him; he reminded her of the actor John Travolta. Johnny also told Allison he loved her, calling her at all hours of the night, usually from a neighborhood bar, slurring his words as he professed his undying love for her. Despite this inebriated declaration of true love, his drunken avowal always ended with a plea for her to sleep with him.

Which is why Allison deliberately dated sparsely and avoided long-term relationships, even though several of the men she had gone out with were each considered to be a great catch. Well, at least that was the consensus by some of the women in her office. Allison, however, didn't have a clue as to what they saw in these guys. In her mind, once you really got to know them, they just didn't measure up. But Allison never disclosed her own final analysis of these men with her coworkers, fearing she would jeopardize their working relationship and only amplify what she perceived to be the ambiguous opinions they already had about her.

Allison carefully examined the left-over meatloaf from the night before and decided it was still free from mold and bacteria. She placed it on a cookie sheet and slid it into the oven. While the meat heated up, Allison rinsed off some lettuce and a small tomato, and deftly peeled an onion.

Allison was quite mindful of the distance she kept from the opposite sex, having been strongly influenced by her parents' ruinous relationship that ended in divorce. She carried painful memories from when her parents were together, going back to her childhood and then as an adult. And later, the loss of her father only reinforced her reservations about the prospects of marriage even more.

Margaret Parks, Allison's mother, was still among the living and resided in Connecticut. Their phone calls were infrequent and they hadn't spent any significant time together since the funeral. "Oh, Alli," her mom chided during their last phone conversation, "you sound just like your father." The disapproving remark echoed in Allison's mind, though she had no recollection of what she had actually said to her mother at the time.

"So what if I'm just like Dad?" Allison questioned herself aloud, almost cutting her finger while slicing the tomato, trying to reinforce her convictions that she and her father had many admirable qualities. "Damn it, Mom," she cried. "You're always judging and rarely approving of anything that either Dad or I would say or do. You're just hateful for thinking that way. Why do you do it? Why?"

After dinner, Allison decided to get to bed earlier than usual. She expected another stressful day at work. The new position she held as associate editor was taking its toll. Not the work itself, which she thrived on, but trying to deal with managing editor Kate Ripley, who had recently been transferred to her department.

Allison's heartfelt confession to her father that evening had enabled her to sleep soundly through the night and the alarm clock startled her awake. It was 7:30 when she bounced out of bed. A mug of strong decaffeinated coffee, a bagel with cream cheese and a few fresh strawberries were all she had for breakfast. Her petite, slender torso had always been the envy of every perpetual dieter she knew, and even overweight strangers seemed to stare at her with contempt. But no one was savvy enough to recognize Allison's anorexic habits. That was her downfall and a well-kept secret.

Her morning routine was usually the same during the workweek. She would turn on one of the local television stations to catch the weather report. *Go ahead ... let's see if you can guess what the weather will be today,* she'd joke to herself, finding their account to be usually inaccurate. And after hearing the report, she decided to wear a light-gray two-piece suit, a red silk blouse and her black, open-toed high heels.

While brushing her brunette hair that reached halfway down her back, she thought of her half-hour drive to work and how it would most likely take longer than usual because of the construction going on at the exit ramp. She was bothered by the long line of cars and the frustration she felt over that particular traffic light at the ramp, changing from green to red much too quickly.

And those construction guys, she'd remembered, *I just hate 'em. There I am, waiting for the light to turn green and they're staring at me like they haven't had any in a month. I can't wait for them to finish the damn job and get out of my life.*

Trying to overcome the tension welling up inside her, she switched her thoughts to her good friend and former coworker Marlene Wills, who had recently relocated to New Jersey. Her decision to move had been spontaneous. It happened shortly after she was fired by the new managing editor, Kate Ripley, when Marlene had not met a deadline for an assignment she had two weeks to complete.

Allison knew for a fact that Marlene had gone to Kate on several occasions to tell her about the probability of not meeting the deadline. Marlene could not get her hands on a required second source to confirm a quote. "Get that second source," Kate kept insisting, "I don't care how you do it. That quote stays in the piece." But in reality, that particular quote was chucked.

The truth can be told in just two words, Allison tearfully admitted to herself on the day her friend was dismissed. *Personality conflict!*

Marlene's move to New Jersey, however, did not jeopardize their friendship. The miles between them were easily overcome with either long-distance phone calls or letters. Allison chuckled to herself, remembering the letter she had received the day before from Marlene when she referred to the Machiavellian managing editor who had fired her. "Is fuckingbitch one word or two?" Marlene had written.

The drive to work had its delays just as Allison had anticipated earlier that morning. But she still arrived ten minutes early to be greeted by Jeff Bonstell, a copy editor whom she had dated on several occasions. "Good morning," he said, giving her a wink and a smile. Allison nodded and smiled back politely, trying not to encourage him any further. Besides, she knew he had already switched his manly attention to "Kate the Ripper," as she was more familiarly known around the office. Her day at work went better than the one before because Kate spent most of her time in meetings and had little time to bother her.

After work, while impatiently waiting for the traffic light to turn green, Allison made a spontaneous decision. She turned right and headed toward the local animal shelter that was only several blocks away. She had visited the center just the evening before and on several other occasions, wanting to adopt a kitten, and each time found she was unable to make the commitment. That evening she arrived home empty-handed once again, unaware that her life was about to change drastically. She had just unlocked the door to her East Side apartment when she heard the telephone ringing. Allison threw her purse on the sofa and grabbed the phone.

"Hello?" she answered, a bit out of breath.

"Hey, girlfriend. It's me," Marlene said cheerfully. "Come on, get yourself together."

"Marlene? What's going on?" Allison asked, surprised to hear from her.

"I'm ba-a-ack. Got here about an hour ago," she teased.

"You're here in Manhattan?" Allison asked excitedly, knowing full well by the tone of her friend's voice that she really was.

"I'm calling from Charlie's," she said.

"Charlie? Someone new in your life?" Allison joked, knowing she meant the watering hole.

"I'm gonna give you just enough time to change into something comfortable. Then get yourself over here, 'cause I'm treating you to dinner," she declared empathically, expecting no excuses to the contrary.

"So you've decided to spend the weekend with Pete Hines?" Allison asked, guessing that was Marlene's primary reason for making the trip back to the city.

"You got it," she admitted. "Now, get yourself over here. Lover boy is still at work, and I need my best friend. Here. Now."

Chapter Six
Danny meets Allison

Danny felt a familiar, comforting warmth settle over him as he stepped through one of the double doors of Charlie's Bar and Grill. "The Clubhouse," as it was referred to by Brightside veterans, was a place of both solitude and excitement. Prominent was the long, mahogany bar that seemed to stretch endlessly along the right wall toward the rear, finally ending before a large room full of tables and chairs.

Along the left wall were a number of well-upholstered booths that continued toward the back, ending where the bar ended. The room in the rear dog-legged to the left and included yet another series of snug, comfortable booths for drinking and dining patrons.

The subdued lighting cloaked the place in a kind of semi-darkness, which always gave Danny a feeling of being warmly embraced and protected.

He at once saw the grinning face of Carlos, the Cuban bartender.

"Danny!" Carlos yelled from behind the crowded bar. "Over here," he directed, placing an ice-filled glass on a cocktail napkin at the very far end of the bar.

Danny squeezed in alongside two construction types and held the glass while Carlos poured a generous amount of vodka over the ice and topped it off with a splash of tonic water.

"How 'bout some vegetables?" Carlos quipped, dropping in a wedge of lime.

The ironworkers next to Danny were ogling the two women sitting in one of the booths across from the bar. Danny found himself transfixed, unable to keep from staring himself. The blonde was doing all the talking, and she was pretty enough. But Danny couldn't take his eyes off the stunningly attractive brunette whose beautiful long hair, flashing brown eyes and full, pouty lips erased for the moment all memory of his dad's passing, work, and Peterson's badly conceived story. The sonofabitch had dogged it this time, coming in late and turning in eighteen pages of gibberish. It had taken Danny several hours to blue-pencil it into shape. If not for the deadline, he would have tossed it back at him for a complete rewrite.

For a brief moment, Danny thought of his dad, felt that familiar sinking feeling in the pit of his stomach. But he quickly pushed the thoughts out of his mind. It was how he had dealt with all things painful in his life, ever since he could remember. When Dad would come home drunk and his mother would go nuts, screaming and yelling, one time even pulling a butcher knife out of a kitchen drawer and threatening his dad with it, Danny would automatically suppress the memory of the experience, file it away in the farthest recesses of his mind. And when Danny got older and started taking up the habits of adults, he found that the use of liquor would hasten the act of *filing* the memories of unpleasant experiences.

Maybe it was the rapid effect of the alcohol re-entering his system that night, but Danny was able to quickly dispel all unpleasant thoughts and concentrate solely on the lovely woman sitting in the booth across the aisle. He found himself compulsively gazing at her, as if trying to memorize how her short skirt revealed beautifully curved thighs and legs ending in black, stiletto-heeled shoes.

It wasn't the first time Danny had fallen in lust, but for some reason he felt this one was different. He also knew intuitively that the standard pickup lines were not going to work for him with this gal.

The brightly colored jukebox near the front door blared forth with the strains of Manfred Mann. "Blinded by the light …"

Allison Parks listened politely as her friend Marlene droned on about her life, her career and her torrid, on-again-off-again relationship with Peter Hines. The bar was pretty crowded for a Thursday, she noted, figuring it had to be all the construction guys working on the building going up around the corner. But she couldn't help but notice the cute guy in the dark blue blazer and jeans standing at the very end of the bar. *He's no construction guy,* she thought.

As Marlene went on about her current love affair, Allison decided to make a game of guessing what Danny did for a living. She was careful not to let him see her looking at him. She studied his clothes, the light blue buttoned-down shirt open at the collar, the faded blue jeans, the polished oxblood half-boots, and the well-pressed blazer. A man who played the establishment game, she decided, but with a streak of nonconformity in him. A rebel at heart. She liked him already.

He was boyishly good-looking, with short brown hair she was sure he teased with a blow-dryer and brush. Cute, perfectly shaped nose, a small mouth but sexy lips. Brown eyes like hers. And a full, neatly trimmed beard. Allison felt a surprising tingling. *Talk about waking the dead,* she thought.

Briefly, their eyes met. A warning bell went off inside Allison's head. But she was compelled to study Danny's eyes for a few more moments, becoming aware of the complex intelligence behind them. And possibly a hint of sadness. She had to work very hard to finally look away.

Danny felt the spark between them. He knew he had been staring too hard at the brunette, but he also realized she had been sneaking peeks at him, too. But how was he going to make a pitch without scaring her off? It was a puzzle, Danny decided, that might need a few more vodka and tonics to solve.

Allison concluded that Danny had to be in publishing. Either he was an editor or an art director. She was sure of it. But how was she going to meet him? She couldn't just ditch Marlene, and besides, she didn't know this guy from Adam. He could be New York's version of the Boston Strangler.

What neither Danny nor Allison was aware of was that there were other forces at work here, forces of a spiritual nature that would ultimately bring them together.

Danny realized he had to use the men's room. He maneuvered around the ironworkers and made his way down the aisle toward the restrooms in the rear. Allison saw him coming and as he passed her booth, she found herself looking up at him. She hadn't planned it; she heard the words, but wasn't even sure she was the one saying them.

"What magazine?" she asked.

Danny stopped in his tracks, wondering if the alcohol was causing him to hallucinate. Was this gorgeous brunette really speaking to him?

"Pardon me?" Danny said.

"I asked you what magazine you worked for," Allison said.

Danny smiled, not sure how he should respond. The men's magazines he worked for were anachronisms, dinosaurs, holdovers from an era long gone. Years ago the mainstay of the magazines had been stories like "I Found the Lost Tribe of Skull Valley," or "Trapped on the Island of Flesh-Eating Wombats." Today's version still had adventure stories, war battles, fights with Hell's Angels types, but there was now no small infusion of sex-oriented material. A poor man's version of *Playboy* and *Penthouse*.

Consequently, when someone would ask him what magazine he worked for, he would half cover his mouth with his hand and try to garble the verbal response.

"How'd you know I worked for a magazine?" Danny finally answered.

"Just a hunch," Allison replied. "So which one?"

"*Mausho*," Danny said, covering his mouth and trying to slur *Macho* as much as he could.

"Oh, one of those hairy-chested men's rags," Allison said, immediately regretting her unkind remark.

Marlene was suddenly at a loss for words. She sat there flabbergasted, astonished by her friend's uncharacteristic boldness with Danny.

"Ouch," Danny said, trying to make light of Allison's offending words, which really did hurt. Danny knew most people didn't think much of his kinds of magazines, and many times he had been accused of taking his work too seriously, but Danny had always maintained a solid work ethic. Something his mother had instilled in him from the time he had first started working, shining shoes and delivering newspapers.

So he worked on what most people would refer to as smut. So what? For years, all through the '40s, '50s and '60s, the magazines had promised a lot more than they delivered. Now, in the enlightened '70s, the magazines were finally giving the readers what they really wanted. But as objectionable as some people found the material, Danny plied his trade with as much diligence and careful crafting as he would have done had he been editor of a scholarly journal.

"I'm sorry," Allison said. "I apologize for the put-down. I was just kidding. I'm Allison and she's Marlene." Marlene smiled at Danny, her lively green eyes blatantly sizing him up.

"We're in the publishing business, too. I'm an associate editor for *Home and Hearth* magazine. Marlene used to work with me, but she's doing real estate in Jersey now. Why don't you join us?"

"Why not," Danny said. "Give me a minute and I'll be right back."

After he left, Marlene confronted Allison, putting her face in Allison's face.

"Excu-u-use me," Marlene said, grinning. "Are they putting Spanish fly in the drinks here or what? What's up with you?"

"He's cute," said Allison. "I don't know, it was compulsive, I guess. I didn't even know I was going to say anything until I said it. C'mon, relax. Pete'll be here any minute and then you won't have that three's-a-crowd feeling."

Danny returned from the men's room, grabbed his drink and change from the bar, and told Carlos he'd be in the booth. He slid in next to Allison and she immediately felt his thigh pressed up against hers. The tingling feeling returned.

"I'm Danny," he said, "Danny Wallace."

"Pleased to meet you, Danny Wallace," said Allison, pointedly keeping her leg exactly where it was.

When Pete Hines showed up twenty minutes later, Marlene became less distracted by Danny the newcomer, instead focusing her attention solely on her extended weekend shack-up. Pete was as blond as Marlene, with similar dancing green eyes and rugged he-man handsomeness. The two had trouble keeping their hands off each other, which left Allison and Danny to get further acquainted.

Later, there was small talk among the four of them. Some good-natured kidding about what a dump Charlie's was and how the roaches appeared well-fed. Probably uptown roaches, Pete had concluded, suggesting that several had hitched a ride in someone's luggage and had reproduced at the small hotel that was adjacent to Charlie's, eventually migrating into the nooks and crannies of Charlie's Bar and Grill.

"Where do you live?" Allison asked Danny, her hand brushing against his as she reached for the ashtray.

"West Eighty-sixth," he said.

"Pretty nice neighborhood," Allison commented.

"Rent-controlled," Danny explained. "Took it over after a friend of mine decided to quit his nine-to-five drudgery and take a few years off to write a novel. He went to Paris about two years ago and I haven't heard from him since. Which reminds me, one of these days *I'm* going to find time to write a book."

"Mind if I smoke?" Allison asked.

"Go ahead," Danny said. "I gave 'em up a couple of years ago, but it doesn't bother me if other people want to smoke. It's a free country."

"Thanks," she said, lighting up and taking a long, deep drag. "Big apartment?"

"Mine? Yeah," he said. "Pretty roomy actually. Living room, kitchen, bedroom. And there's a small room off the living room that I use for my studio, my den."

"No bathroom?" Allison joked, feeling playful.

"No," Danny said, playing her game. "There's a communal outhouse we all use on the roof."

"Touché," Allison said, laughing. "So it's just you rambling around in that big upper West Side apartment?"

"Not exactly," said Danny. "I've got Bratly."

"What's a Bratly?" Marlene spoke up, oblivious to Pete's face buried in her neck.

"Bratly's my two-year-old calico cat," Danny said.

Gong! Danny had hit one of Allison's primary response chords. *He has a cat! I love this man already.*

"I've always wanted a cat," Allison said aloud. "I'm jealous. I keep thinking about maybe adopting a kitten. But calling him Brat … and what's with the adverbial 'ly'?"

"He's a she, as most calicos are. She was such a little thing when I got her, with a big mouth. She scolds me constantly. It seems like she holds her breath and draws out her meowing as if she's singing. She's always into mischief, so I called her a brat and the name stuck. I added the 'ly' to make it two syllables. It just sounded better."

"How 'bout we order some dinner," Pete suggested, finally coming up from Marlene's neck for air. A suggestion to which all parties readily agreed.

Later, after dinner, Marlene and Pete excused themselves and went next door, deciding to take advantage of the hotel's convenient proximity.

Danny offered to get Allison a cab so she didn't have to take the subway downtown late at night.

Allison declined, explaining, "I've got my own car. It's parked in the garage two blocks over."

"What's with the car?" Danny asked her. "Most people who live in the city don't want to be bothered."

"What's with the cat?" Allison countered. "Most men don't want to be bothered."

Danny laughed. "You're right," he said. "We're even. No more questions."

"How about I drop you off?" Allison offered, but Danny said he would take a cab.

"Will we see each other again?" she asked.

"Of course," Danny said. "I'll call you."

"There's a cliché."

"Yeah, but I mean it. I've got some business to take care of and I'll be tied up for a few days." Danny didn't know why but he couldn't share his grief with Allison, or anyone, just yet. He knew he had to call his mom, and that would be difficult enough.

"Why don't we exchange business cards? You write your home phone number on yours and I'll do the same on mine. Then I'll walk with you to get your car," Danny said.

Allison smiled and nodded, fishing in her purse for her cardholder. Somehow, she believed Danny. She knew he was troubled, and she also knew it was none of her business. *Let me give him his space and be respectful,* she thought. *I'm sure he'll call me when he's ready.*

When they reached the garage, Danny said goodnight, again promising to call. Allison suddenly leaned forward and kissed him fully on the lips. It wasn't a long or passionate kiss, but it had feeling behind it, which they both sensed.

Neither of them had any idea of the future events that were about to unfold, nor who would be guiding those events ... at least not yet.

Chapter Seven
Experiment in the Data Room

Lloyd motioned to Mickey to take the seat in front of the computer in the Data Room, making sure to close the door behind them. "Do you remember how to turn it on?" he asked.

"I feel like a fish out of water," Mickey replied, trying to ease the tension he was feeling. "Where the hell is it?"

Lloyd leaned over and flipped the switch. "Go ahead. Type in your name," he said. When Mickey began to diligently search for the letters on the keyboard, hitting each key with just one finger, Lloyd asked, "So what did you do for a living, Mick? Were you a musician?"

"Antiques," he answered, still trying to finish typing in his name. "Bought and sold antiques. Mostly furniture. I even repaired or refinished them. It was a tough business."

"Antiques, huh. I love antiques. My room here even has some exquisite pieces."

When Mickey had finally completed typing in his name, Lloyd had him hit the enter key. "Are you ready to type in your daughter's name?" he asked.

"Have you got all day?" Mickey teased, searching again for the right letters. "And why in the hell are these letters all mixed up? Don't they know how the alphabet goes?"

Lloyd just laughed and didn't bother to give him any explanation to his questions.

"A date? Now it's asking for a date," Mickey said after finishing Allison's name and hitting the enter tab again. "I'll do yesterday's date ... today isn't even over yet."

Allison slipped a blank cassette into her tape recorder.... My tears just won't stop and I need you to give me just a little more time. I love you, Dad ...

Mickey read the day's journal on the wall from beginning to end. Though it took him only a short period of time to read, he felt as though he had just spent the day with her. At home. At work. At the animal shelter. "I love you, too," he said aloud. For the first time in three years, there were no tears, just a wonderful, warm feeling.

Lloyd had also read the day's events that were so boldly projected on the wall. *Allison was indeed a lovely young woman. Perfect for my son, Danny,* he thought.

"Is Allison still in the city?" he asked, wondering if Mickey could come to this conclusion from what he had just read.

"She sure is. Same apartment, too," Mickey replied with an air of excitement. "Now what?" he asked, not forgetting what Lloyd had said about having some ideas up his sleeve.

"Go ahead and print this journal out first," Lloyd said, and Mickey hit the option one key.

"Now type in today's date and see what happens."

Mickey looked at his wristwatch. "But it's only two in the afternoon back on Earth. See this watch?" turning his wrist for Lloyd to get a closer look. "That nice fellow, Joe Patrick, told me my watch was set to Eastern Daylight Time. That's Earth time, you know. Pretty damn good, don't you think? And it's just like the one my daughter gave me."

"Go ahead ... type in today's date anyway," Lloyd said, smiling, anxious to test the computer. "Just for the hell of it ... let's see what happens."

So Mickey typed in the day's date and hit enter. The two men watched the words from the previous day's journal disappear. They both kept their focus on the wall. They waited. And waited ...

"Nothing," Mickey said.

"No, wait. Look. The screen's still lit up. There just aren't any words yet. Let's switch seats," Lloyd said, not quite ready to explain what was running through his mind.

Mickey obliged his partner and they maneuvered around each other, exchanging seats. Then he watched in amazement as Lloyd's fingers began hitting different letters on the keyboard at an unbelievable speed. The words, as he was typing them, were actually showing up on the double side-by-side wall screen:

Today, my new friend Mickey Parks broke the barriers between his isolation here at the Manor and that of his daughter's life back on Earth. For a few precious moments they were together. But yesterday's journal was only a mere glimpse of the past and cannot compare with what the future could unfold. Not only for Allison, but for Danny, too. It's just providence that they both happen to live and work in Manhattan. It would be wonderful if they could meet. Somewhere. Somehow. Let today be their new beginning. It's time these two young adults—unattached, deserving, should be the players in a new and meaningful, loving relationship. Not through their fathers, whose earthly spirits are destined for parts unknown. But through each other. Their future should not be clouded with sadness and grief. Mickey and I, Lloyd Wallace, send our love and best wishes to Danny and Allison.

"Do you see what you've done?" Mickey chimed. "Look up at the wall."

"Hold on to your hat," Lloyd said, already aware of it. "Let me try one more thing." Then Lloyd tapped the enter key. "Look," he said, feeling exceptionally pleased with himself, "when I hit the enter key, the program accepted what I just typed."

"What do you mean?" Mickey asked, still reeling from the high-tech crash course.

"Look at the computer screen. It's gone back to the three options. Watch. I'm going to pick the first one and print us a journal."

Lloyd reached for the small white-covered daily diary as it came out of the slot from the base of the computer. And when he opened it up, all the words he'd just typed were printed inside.

"Here," he said, handing it over to Mickey, "this one's for you. I think you should take it back to your room and keep it as a memento of what you accomplished today."

"Yeah … uh … thanks. I guess it'd be okay to keep this one," he said with a tone of innocence. "After all, today's journal on Allison won't really exist until tomorrow."

"So … do you want to type in any more dates or have you had enough for today?" Lloyd asked, satisfied with what they had both accomplished so far and willing to accommodate his friend's wish.

"I'm feeling too good right now to mess with it anymore," Mickey answered. "But could we come back up here tomorrow?"

"Oh, absolutely. How about right after breakfast?" Lloyd suggested. And the two men left the Data Room.

Lloyd and Mickey did return to the Data Room that following morning. They were stunned when they found that Allison's journal had revealed her first encounter with Danny took place the previous evening at Charlie's Bar and Grill. Both men wondered if Lloyd's experiment on the computer the day before was the reason why this incredulous get-together took place.

"Damn. This is unbelievable. Did we do this?" Mickey asked, feeling somewhat unnerved by the possibility.

"Hell if I know. It was pure speculation on my part that we could have any effect on what goes on back on Earth. But it sure looks like we did."

Lloyd quickly printed out the copy for Mickey, and then proceeded to call up his son's journal for that same day. "I'll be damned. It really looks like Danny and Allison could be moving right along into the relationship that I wrote about yesterday."

Then, noticing that Mickey still had a look of panic on his face, Lloyd whispered, "Hey, buddy, everything's fine. The kid's are happy with each other. You can't deny that after what we've just read. They swapped phone numbers. And that goodbye kiss. Why, they're a couple made in Heaven. Get it?"

Mickey knew Lloyd was trying to lighten his mood. "But this place isn't Heaven, is it? We're at Midway Manor, and we're foolin' with something we shouldn't be foolin' with."

"But we don't know that, Mick. This whole thing can be one hell of a coincidence. Besides, if we were doing something we shouldn't, don't you think we would've been called on it? They seem to know everything around here, right down to what size I take in goddamn underwear."

Feeling satisfied with his theory, Lloyd was willing to take the next step. "So ... how about I go ahead and type in something else for today? That's really the only way we could find out whether or not we're fooling with the future. Are you with me, or do you want me to try something entirely different?"

"I don't know. I need some time to think. I certainly didn't expect to read that my daughter would meet your son last night. Don't misunderstand me, please. I'm happy about their getting together. Your son seems to be quite a fine young man. But I'm going with my gut on this one. The words you typed into the computer yesterday caused it to happen. And—"

"And what? What's troubling you about it?" Lloyd asked, trying to show some respect for his feelings.

"I don't know," he said, searching for an answer. "I'm feeling like it has something to do with one person having power and control over someone else. And that doesn't sit well with me. It reminds me of my ex-wife and the really bad marriage we had."

Mickey shook his head and sighed, remembering how it was back then. "If things didn't always go her way, it'd lead to a shouting match. And when we'd argue, it always ended with her having the last word. The scene was always the same. Always. Then I'd go off and play my guitar in another room. I'd resigned myself to letting Margaret have the last word 'cause I was sick and tired of the bickering. I hated myself for being so damn submissive. And obviously she didn't like me much either because she eventually left and filed for divorce."

"I'm sorry, Mick," Lloyd said with sincerity. "I guess my own short-lived affairs with so many different women actually spared me from that kind of heartache and grief. When I was still married to Dorothy, my ex-wife, I didn't spend a whole lotta time at home, so there wasn't much opportunity to bicker. Not that I didn't give her good reason to give me hell. Maybe we did argue and I was too drunk to be aware of it. Anyway, I don't recall. For the most part, when Dorothy and I were together, things were pretty calm."

"But you got divorced for a reason. She must have been upset about something."

"Yeah, when she became aware of my ... uh ... indiscretions, the confrontation was actually civilized. She asked me if I'd been unfaithful, and I said yes. True, she'd been upset about it, and she cried a lot at the time. Then she told me she couldn't go on living like that … that we had to get a divorce. But aside from my own marriage, there were times when I envied certain couples whom I knew quite well. They seemed to be really close and loving in their relationships. From my perspective, their good days outweighed the bad a thousand to one."

Lloyd continued, referring back to Mickey's original concern about any one person having power and control over another. "But hey, we love our kids and neither one of us would do anything from this end to hurt them."

"I know you're right about that … but if you don't mind, I'd rather not do anything more for today. Maybe tomorrow."

The two shook hands and Mickey left the Data Room. Lloyd stayed on and found himself reading his son's journal from the day before over again. Perhaps Mickey didn't notice it but Lloyd was quite concerned, realizing that his son Danny hadn't shared his grief with Allison.

"Well, Mick, old buddy," Lloyd said to himself, "you didn't want us to do anything more with your daughter, and that's okay. But there's no one here to stop me from typing in today's date and foolin' around with a blank journal that belongs to Danny." Then he entered the date. And when the lighted screen went blank, he began typing:

Yesterday, my son Danny met a wonderful young woman. He should know that sharing his grief with Allison Parks would not jeopardize his new relationship with her in the least. In fact, his openness would bring them closer together. After all, she's lost her father, too. Together, there won't be time to dwell on their sorrows. Yes, their time well-spent with each other will bring them only joy.

Chapter Eight
Danny prepares for the funeral

"Brightside Publications. Look at the bright side."

Danny cringed as Jeanie's all-too-familiar words echoed in his ears. He quickened his pace down the hallway, his mind racing, trying to sort out his priorities for the day.

He stopped at the bullpen and called out to Harold Waters, the assistant managing editor, motioning for him to join him in his office. Harold was a short, wiry man with overly large hands. Danny wouldn't let more than a couple of weeks go by without kidding him about being the only guy he knew who could play baseball without the need for a glove.

But Danny depended heavily on Harold for keeping the flow of traffic going, for making sure that the other editors maintained a high quality of proofreading and copyediting, and for just generally making sure that all things ran smoothly.

He would also use Harold to bounce story ideas off of, and he was a whiz at headlines and cover titles. Also invaluable was Harold's "secret file" of photos he would get from the different wire services. He would have hundreds of photos sorted by category, and when Danny needed to illustrate a particular subject or theme, Harold was the man to call. "I need a guy in a speedboat with two bikini-clad girls flanking him," Danny would tell Harold, and Harold would come up with the photo. And if the guy in the speedboat had to have a beard, Mel the retoucher would oblige with his handy airbrush.

When Harold sat down in the chair facing Danny's desk, Danny wasted no time going over the running sheets for the three magazines that Harold handed him. On these sheets were the lists of articles for those particular issues, the various writers' names, the due dates taken from the master schedule for each phase of production, and the penciled-in dates as each task was completed. In other words, the dates when a manuscript arrived in house, when it was copyedited and sent out to the typographer, when first galley proofs were received, when proofs were corrected, when a layout went to the art department, when it was returned, when paste-ups were done, ad infinitum.

"Everything looks good," Danny said. "You have any problems that you need me for?"

Harold shook his head. "We're fine, Dan. Don't sweat it. I know you've got your hands full."

"Yeah, well, I've still gotta call Mom and break the news. And I've got to call Dad's girlfriend and find out about the funeral. She's taking care of all the details, thank God."

Harold nodded and left then, his big hands clutching the running sheets.

Danny decided to bite the bullet and get the hardest task over with first. That was the way he usually did everything. Take care of the most difficult or uncomfortable things first, then whatever comes after that will seem easy in comparison.

Danny's mother's voice sounded tired. "How are you, darling boy?" she said, perking up when she realized it was one of Danny's infrequent phone calls.

"I have some bad news, Mom," Danny said, trying to keep his voice from quavering. "Dad passed away on Wednesday."

There was silence at first as Dorothy Wallace digested the information. A panorama of her life flickered through her brain. She saw Lloyd Wallace as a young man, a handsome, ambitious newspaper reporter who kept himself immaculately groomed, who even wore a jacket and tie when he went to the beach. She saw him clearly as he swept her off her feet, wined and dined her, made incredibly passionate love to her, promised her the world.

She also saw him drinking to excess, coming home one night and scattering prophylactics across the front lawn. She saw him drunk often, turning up the radio to full volume, reeking with the strong smell of whiskey.

But worst of all, she saw the lipstick stains on his clothes, the evidence of his frequent transgressions with other women. And she remembered the hurt she felt, the betrayal.

"I'm sorry," Dorothy said finally. "Your father was my one and only true love." She paused for a moment. "I guess he'll be buried in Springtown, right?"

"Yes," Danny replied. "I'm in the process of working out the details now." He carefully avoided mentioning his father's girlfriend. "You wouldn't be interested in attending the funeral, would you?" he asked his mother warily.

"No," she said. "You know how bad my knee is. I wouldn't be up to traveling."

Danny breathed a sigh of relief after he hung up with his mother. Her presence at the funeral with Lloyd's girlfriend would have been a little too much to take. He now had to deal with his father's girlfriend.

"Hello, Susan," Danny spoke into the phone. "How you holdin' up?" He knew Susan Keating had been his dad's last sleep-in pal. She had been with his father for the last year or so, and had actually moved in with him, though his father had been more in the hospital than out of it over the past three years. Danny had only spoken to her twice, once when he had met Lloyd for a rare lunch date, and a second time on the phone.

"I'm okay, Danny," she said, "once the Valium kicks in. Are you all right?"

Danny stifled a choking reflex, faked a cough, and said he was hanging in there.

"As you may have been aware, your dad had wanted to be buried next to his parents back in Springtown," she said. "I'm on my way out the door to catch a plane. I've made all the arrangements by phone. He'll be laid out at Wilson's Funeral Home on State Street, and the funeral service will be held Sunday at the First Baptist Church on Puckett Avenue." She paused briefly, and then added, "It'll be closed casket, of course. He was pretty bad at the end ..." Her voice trailed off.

Danny swallowed hard, finding it difficult to speak.

"Danny," Susan said, her voice rising, "are you okay?"

"I'm good," Danny lied. "I'll fly out in the morning and see you at the funeral home."

He said goodbye and hung up, the image of Allison suddenly big in his head. The thought of her excited him, but he knew all of that would have to wait until he got back from Springtown.

Danny remembered the cheesecake spread and wondered how that was progressing for *Macho*. He walked down the hallway to the art department and entered the art director's large office. As usual, there were a number of people sitting or standing around.

Larry Roberts, the art director, stood behind his desk, talking on the phone and shuffling through sets of four-color progressive proofs, or progs, and making notations on them with his red pen.

In the old days, the magazines' cheesecake sections consisted of nothing more than black-and-white pinups in bikinis, standing next to a tree or running on the beach. Photos of women with exposed nipples was unheard of in the 1940s, '50s and early '60s, much less spread shots of full frontal nudity. Even *Playboy* didn't show pubic hair until the advent of *Penthouse*. And when *Hustler* showed up, well, the cat, or pussy, was out of the bag, so to speak.

A vendor from one of the stat houses was sitting in front of Larry's desk. When Larry laid out a new set of progs, the young vendor looked them over, smacking his lips as he gazed longingly at the gaping vulva in front of him.

"God," the vendor said, "could I eat that."

Without even blinking, Larry replied, "Go ahead. I've got an extra set of proofs."

Everybody laughed then and Danny slipped out, confident that Larry had the visual front under control.

Back in his office, Danny fought the urge to call Allison at work. He still had a lunch date with a writer that he didn't want to break. And he still had to make airline reservations, not to mention packing. Maybe he would call her from home later that night.

The day wore on. Lunch turned into three martinis and a very bad headache by 3:30. He sweet-talked Anna, Ralph Corona's secretary, into booking his flight to Chicago. He would rent a car when he arrived and drive out to Springtown from there.

Danny wrapped up a few last-minute loose ends and was able to leave the office by 5:40. He flagged a cab and headed uptown. By 6:20, he was in his apartment and Bratly was rubbing up against his leg, scolding him in her unique singsong feline voice.

Danny opened a can of cat food and spooned it out into Bratly's personal dish. It was tuna, her favorite, and she began lapping it up noisily, sounding more like a dog than a cat. Danny smiled, relieved that his cat was content, and thinking how nice things would be if people were so easily satisfied. He washed his hands at the kitchen sink, dried them with a paper towel, and walked into the bedroom to pack.

Later, Danny called Allison at home.

"Glad to know you made it through Friday," Allison said, happy to hear from Danny so soon.

"Just wanted you to know I'm leaving for Chicago in the morning and won't be back in town until Tuesday."

"Okay," said Allison. "Should I know what's in Chicago?"

"Actually, I'm going to Springtown, Illinois, to bury my dad," Danny suddenly blurted out. He tried to stay composed but he was aware of the trembling in his voice.

"I'm sorry, Danny," said Allison softly. "I didn't know …"

"It's all right. I'll get through this. But I really want to see you again. I'll call you after I get back, okay?"

"I'll look forward to it, Danny."

"Good night, Allison." Danny hung up, aware of the emotional roller coaster ride he'd been on since Wednesday, full of highs and lows. He wondered what would happen next.

Chapter Nine
Reflections of loved
ones left behind

The words that were typed into Allison's blank journal on Thursday had, as predicted, been replaced by the authentic version. For that reason, when Lloyd finished typing his excerpt that had gone into the blank journal belonging to Danny, he then printed out a copy of the faux white-covered diary.

Lloyd had planned to share what he had just finished writing with Mickey, and also hoped it would show some similarity to his son's actual activity for that Friday. As far as he was concerned, a second coincidence would further reinforce the theory that he and Mickey had the means to influence the future of their grown children. But this journal wouldn't be available for hours.

Lloyd remained fixed in front of the computer, his thinking now hampered by anticipation. After more than twenty years of sobriety, he still had that persistent voice inside his head urging him to have a drink whenever he felt anxious. Yet in the past, despite the fact that a drink was so obtainable in comparison to his rampant assignations, the promise of a woman who could give him that same heightened sense of gratification had always been worth the wait.

Worth the wait, he reflected, thinking of the many women he'd been with over the years. *But not worth the pain that it caused Dorothy.* He had never forgotten that very first time. The time when he had broken his promise to remain faithful to the woman he had married. *Dorothy never knew about that first time,* he remembered, *or that I'd vowed to myself at the time to spend the rest of my life making it up to her.*

But five years later, when Lloyd had faced the fact that the drive of his desires went far beyond both his will power and his idealistic intentions, he had packed his suitcase and left her for good. It had been the second of two choices Dorothy had given him in her ultimatum, the first being the impossible task of remaining sexually faithful to her.

I had to leave you, my dear sweet Dorothy, Lloyd admitted to himself. *It was the only way I could stop hurting you. And Danny, my God, that innocent little boy who'd already witnessed way too much. I still believe that my leaving gave both of you a second chance for a better life. A life without me and all the pain I had caused.*

Lloyd, though he had still believed that the separation from his wife and son had been for the best, now ached to be an integral part of his son's future. He focused back at the computer screen and began typing in dates and printing out Danny's daily journals that covered the previous two weeks. When he had finished printing the last journal, he shut down the computer. He carefully gathered together all the diaries and then headed off to the confines of his private room on the first floor.

Earlier, Mickey had returned to his own room after leaving Lloyd in the Data Room, bringing back with him the copy of Allison's diary for that Thursday. He had kept the first diary, the one from Wednesday, and also saved the journal in which Lloyd had typed in his own words.

Mickey read each of the three journals over and over again. *We did it. We made it happen,* he thought to himself, still convinced that he and Lloyd were responsible for bringing Allison and Danny together. He then picked up one of the journals and pressed it against his chest. *My dear Allison, forgive me for interfering in your life,* he thought, *but I'm delighted you've met Lloyd's son. You should have someone in your life. Someone you can love and who will love you in return.*

Mickey moved the diary away from his chest and attentively placed it back on the desk next to the other two journals. With his right hand still in contact with the white cover, he frowned when he recalled what he had read about his daughter having some concerns working with a new managing editor.

"You know," he said aloud, wishing Allison could really hear him, his parental role awakening, "you've had more than enough grief dealing with your mother's neurotic attitude. You really don't need to be working with someone like that Kate person if she isn't going to treat you with respect. You're too damn good at what you do and you deserve better."

Mickey also remembered what he had read in Danny's journal, having had the opportunity to examine his day's events when it was displayed on the double-sided wall screen. He had read it from beginning to end before Lloyd printed a copy for himself. *Danny actually works for some men's magazines,* Mickey recalled. *But Lloyd told me ... the first day I'd met him ... that his son is real smart. So why the heck is Danny wasting his time on that sex trash? Lloyd can't be feeling any too good about this.*

Mickey had dismissed the idea that Allison should consider getting away from Kate Ripley and relocate to New Jersey to be near her friend Marlene. *No. Not a good idea,* he had thought, *not a good idea at all. I really want to see Allison and Danny spend more time with each other, and if she moved to Jersey, that would just ruin everything.*

Mickey didn't quite understand why he had such positive feelings about Danny. After all, he didn't really know him. He had concluded that it probably had to do with the strong bond that so quickly developed between Lloyd and himself.

Ain't it something that Danny lives with that little cat? he thought, smiling to himself. *Allison's always wanted one, even when she was a little girl. But her mother hated cats.*

Yeah, that's right, he remembered. *I had forgotten about that. Margaret hated cats. She was the only person I ever knew who actually used the word hate whenever anyone even mentioned the furry little creatures.*

Mickey turned in his chair to face Allison's photo that was sitting on top of his dresser, clearly remembering what happened when Allison was older and had moved into her own apartment. "You were so adamant about my moving in with you after Margaret left. And you still didn't get yourself a cat because you were too worried about my allergies acting up. Bless your sweet heart," Mickey said, kissing his fingers and then blowing the kiss across the room directly at her photo.

Mickey realized he was actually feeling more at peace with himself. Spending time in his room reading Allison's journals and reflecting on everything that had taken place since Lloyd's arrival on Wednesday did make a difference.

He suddenly became aware that he was hungry. *Dinnertime*, he thought. The Manor had even seen to it that its residents still experienced an appetite. He looked forward to treating himself to a large, juicy T-bone steak and departed for the dining room.

As usual, there were only a few residents scattered throughout the banquet room. Mickey stopped by Mary Jenkins' table to say hello. "How ya doing this evening?" Mickey inquired.

"I'm doing well, thank you," Mary responded, her tight silver curls gleaming as brightly as her smile. "Another long day for me at the computer. Thought I'd take a break before going back up there," she said, knowing that Mickey was always respectful of her daily, all-consuming schedule in the Data Room.

Mary had chosen Midway Manor as her destination because of her forty-year marriage to Max, her lifetime companion who was still in a coma at Larkin Hospital, in Minnesota.

Max and Mary had been in a car accident. Mary was pronounced dead before the ambulance arrived at the hospital. Her husband had fallen into a coma right after emergency surgery was performed, the doctors reporting a very slim chance that he would ever come out of it. Ironically, Mary spent hours at the computer every day because Max's daily diaries would record all his thoughts.

Mary would read all about the different thoughts and memories that ran through Max's mind while he himself remained lifelessly asleep in his hospital bed. Most of what she had read about each day, however, were memories that she herself had long forgotten. And thus, Mary would spend hours researching their past until she found exactly what he had been thinking about.

"I'm going to have the T-bone tonight," Mickey said, but his thinking followed a different course. *How lucky your husband was, Mary, to have lived with a woman who was so loving and sweet. And still quite attractive for her age of seventy-two.*

"Good for you," Mary replied, smiling. "Isn't it wonderful that we don't have to worry about calories or cholesterol or any of those things anymore? And as far as the meat is concerned, they told us no animals were actually slaughtered."

"That's so true. And now I'm even able to enjoy a good steak without worrying about my dentures slipping," Mickey added. He would never forget what had happened that first morning after arriving at the Manor. Those same dentures that had flopped around in his mouth while back on Earth had become permanent fixtures. It was quite a scene that morning, watching himself in the mirror as he kept tugging at his new permanent set of teeth and saying to himself, "What the hell?"

Mickey called out a friendly hello to several other residents as he walked over to his usual table, not realizing that Lloyd had come in while he chatted with Mary and was already seated at Mickey's table.

Mickey was pleased to see Lloyd. "Let me get my dinner and then I'll join you," he said as he passed by him, heading for the buffet. Lloyd had already filled his plate and waited for Mickey to return.

"The steak is excellent," Lloyd said, noticing that Mickey had made the same choice, "… and that woman you were talking to when I came in? Has she been here a while?"

"Ah, yes, you mean Mary Jenkins. I'd say about a year. Her husband's in a coma back in Minnesota, and she spends most of her time at the computer."

Mickey continued, assuming that Lloyd would want to know who was who in the dining room that evening. "You see those two guys sitting at the table over there? Well, the one wearing the blue sweater is Sam and the young fellow sitting with him is Jimmy.

"Then there's that group of ladies. The four of them are sitting all together. Trish is the redhead. Jean's the one dressed in black. Myrna's the one doing all the gesturing with her hands. The fourth is actually Myrna's sister, Tina, the real quiet one. Oh, yeah, and the old fellow sitting way back there by himself is Burt."

"What about that white-haired couple over there?" Lloyd inquired, pointing to an unusually attractive older man and woman sharing a table together. They sat deeply engrossed in an intimate conversation, seemingly indifferent to the people around them.

"Yeah. The Holloways. I don't really know their first names. Awful thing that was … the two of 'em suddenly showing up here at the same time. Some kind of accident, but I don't know much about the details. They haven't been around very long."

Mickey, having been a three-year veteran, thought he would eventually find out about the Holloways, but that opportunity never came as the couple would disappear as suddenly as they had arrived. Since his own arrival, he had gotten acquainted with just about everyone who had come to the Manor. He not only knew their names, but each of their personal histories, too. He could easily say he liked everyone he had met, or at the very least felt comfortable talking to them.

For Mickey, this pleasant social opportunity had rarely presented itself back on Earth. He had spent the better part of his life feeling isolated and inadequate. He often defended himself to family members and friends, to his ex-wife, and even to contemporaries in the business world. But he remained fixed and determined that the one thing he did right in his life was to raise his daughter with love and understanding, to be there for her under any circumstances.

"You know, Mick," Lloyd said with sincerity, "Maybe I haven't been here long enough, but I look at myself and I look at you. Then I look around at everyone else in this room, and I just can't get used to the fact that we're all dead."

Chapter Ten
Journal tampering

"You what? You can't believe we're all dead?" Mickey had said to Lloyd while they were having dinner together the previous evening. "Let me enlighten you. No one here is *dead*. You need to take a look in your copy of the Manor's dictionary. Everyone's got one. Don't you have a set of books in your room?"

"Why yes, as a matter of fact I do," Lloyd had answered, recalling that first evening when he had not been able to satisfy his curiosity about what books were on the shelves. "You know, I was going to check them out when I first arrived, but I'd fallen asleep on the recliner after that fabulous scent of lilacs had floated through the room. And, to tell you the truth, with all this business with the computer and the kids' journals, I just haven't found the time to look them over."

It was early Saturday morning when Lloyd finally pulled out his copy of the Manor's dictionary. He carefully flipped the pages until his finger had come to rest at the word "death." The definition read:

A term used on Earth for the termination of a life form. The proper description of "death" should unconditionally be translated in The Scripture as the pure and simple act of the natural transformation from the physical body to one of a complete spiritual nature. There are, however, destinations in the hereafter such as Midway Manor, Reunion Valley and the City of Lights that will grant the spirit the perception of the physical earthly form.

Lloyd was not entirely in agreement with the definition. Death was much more than a natural transformation of his life form. It was a permanent and final separation of the accumulation of sixty-three years—his family, friends, coworkers, and his life's work in publishing. And Danny.

"I don't have time for any more of this," Lloyd said aloud to himself, his son's image filling his head. He replaced the dictionary on the shelf, noticing the titles of some of the other books: *Earth's Unsolved Mysteries Revealed (For Manor Residents' Perusal Only)*, *Basic Guidelines for Using Midway Manor's Data Room Computers,* and *Destinations in the Afterworld, a Manor Resident Primer.* Lloyd made a mental note to examine these books in depth at a later date, and hurried off to the Data Room. He was anxious to find out whether anything he had written in Danny's blank journal for Friday had actually taken place.

"I'm proud of you, son," Lloyd declared as he read Danny's journal. "Telling that sweet girl *why* you'd be out of town until next Tuesday was exactly what I wanted you to do. And she'll be earnestly waiting for your return. I guarantee it."

Then, one by one, Lloyd called up blank journals for the next few days and proceeded to type in his heartfelt desires and some guiding principles for Danny to follow. He reasoned it was imperative that his son get through the long weekend and the funeral with a minimum of stress and sorrow. Lloyd typed in a few memories for Danny to conjure up that would bring a smile to his face, in spite of the tears. He had also added a line that his son should find it in his heart to comfort Susan, Lloyd's girlfriend, who had been there for Lloyd during such difficult times in the past months.

Lloyd deliberately didn't retrieve a blank journal for the following Tuesday, the day his son would be returning to Manhattan. He had wanted to check with Mickey first. "Damn," he said aloud, realizing how long he had been sitting at the computer and that he had completely forgotten Mickey was waiting for him in the dining room. He shut down the computer and hurried off.

"Well, I'm a believer, now," Lloyd said, sharing the results of Friday's events with Mickey, who sat at the breakfast table with him. "We can definitely influence the direction of Danny's and Allison's lives."

"Glad you finally caught up with my own thinking," Mickey responded with a grin and a tone of approval. "I figured it out when the kids met each other two days ago."

Mickey poured himself a second cup of coffee, taking a moment to gather his thoughts. "You know," he said, "I've read Allison's diaries dozens of times and one thing I'm not happy about is my daughter's having to work for some managing editor who fires people for no good reason. I've thought long and hard about what I can do for her to make things better, but I haven't been able to come up with anything that seems right. The only thing I'm sure of is that I'm real happy Danny and Allison have met and I want them to keep seeing each other."

"I agree," Lloyd said. "But Danny's left today to attend my funeral in Springtown, Illinois, and he won't be back until sometime on Tuesday. I figured, if you want, we both could write something in the kids' blank journals for that Tuesday to be sure that they get right back together again. Are you with me?"

"Absolutely," Mickey answered. "You said Springtown, Illinois? Well, ain't that something. I'd lived just a couple of hundred miles from there with my wife for almost a year before we moved to Connecticut. In fact, Margaret had just found out she was pregnant with Allison when we'd left. But getting back to the kids, do we have to wait until Monday to write anything up?"

"Oh no, that's not necessary at all. This morning I was able to call up blank journals for the next few days while Danny's away. So I'd say that we could type in any future date we want to get a blank journal."

"So what are we waiting for? Let's do it."

"Yeah, sure. But first let me spell out what I'm really saying about them getting together again," Lloyd said, cautiously approaching the bottom line. "All right then, first thing we have to do is get into both Danny's and Allison's blank journals. We've got to make sure they wind up as a couple."

"I already got that part," Mickey interrupted. "And what?"

"We have them ... well ... how can I put it delicately? We get them to, uh, consummate the relationship."

"You mean write in their blank journals that they do it, that they have sex?"

"I couldn't have said it more gracefully."

"Well, just because they have sexual relations doesn't mean they'll continue as a couple. People do have sex and then go their own merry way."

"I think we've read enough to prove that the sexual tension is already there between them. Doing what comes naturally may not keep them together, but it will calm them down. After that, I think they'll have a chance to appreciate each other's various qualities, which will nurture the relationship and help it to grow. And, of course, we'll keep up with what they're doing by reading their daily journals and continue to write in the blank ones as we see fit.

"And I hope that first thing Wednesday morning we can confirm Danny and Allison's, uh, merger Tuesday night. Meantime, let's go upstairs to the Data Room and get the ball rolling right now."

Mickey watched Lloyd as he slipped into the chair in front of the computer and began flicking switches and typing in commands on the keyboard. He marveled at how adept Lloyd had become with this new technology in such a short time. For Mickey, who had a difficult enough time with mere typing, the whole thing was simply magic.

"Okay, I've got Danny's journal for Tuesday on the screen," said Lloyd. "Let me type in the scenario."

On the evening of Danny's return to Manhattan, he should spend every waking moment with the lovely young woman, Allison. Let their encounter begin with his hand gently touching hers. This touch will mark the conclusion of their empty, loveless lives. And the beginning of an endless and deepening love between them. The nightfall will find them united as one.

Lloyd let Mickey read what he wrote in the journal before hitting Enter. Mickey pondered over it for a few minutes, reading and rereading what Lloyd had written.

"Is that what they call purple prose?" Mickey said, chuckling.

"Are you okay with it?"

"Yeah, of course. Punch it in."

Lloyd hit the Enter key and then called up Allison's blank journal for that Tuesday. The men exchanged seats and Lloyd patiently waited and watched as Mickey typed in a similar scenario, one letter at a time.

After he was done, Lloyd sat back down and printed out the journals, handing Mickey his daughter's version.

The manipulation of Danny and Allison had begun. And the most important, life-altering intervention still lay ahead—an extraordinary gift intended to eventually secure their future happiness forever. But the dads never figured on danger from the Dark Side.

The ominous, dark storm clouds filled the night sky, threatening to empty their contents on the small town of Hobart near the eastern border of Tennessee. Flashes of lightning shot across the sky, followed quickly by claps of thunder. The loud booms muffled the screams of the little boy in the weathered, one-bedroom cabin isolated on the outskirts of town.

"No! Daddy, don't hit me!" *pleaded ten-year-old Caleb. The fiery redheaded boy cowered in a corner, his small arms failing to protect his young body from the blows of his enraged father.*

"Lyin' little heathen!" *the boy's father bellowed.*

"I'm not lying," *Caleb yelled, sobbing.* "I saw Mommy again … she comes to me when I'm sleeping. She … she says she's in a place called Midnight Manor and that she's watching over me."

"Blasphemy!" *roared the father, lashing out at the child.* "There's no such place, you hear! I'll beat you 'til you're dead!"

"But it's true, Daddy!" *Caleb continued to sob uncontrollably.*

"You hear me, boy! I'll beat you 'til you're dead!"

Chapter Eleven
Danny buries his dad

Danny's flight got him back to LaGuardia Airport late Tuesday afternoon. He barely listened to the cab driver going on about the state of the economy and how it was getting harder and harder to make a decent living.

Danny played back the weekend's events in his mind, how he had suddenly developed a cough during the service and couldn't stop hacking until it was time to leave for the cemetery.

Lloyd Wallace's funeral had indeed been closed casket, and the church was packed with Springtown natives who had known Lloyd when he lived there in his earlier years. There were a few people from Lloyd's newspaper who had made the trip out from New York. And, of course, Susan, his dad's girlfriend, was also there. She showed no emotion until they had arrived at the cemetery. It was then that she had broken down and wept.

Danny had stood alongside Susan, his arm around her in an attempt at consolation. He barely knew her but he felt it was the right thing to do. Later, after Susan and everyone else had left, Danny had remained at graveside. He had stood there alone, head bowed, hands clasped in front of him, his thoughts tracing the earlier part of his life.

He remembered the expression on his dad's intense but smiling face as he would literally bang out a song on the piano. Danny knew his dad played mostly by ear but he could not recall whether he had actually been able to read music.

Lloyd Wallace also used the typewriter in much the same way he played the piano, though not with all his fingers. He would jab fast and furiously at his beat-up old Royal with two or three fingers of each hand. Danny had never learned how to play the piano, but his typing style was the same as his dad's. Over the years, coworkers would tease Lloyd, and subsequently Danny, about their typing abilities, but in fact both were faster and more accurate than most of their contemporaries.

Danny remembered the last time he had been to Springtown. They were there to bury Lloyd's mother, Danny's grandmother. They had driven back to Chicago after the funeral with Lloyd's brother, Uncle Edward.

Edward Wallace was ten years older than Lloyd and several inches shorter than Lloyd's five-foot-ten-inch frame. But what Edward lacked in height, he made up for in his distinguished appearance and reserved demeanor. The antithesis of Lloyd's glad-handing, free-speaking manner, Edward never spoke unless he had something to say. Which no doubt was helpful in his job with a hush-hush government agency.

But Edward's quiet reserve belied a wonderfully dry, almost mischievous sense of humor. Danny recalled the morning of the funeral. The three of them had stayed at the Windsor Inn, Springtown's fifty-five-year-old downtown hotel. Danny and his father had shared a room, while Edward had taken a room across the hall. On the morning of the funeral, Danny and Lloyd left the room dressed appropriately in dark suits and ties. They had walked across the hall and knocked on the door of Edward's room.

"What? What time is it?" the muffled voice on the other side of the door said. And Danny remembered how rattled his father had been that Edward had overslept and wasn't ready to leave for the funeral.

"My God, Ed," Danny's father had yelled through the door. "How could you do this?"

Danny smiled as he remembered how the door had swung slowly open then, revealing Uncle Edward standing there, fully dressed, resplendent in dark suit and tie, long open dress coat, wide-brimmed hat, and the longest cigar Danny had ever seen protruding from his mouth.

"You guys ready?" Uncle Edward said, an impish grin on his face.

Danny also recalled the scene at the airport waiting room. It had been extremely crowded as usual, and many attractive women passed by the three men who sat together. Lloyd noticed how intently Danny eyed each of the passing young women and had commented, "You can't ball them all, Danny."

This from a man who had certainly made a valiant attempt to do just that. Danny had smiled to himself when he remembered the incident, thinking how that had been the last time the three of them were together. He also thought about how interested his dad had been in so many things: music, especially Dixieland jazz; outer space, and how excited he had been when Russia put Sputnik into orbit; being a ham radio operator and talking with people all over the world. And his writing—he suspected his dad probably had an unfinished novel lying around someplace.

"Goodbye, Dad," Danny had said finally, not bothering to wipe the steady stream of tears from his cheeks. "I love you. Maybe I'll see you again in another life."

The taxi lurched to an abrupt halt, bringing Danny back to the present. He peered out through the cab window and saw that they had arrived at his apartment building. He paid the cabbie the fare, which Danny considered the equivalent of a sizable ransom, then waited while the driver took his suitcase from the trunk and placed it on the sidewalk.

"How ya doin', Mr. Wallace," said Neil the doorman as he grabbed Danny's bag and opened the large glass door for him. "How was your trip?"

"Just fine," Danny said. He hadn't told Neil about his father. The last thing he needed was a bunch of people telling him how sorry they were. Danny preferred to grieve in solitude.

Upstairs, after closing his apartment door, Danny's whole body seemed to cave in. He took off his jacket and draped it over the back of a chair, then let himself fall backward into the couch. Bratly jumped up next to him and began her scolding tirade, telling Danny how awful it had been for the past three days. He pulled the little cat closer to him and began to cry softly, telling her that everything was going to be all right. She began to purr, her small body vibrating in his arms, and Danny wept until he dozed off.

The phone startled Danny awake. He listened while the answering machine took over. "You've reached me but I'm not here. You know what to do after the beep."

"Hi," the feminine voice said. "It's Allison. Maybe you remember me from last week. Just wanted to know if you were okay. Give me a call when you get in." There was a long pause. "I know this sounds weird, since we hardly know each other ... but I ... uh ... miss you." Click.

Danny smiled as he remembered Allison's long dark hair, flashing brown eyes and pouty lips. He felt a stirring in his loins as he envisioned the rest of her exquisite body pressed up against his. *Nothing like a woman to get your mind off unpleasant things,* he thought.

Bratly's incessant whining brought Danny back to reality. He went into the kitchen and took a can of cat food from the cabinet. Bratly rubbed up against his pants leg as the can opener noisily sliced open the metal container. He spooned out the contents into a clean dish and picked up the old cat dishes encrusted with bits of dried up cat food. He made a mental note to thank Vickie from 6A across the hall for coming in and feeding Bratly while he was gone.

While Bratly lapped up the cat food as if she hadn't been fed in a week, Danny tossed some ice cubes into a highball glass and poured himself an overly generous portion of vodka. There wasn't any more tonic water left in the fridge, but that didn't deter Danny. He was drinking for effect, not taste.

The alcohol did its job quickly and Danny relaxed as he felt the warmth spread throughout his body. He went back into the living room and fished out his wallet from the inside jacket pocket. He found Allison's business card and dialed her number.

"Hello." Her voice sounded scratchy, as if she hadn't been able to clear her throat.

"Hi, it's Danny. Is this a bad time? I hope I didn't interrupt your dinner."

"Oh, hi, Danny. No, I was just thinking about dinner and how much I don't feel like cooking." Danny noticed her voice had immediately lost its scratchiness. She suddenly sounded alert and excited.

"Well, that makes two of us," Danny said. "You wanna grab a bite together?"

"Are you asking me out on a date, Mr. Wallace?"

Danny chuckled. "Yeah, I guess I am."

"Where and when?" Allison asked.

"Do you like Italian?"

"What's not to like?"

"Great," Danny said, smiling into the phone, his grief almost forgotten for the moment. "There's this wonderful Italian restaurant on West Forty-fifth, Johnny's, right across from where the old Peppermint Lounge used to be. Know the place?"

"I'm not familiar with Johnny's, but I had a drink at the Peppermint Lounge once."

"Well, that's long gone. It's just another run-of-the-mill watering hole now."

"My car's in the shop, Danny. Do you want to meet at Johnny's? I could take a cab."

"Why don't *I* get a cab and come to your place and pick you up?" Danny said.

"Nah. That's not necessary. You can take me home in a cab *after* dinner."

Danny was instantly aroused. *Green light,* he thought. "Okay," he said, checking his watch. "I'll meet you there about seven-thirty."

Johnny's was a small, intimate Italian restaurant known for its good food. There were fewer than two dozen small tables, but they were covered with immaculate, bright red tablecloths and matching cloth napkins. In New York, this is one of the standards by which all restaurants are measured. A place could have good food, but paper napkins earn it a negative vote. This is not to say that cloth napkins alone will render a place "in." The food also has to be excellent, and Johnny's fit the bill and then some. The lighting was subdued, offering a pleasant ambiance that complemented the excellent culinary experience.

In the front near the door there was a small bar with five or six well-upholstered bar stools sporting comfortable backs. Danny had spent many lost afternoons and evenings sitting at this bar, swapping sea stories with Big Red the bartender. Whenever he would try to leave, Red would offer him another drink. "Hey, Dan, have one more with me," Big Red would say. And Danny would shake his head and mumble something about having to get back. But Red would already be pouring the vodka freely into a glass and saying, "A taste, Dan. Just a taste." And Dan would be hooked. He'd sit there and drink until his legs went numb.

Allison was sitting at the bar when Danny arrived. Big Red had served her one of his patented dry Manhattans and she was already feeling giddy.

Danny sat down next to her, trying to identify the strange feeling that had taken over his mind and body. This woman was different, he knew. He felt an attraction to her unlike he'd had with any other woman he had ever known. He had felt compelled to call her when he got back, and would have done so even if she hadn't called him first. In fact, everything he had done so far with her, everything he had said, every move he had made was compulsive. He was addicted to Allison, for God's sake, and he hadn't even slept with her yet.

Danny smiled and said hello. Allison smiled back, her right hand holding the bar cushion. Danny placed his hand over hers. He looked up at Big Red and ordered an extra dry vodka martini, straight up with an olive.

"I took the liberty of telling them we were dining here tonight," Allison said as the maitre d' approached. Danny nodded his approval.

"I'll have your drinks brought over right away," said the maitre d', and they followed the man to their table off in the corner.

Two Manhattans and two martinis later, Allison and Danny were holding hands and gazing intently into each other's eyes. They both had ordered Veal Oscar and, as promised, the meal was exquisite.

"You may not want to talk about it, but I have to ask," said Allison softly. "Did the funeral and everything go okay?"

"Yes ... I got through it."

"I lost my dad three years ago. We'd been very close." She paused for a moment, hesitating, not sure if she should continue. "I ... uh ... I think ... I've got this feeling he's trying to contact me now."

"What do you mean?" Danny wasn't sure he heard her correctly.

"It's little things. A song on the radio. A candle flickering. That sort of thing. But lately, I've been feeling he's right nearby."

Danny laughed nervously. He didn't want to insult Allison, but he wasn't one to buy into, as he put it, all that ghostly hocus-pocus. He tried to be respectful. "What's he saying about me?"

"Nothing yet, but I'm sure he'd approve."

"I think my dad would do a thumbs-up on you, too."

Later, in the back of the taxi, Danny held Allison close. They kissed finally, long and passionately, their tongues fencing, exploring the newness of each other.

I can't believe I'm feeling the way I feel, Allison thought. *This isn't just a physical attraction. There's something else going on.*

They resumed the kiss when they got inside Allison's Victorian-decorated apartment. Allison finally managed to break free and push Danny down onto the sofa. "Let me get us something to drink," she said, kicking off her high heels and heading for the kitchen. She retrieved a bottle of brandy she had been saving for a special occasion and handed it to Danny along with two brandy snifters.

"You like Paul Whiteman?" she asked as she padded over to the stereo.

"Love the guy," Danny fibbed, not sure of the name.

Allison put on a stack of records and flicked the switch. She came back to the sofa and cuddled in close to Danny as the dulcet strains of Whiteman's "Old Rockin' Chair" filled the room.

What is it with this man? Allison thought. *Why am I so attracted to him? It's not just sex. I actually feel something else for him, something stronger than mere sexual attraction. What's happening to me? Why do I just want to hold him and never let go?*

Danny held on to Allison tightly, feeling her softness as she snuggled into the crook of his arm. Despite the alcohol both had consumed, he could smell the fragrance of her and it almost made him swoon. *My God,* he thought. *What's going on with me? Sure, I want to go to bed with her. But this is something very different. I've never felt anything like it with any other woman. Is this love?*

Allison thought her heart was going to explode. Danny was making her tingle all over. At the moment, she felt there was nothing more important in her life than being with Danny. She opened her mouth over his, kissing him deeply. She knew she had crossed over the point of no return, and wanted Danny inside her more than she had wanted anything in her life.

Danny looked into her beautiful dark brown eyes and saw her desire. He realized they had gone too far to make it to the bedroom. In the state they both were in, the bedroom may as well have been in Central Park.

He began unbuttoning her blouse, trying to restrain himself from moving too fast. *What was this girl doing to him?* His thoughts were racing, competing for dominance with his hormones. And then Allison was helping him slip off her skirt. His eyes drank in the loveliness of her beautiful skin covered only by the black-lace bra and sheer bikini panties. He literally tore off his shirt as Allison fumbled with his belt buckle.

She unzipped his pants, emitting an "Oh!" when her hand inadvertently brushed against the hardness hidden only by the thin cloth of his jockey underwear. *What the hell is happening with me?* Allison wondered. *I'm the gal who wasn't going to let any man get close to me.*

Danny thought he sensed a hesitation in Allison, an ever-so-subtle pulling away. He kissed her gently then, letting the warm, loving feeling he had for her translate through his lips. He felt it, and hoped she would feel it, too.

When they were both naked, Danny could see, even in the dim light, that Allison was more beautiful than he had imagined. He turned on his side and wrapped his arms around her, delighting in her cool, bare skin touching his. Allison trembled as she felt Danny's engorged manhood throbbing against her.

Danny began to explore Allison's body with his mouth, first nuzzling her neck, then moving down to kiss her breasts lightly. When his lips and tongue finally found the soft, downy mound between her legs, Allison moaned softly.

"Now!" she gasped, and Danny moved over and entered her, slowly sliding his rigid manhood deep inside her. *This isn't happening,* Allison tried to convince herself. *It's just a dream.*

Danny's thoughts had conceded to his hormones. He began to thrust gently, building to a steady rhythm. He looked into her eyes and saw that they were wide open with undisguised joy, and he kissed her then, tasting the sweetness of her lips as he continued thrusting.

Allison met Danny's deep thrusts with her own, and when they reached a climax, it was in unison, with wave after wave of pure ecstasy rippling through their bodies.

"Danny!" she cried out softly. *God, I've never felt so loved by a man.*

Danny was too exhausted to think clearly, but he knew in his heart that this woman—this complex bundle of beauty and passion and intelligence—was indeed his soul mate.

And then, locked in each other's arms, they both fell into a deep, satisfying sleep.

Destiny was in firm control, and Destiny's real name was Mickey Parks and Lloyd Wallace.

Chapter Twelve
Look at the Bright Side

The aroma of freshly brewed coffee made Danny instantly aware of his strange surroundings. Obviously, Allison had gotten up early and was in the kitchen. He got up, pulled on yesterday's jockey shorts and padded barefoot into the bathroom, making sure to lift the toilet seat before he relieved himself. Though still only half awake, Danny took note of the antique porcelain figurine of an angel sitting on the Victorian lacework covering the top of the toilet tank.

He moved to the sink and washed his hands, splashing water on his face before reaching for a hand towel. Looking into the mirror, he winced when he saw the bloodshot eyes and splotched red face peering back at him.

He walked into the kitchen and saw Allison standing at the sink, rinsing off two coffee cups and placing them in the dish drainer. He walked up and wrapped his arms around her from behind. She had already taken a shower and was fully dressed in black slacks and a red velour top.

"Good morning, sunshine," he said, kissing her on the side of her neck.

Allison smiled and kissed him back. "You look like you've been through a hurricane," she said. "I guess you need a cup of coffee. Milk and sugar are on the table."

"I'll tell you what I need," said Danny. "Got any vodka?"

Allison wasn't very shocked by the question. She'd dated a few heavy drinkers in her time and knew all about the hair-of-the-dog remedy.

"You want it straight, Binky?" she asked almost mockingly, "or do you need to mix it with something."

"Tomato juice or OJ would be good."

"I've got both in the fridge. Help yourself." She opened one of the cupboards, took out an almost full fifth of vodka and placed it on the table.

Danny chose the orange juice and poured it into a glass, mixing it with a hefty shot of vodka. He chugged half of it down immediately and waited for the warming glow that would follow momentarily. In a few minutes he felt better.

"Put the vodka away, please," he said. "I'm okay now and I don't want to overshoot my mark. I've got to get into the office and get some work done."

"Let me show you around the apartment first," Allison said, proud of the Victorian motif and her decorating abilities.

She took him by the hand and led him into the living room. Danny couldn't help but wonder how he and Allison had actually made love and then slept on the stiffly upholstered Victorian sofa. No wonder his back hurt.

Allison picked up the needlepoint throw pillows and placed them back on the red sofa, then retrieved the black velour throw, folded it and draped it over the arm of the sofa. On a table next to the sofa was an antique gold-framed photo of Allison and a man whom Danny guessed to be her father. Next to that was a large white candle.

Danny smiled his approval when Allison pointed out the curio cabinet housing her collection of porcelain cats, then noticed there were doilies everywhere, with velvet and lace curtains on all the windows.

Danny appreciated the décor. His mother had been very fond of antiques and had filled their home with them.

Danny also noticed the piles of audiocassette tapes next to a tape recorder.

"That's what I use to talk to my dad in a kind of self-help therapy," Allison explained. "I know you won't believe this, but I thought I felt his presence the other night. I had told him I loved him and the candle had flickered right at that moment. The lights also dimmed and I heard a snapping sound like electricity. I swear he was with me then."

"I try to keep an open mind," said Danny, "but ghostly spirits aren't part of my set of firm beliefs." Danny tried hard not to say anything that might offend Allison, but he didn't want to pretend he believed in something he didn't.

"I'll tell you something else," said Allison. "I think he's somehow influencing my life."

"C'mon now, you know how crazy that sounds?"

"I'm serious. Lots of people, including yourself I'm sure, wonder why they do certain things, why they make certain decisions. Don't you ever wonder about fate and why events happen the way they happen?"

"Yeah, I do, but the only spirits I blame are those that come in a bottle. Usually it's because I drank too much, like last night."

"Oh, so what happened last night was just a drunken mistake?" Allison seemed hurt.

"God no, Allison." He put his arms around her and kissed her tenderly. "What happened last night was the most wonderful thing I've ever experienced."

Allison melted in Danny's arms, relieved to hear his soothing words. *I don't know what's happened to me,* she thought, *but I'm absolutely hooked on this guy.*

"Mark my words, **Danny Wallace**, there's something going on and Mickey Parks, my **father, is** involved."

Danny chased the alcohol with a cup of black coffee, showered and got dressed, not too happy with wearing the previous day's underwear. He kissed Allison goodbye and promised to call.

"I'd like you to come over to my place and meet Bratly," he said, and Allison nodded her agreement.

Danny hit the street just before 9:00, miraculously flagging down a cab within minutes. He arrived at Brightside Publications about twenty minutes later, whisking right by Jeanie with a talk-to-you-later wave. He sat down in his office and put his head in his hands, again recapping the events that had transpired over the last few days. It was hard to shake Allison's beautiful Natalie Wood face from his mind.

He began to sort through the memos, while-you-were-out slips and several pages of titles, blurbs and captions Harold had left on his desk for approval.

Danny looked up when he heard the knock on his open door. Gary Felson, one of the associate editors, stood in the doorway.

"Hi, Danny," Gary said. "Sorry to hear about your loss."

"Yeah ... well ... thanks, Gary. C'mon in."

"I hate to start your day off bitching, but I've had it up to here with this goddamn writer."

"Which writer would that be, Gary?" Danny asked, aware that there were more than a few of Brightside freelancers with idiosyncrasies that irritated the hell out of his editors.

"Bob Hanover, the sonofabitch. He never leaves any margins on the sides, he types right down to the very bottom of the goddamn page, and he hits the keys so hard that they bang right through and all the O's make holes in the paper, for crissakes. How am I expected to copyedit the damn thing? Can't you talk to him?"

"I have, Gary. Many times. But I'll give it another shot."

After Gary went back to the bullpen, Danny made his first call of the day. He needed to confirm his lunch date with Samantha Hodges, an agent who provided Danny with at least a third of the manuscripts he needed each month for his magazines. She was a nice woman with orange hair, whose ability to juggle sentences on the order of "I know you think you understand what you thought I said, but what you don't understand is that what you heard is not what I meant" would seem to qualify her for a high-ranking position in the federal government.

"Hi, Sam," Danny said into the phone. "Are we still on for lunch at Chances?"

"Yes, dear," replied Samantha. "But we'd better make it for around twelve-thirty instead of noon because my car's in the shop getting a new water pump and I can't pick it up before noon because—"

"Sam," Danny interrupted, "twelve-thirty is just fine. I've gotta go. See you at Chances." Danny hung up then, suddenly realizing he was thinking about a martini. Samantha and Brightside are prime candidates for lending incentive to alcohol consumption.

Samantha was another one of those New Yorkers who insisted on getting around the city by automobile, which in Danny's opinion was sheer insanity. What with the crowds, the congestion, the difficulty of street parking, or the cost of paid parking, what would be the point? No point when one has the availability of subways, buses and taxis.

Samantha's car problem reminded Danny that Allison also drove a car in Manhattan, and for a few moments, Danny's mind was again filled with the image of Allison and the events of the previous evening.

The publisher's austere appearance in his doorway brought Danny back to reality. "We just got the latest figures on *Macho* for May," Walter Ashburn said, smacking a copy of the magazine with the back of his hand. "They're dreadful!"

Walter was not a big man, about five-eleven, but he carried himself with a quiet, distinguished, self-satisfied arrogance that often struck fear in the hearts of most of the men and women who worked for him. They all addressed him as Mr. Ashburn, and it was rumored that even Walter's two brothers called him Mr. Ashburn.

When Danny first interviewed for the job, the silver-haired Walter was wearing sunglasses, which he always wore whenever he left the office. This had an intimidating effect on Danny that left him uneasy for the rest of the interview. But Walter hired him anyway and for several years Danny's books sustained above-average sales, which solidified his relationship with Walter Ashburn and enabled him to feel comfortable addressing him as Walter.

Now, however, in the waning days of the men's adventure magazine field, sales were dropping and the relationship between Danny and Walter had become strained, to say the least.

"I think it's the color red," Walter said firmly.

"Pardon me?"

"Red. I think we use too much red on the covers. Red's a turn-off. Bulls get angry when they see red. Red cars get hit more often than any other color, according to the insurance companies."

"If you say so, Walter."

"I say so," Walter said, chillingly. "Tell Larry to cut back on the use of red and we'll see if maybe that'll improve the numbers." And then he slipped on his dark sunglasses and walked silently back down the hallway.

Danny checked his watch and saw that it was nearly 11:00 AM. He still had time to run through the titles, blurbs and captions; read through two manuscripts; call one of the writers; and run over to bookkeeping to make sure Doris credits him with funeral leave and doesn't take away his sick days.

Jeanie called then to tell Danny the coffee wagon was out by the elevators. Danny considered another cup of coffee for a moment, and then remembered his lunch date with Samantha and the great martinis they made at Chances. His mind was starting to get cluttered with thoughts of booze, work, Samantha, Allison, his dad, Walter—all of them vying for the lead spot in his head.

Chances was a second-floor bar and restaurant on Fifty-eighth Street, between Madison and Fifth. As soon as Tommy the bartender spotted Danny coming through the door, he began pouring the vodka. Samantha was waiting at the bar, her orange hair standing out in the darkened room.

Danny grabbed the stool next to Sam and sat down, keeping one eye on Tommy as he stirred the martini, poured it into the long-stemmed glass and added an olive.

"Here's looking at you, Sam," he said, taking a long sip of the chilled liquid. And Samantha raised her glass, a plain Coke. She never drank when she was driving her car. Which was probably a wise move since walking in New York was dangerous enough much less driving under the influence.

"I'll cut to the chase, Sam," Danny said. "Things don't look good. I give these magazines maybe another year, at best. And then we'll all be looking for work. But for now, I'll take the stories we spoke about, and anything else you think I can use."

"Pretty gloomy news, Dan. What's up?"

"Sales have been dropping every issue, with all the men's magazines, and it doesn't look like they're ever gonna get better. The only ones doing well up there are the movie mags."

"Yikes. I'd better let my writers know. To be forewarned is to be forearmed ... and forearmed is half an octopus."

"It's not funny, Sam."

"I know, believe me, I know. I'm writing a book on humor and I was just trying that one out on you."

Artie, Chances' manager, came over to tell them their booth was ready, and Sam and Danny followed him with their drinks. The food was good and reasonable at Chances, and they both ate with relish. They didn't know it then but it would be the last lunch they would have as editor and agent for a while.

Allison couldn't wipe the smile off her face as she made her way to her office. She tried to convince herself that it was because she had finally been promoted to *associate* editor and had moved from a desk in the big room to her own office with a window and a door, but she knew the night with Danny had a lot more to do with it.

As she settled in at her desk and rolled a fresh sheet of paper into her typewriter, trying hard to keep Danny's image out of her mind, Jeff Bonstell stood in her doorway grinning like a Cheshire cat.

"What're you grinnin' at, Jeff? You look like a cat that just swallowed the proverbial canary."

"I don't know exactly," he said. "I guess it's because I noticed you when you got off the elevator. You looked positively radiant."

"What on earth are you talking about," Allison replied, both flattered and flustered that Jeff had been watching her.

"You know. You've got this special glow about you. Who's the lucky guy?"

"Get outta here, Jeff Bonstell," Allison said, blushing now.

Damn. Is it that obvious? She felt herself smiling again and she knew it was going to be real difficult to get any work done. *Danny, you gorgeous bastard, what have you done to me?*

When Danny got back to the office, Paul Hymoff was sitting in the chair in front of his desk, waiting for him. Paul was a freelance writer who drove every men's magazine editor in New York nuts. His specialty was compiling facts for pieces like "50 Ways to Please Your Lover" or "35 Tricks Car-Repair Hustlers Use to Scam You" or "40 Fast-Track Tips on How Furnace-Repair Vultures Cheat You Blind." And the material always turned out to be excellent.

Paul's problem was that he would jot down thoughts on little pieces of paper of all shapes and sizes. He'd type up a lead and maybe a few pages, and then he'd paper-clip the small pieces of paper to the abbreviated manuscript and turn the whole shebang over to the editor. To add insult to injury, the manuscript pages, as well as the little notes, often had food stains on them. And Paul himself, obviously not a frequent bather, usually showed up disheveled in soiled, wrinkled clothing.

"Hi, Paul, how are ya," Danny said, moving swiftly behind his desk and shuffling papers to avoid actual physical contact with Paul, who began going through his pockets and extracting bits of paper and placing them on the desk.

"Hi, Danny. I've got that piece on ways to beat the IRS you wanted," he said, continuing to rifle through his pockets. "I've got a few more tidbits here—"

"Paul," Danny said as gently as he could, sighing between sentences. "My editors are complaining about how they're always having to type up all those notes you clip to your articles. You really gotta type it all up at home before you bring the piece in."

"Will do, Dan. I promise," Paul said, peering up at Dan over the top of his smeared glasses.

"Seriously, Paul. You might also consider mailing your articles in. It'd save all of us some time and effort."

Paul nodded and left, but not before he insisted on shaking Danny's hand. Danny, of course, promptly hurried out to the men's room and washed his hands vigorously.

The day wore on as Danny caught up with the work. Allison called at 4:30 to confirm that she'd be leaving work a little after 5:00 and how about meeting at this little German restaurant she knew over on Sixty-fifth and Third. Danny agreed, excited that he would soon see her again.

Later, after dinner, Allison drove Danny back to his place.

"You know," she said as he opened the door to his apartment, "I'd love to eat at home once in a while."

"How's your cooking?"

"I'll knock your editorial socks off," Allison said. "How 'bout a nice intimate dinner at my place this weekend?"

"You're on," he said. "And I'll return the favor as soon as I can get to a grocery store and lay in some supplies."

"Lay being the operative word here," Allison said playfully, and Danny pulled her close to him, his lips gently grazing across hers. She tasted sweet and he felt her body go limp against his.

"I want to pick you up and carry you into the bedroom," Danny said, "but I'm afraid I might get a hernia." They both laughed.

"Oh, thanks," Allison said. "Is that your way of telling me I'm too fat?"

"You're hardly fat, sweetheart. It's just that I'm not much for working out and lifting weights. My muscles are all up here," he said, pointing to his head.

"Which means you're too smart for your britches, right?"

"Then we'll just get rid of the britches, yours and mine," he said, taking her by the hand and leading her into the bedroom. They undressed each other slowly, their eyes locked on each other's. Allison's heart was pumping so hard, she thought it would explode. *What is it about this guy that gets my juices going? I can't get enough of him.*

Danny kissed Allison all over, everywhere his lips could go, arousing her to a level she never thought possible. This was something Danny had never done before, taking the time to pleasure a woman the way he was pleasing Allison.

He entered her then, fusing his body with hers. Thrusting slowly at first, he began pumping faster, deeper, until he heard Allison gasp and cry out. He let himself go, releasing a flood of energy and passion and emotion deep inside her.

Moments later, Danny carefully rolled over and gently pulled Allison with him, remaining inside her. He held her closely, kissing her face and whispering how much he loved her.

Allison held on to Danny tightly, clinging desperately to him as if he might at any moment leap up and bolt for the door, deserting her forever.

"I love you, too, Danny Wallace," Allison whispered back, "with every fiber of my heart and soul."

Later, in the kitchen, Bratly made her appearance, cautiously approaching the unfamiliar Allison.

"Oh, how beautifully adorable you are!" Allison said, scooping up the petite calico and holding her against her cheek. Bratly began her singsong meowing and Allison put her down on the floor, knowing the cat was hungry.

After Danny fed Bratly, they went into the living room and sat close together on the couch. Allison reminisced about her father, and Danny spoke at length about his dad.

"My dad loved antiques, old things," she said. "He loved the way people took pride in their craft, in what they made. That's why he opened an antique store. I loved that about him, his passion for exquisite, well-made things. And that passion rubbed off on me, obviously, if you remember the Victorian motif in my apartment."

"Remember it?" Danny said playfully. "How could I forget? And I've got the backache to prove it." Allison smiled at the not-so-subtle reference to their making love on the rigid Victorian sofa.

"Well, if you hated it so much," Allison said with a grin, cupping his face in her hands, "I'll make sure you don't get to sit on it ever again."

Danny laughed and held her hands, kissing her softly on the lips.

"Sweetheart," he said, "I'd make love to you on the sidewalk if there was nothing else available."

"What a sweet thing to say." She paused. "What about your father? Tell me about him."

"Well, first of all, I didn't get to see much of my dad for many years. My parents were divorced when I was pretty young ... I'd just as soon not go into that part of my life right now. I'll tell you all about it another time.

"Everyone loved my dad. He had charisma, a way about him that attracted people. Public relations was so perfect for him. And he was such a kindred soul, so kind and gentle. There wasn't a mean bone in his body. When I was a kid, his idea of discipline was to say, 'Now, Daniel, you mustn't do this or that.'

"He never once hit me, never spanked me."

"So you were a spoiled brat?"

"No. My mother took care of the discipline. Not that she hit me a lot. But when I deserved a spanking, she took care of it. And there were times when I guess I deserved a spanking. She believed mostly in punishing me, not letting me watch television or go out to play."

"My dad played guitar," Allison said. "He was really very good at it. He used to get together with friends and jam for hours."

"Really? My dad played the piano. He was also good at it. Too bad the two of them couldn't have gotten together. They probably would've been a super combo."

"Piano? He did? Wow. That reminds me. Remember when I told you about how I've felt my dad's presence now and then?"

"Yeah ... I remember."

"Well, the other evening after I had done my therapy ... you know ... talking to my dad on the tape recorder, I turned on the radio and that song 'Stardust' came on. It's happened before, but this was a version I'd never heard before—a guitar and a piano."

"I've certainly heard 'Stardust' before, but I don't recall ever hearing a guitar-piano version."

"Maybe I'll hit the record stores and see if I can find it." Allison paused, then added, "Wouldn't that be something if your dad and my dad had hooked up and were playing 'Stardust' somewhere together?"

"You have some imagination, Allison."

"Of course I do. I dreamed you up, didn't I?"

Danny laughed. "Yes, and am I glad you did."

They talked for hours, until Allison decided she had better get home.

"Call me tomorrow when you get a chance," she said, and Danny promised he would.

"If I get tied up and don't call you by a reasonable time, then go ahead and call me. You have my work number."

They kissed and held each other tightly for a very long time, realizing this was not just a one-night stand, or even a casual two-week fling. They knew in their hearts that this one was for real, forever.

Chapter Thirteen
The answers to unsolved mysteries

Mickey knocked on the door of the computer room to the beat of the familiar ditty, "shave and a haircut, two bits." Lloyd had just finished reading Danny's journal for Tuesday. Bolting from his chair to open the door that had automatically locked, he greeted Mickey with a bear hug, unable to hold back his tears of joy. "They did it, Mick! They did it! Danny spent the night at Allison's apartment. First they went to an Italian restaurant. And then they did it!"

Mickey tried to focus on Lloyd's news bulletin, but was too aware of his friend's hug that lasted just a few seconds longer than the usual hug between two men. It made him somewhat uncomfortable.

When Lloyd finally released his grip, Mickey realized just how excited his friend had become over the news. "Are they falling in love?" Mickey asked as he read Danny's journal over Lloyd's shoulder.

"I'd say the kids are absolutely on the right track. Let's keep it going. I'll call up some blank journals right now."

"Did you read the part about how my daughter has this feeling that I'm near her and that I'm somehow influencing her life? Is that psychic or what?"

"It sure as hell is," Lloyd said. "And I wouldn't be surprised if she speculated about the two of us playing together. It's like your daughter's watching us."

"It sure seems like it. Listen, when we're finished here, how 'bout we break for lunch?"

"Good idea," Lloyd replied. "I'm starving. You know, for spirits who aren't supposed to even be in human form, they've done a marvelous job in restoring all the needs and cravings we had back on Earth."

"Well, almost all cravings. I don't seem to have any sexual urges," said Mickey. "How about you?"

"No. None. I guess if they allowed that, it would make it all somewhat complicated ... too bad, though."

When they finished typing in the pages of Danny's and Allison's blank journals, they left the Data Room and headed downstairs. As usual, the buffet was fully stocked with a variety of soups, salads and cold cuts. The two filled their plates and easily found an empty table.

"That's another thing I've wondered about," said Lloyd.

"What's that?"

"The lack of crowds here. Back on Earth, that's all we had ... having to wait on line for just about everything. But here, it's like we're back in the forties."

"I asked the director about that a while ago," said Mickey, pausing to take several bites of his Reuben sandwich, "and he explained that there's a big turnover here. People come for a little while, and then move on. And there are so many other destinations. Besides, there are a lot of people who just don't qualify to come here—sociopaths, career felons and cold-blooded murderers, to name a few."

"How about famous people, movie stars, singers, politicians ... people like that?"

"Not a whole lotta politicians," Mickey said, laughing, "but we do get some famous people occasionally passing through. You should have been here a few months ago. Lee J. Cobb, the actor, was around for a few days. Big guy. He didn't talk about who he needed to monitor back on Earth, but while he was here he was a lot of fun."

"Too bad he didn't stick around," said Lloyd, "I would have enjoyed meeting him. He was just terrific in *On the Waterfront*."

Lloyd stopped talking to look up as Burt neared their table. "Scusa me," Burt said.

"Hey, Burt. How ya doin'?" Mickey said. "Have you met Lloyd?"

Lloyd got up from his seat to shake Burt's hand. "Hello."

"Sit. Go ahead, sit," Burt ordered Lloyd, his Italian accent obvious despite his raspy ninety-year-old voice. "I just want to say how I like so much your *musica. Ambedue* ... I say this to the two of you," his right hand waving two fingers in the air. "I hear you play 'Stardust' the other day, and it was *molto bueno* ... very, very good." He paused for a moment, his fragile body swaying ever so slightly. "And I wonder when you play again this *musica*?"

Lloyd looked over at Mickey and knew exactly what was running through his head. "Well, thank you for your very kind words, Burt. Matter of fact, Mickey and I were just getting ready to head over to the Renaissance Room and play a few tunes. How 'bout you join us?"

"Ah, yes. Bless you both," Burt answered, smiling when Mickey took his arm to support him as they walked the short distance down the hall. "I okay. I justa wee bit unsteady."

"I thought Midway Manor fixed every resident's disability." Lloyd said.

"*Si* ... ah, yes ... they do," Burt answered. "If you see me before ... I use walker all the time. It was no good like that. And now ... I no need."

When they reached the Renaissance Room, Burt slowly seated himself at one of the leather-top tables. He took hold of Mickey's hand and said softly, "I know you do this for me and I thank you so much. But I must say more to you, my good friend. My business here ... she's afinished, and soon I leave this nice place."

"All right, Burt," Mickey said, squeezing his hand. "Let's give you a good bon voyage sendoff. I'll be right back with my guitar."

Lloyd was already seated at the piano and had started playing "Stardust." Mickey quickly returned and joined in with his guitar. Sam, one of the other residents who had also been in the room playing chess with Jimmy at the time, stood up and started singing the words to the song.

As several other residents in the room drew closer, Burt grinned broadly, tears streaming down his wrinkled cheeks. Lloyd and Mickey played one tune after another for more than an hour, and then the two men joined Burt at his table. "*Grazie. Grazie.* I mean to say, thank you," he said, forgetting for the moment to speak in English. "You give me a good sendoff."

Lloyd listened intently as Burt explained that his stay at the Manor was for one very particular reason. To wait there until his granddaughter had given birth to her first child. Her last daily journal revealed that his new great grandson weighed in at six pounds, seven ounces and, not surprisingly, had been named after his grandfather. Both the new mother and her newborn were doing exceptionally well. Burt's next destination in the afterworld was a place where he could bring this great news to his wife. The Manor's director, Joseph Patrick, was already in the process of making the arrangements for Burt to meet with her at a location fittingly named Reunion Valley.

"That'd be somewhere I'd like to go," Lloyd said to Mickey after they had said their goodbyes to Burt, who had been approached just minutes before by an attendant and then personally escorted to the administrator's office. "It'd be great to see my mother and father again. And especially my brother Edward. You'd really like him, Mick. He's quite a character."

"I've never really given much thought about leaving the Manor," Mickey admitted. "All I ever think about is my daughter. But I've read my copy of *Destinations in the Afterworld*, and Midway seems to be the only place where I can monitor her life on Earth."

He paused to reflect a moment. "I must admit, though, the options they describe in the book are pretty darn impressive. I've read it, at the very least, more than a dozen times."

"Yeah, I know about this book. The title caught my eye just this morning, but I haven't read it yet. And there are a few others I'm anxious to look over. There was one called *Earth's Unsolved Mysteries Revealed*. Now that information would be worth plenty back on Earth," Lloyd said. "Have you been through that one, Mick?"

"Oh yeah, I have. You wouldn't believe the stuff that's in there. It's incredible. The first thing I went to was the chapter on Glenn Miller. You know ... the famous bandleader who disappeared back in 1944. I just had to find out what really happened to him."

"And ... what happened to him?" Lloyd asked, waiting anxiously for Mickey to continue.

Mickey then told him in detail what he had read about Miller's disappearance and what had transpired.

"No ... holy geez. I don't remember reading any possible scenarios like that back on Earth. Nothing that even came close to explaining why he'd vanished without a trace."

"... and after I read about Miller," Mickey continued, "I couldn't put the damn book down. There were all kinds of good reading in it. I mean really good reading. Like what happened to Amelia Earhart. And Judge Crater. And Jimmy Hoffa. And even—"

"Hoffa?" Lloyd interrupted. "Now hold up a minute. You've gotta tell me, Mick, did Jimmy Hoffa really wind up a hamburger in upstate New York or what?"

Mickey noticed that Lloyd could barely sit in his seat, anxiously waiting to hear the outcome. But Mickey decided it would be more fun to leave Lloyd hanging with the question and said, "Well, now, what's it worth to you if I tell?"

Lloyd thought for a brief moment. "You're a nice guy, Mick," he said with sincerity, "so I'll tell you what. Give me a few hours and I'll get back to you with an answer."

Mickey was baffled by his response. "What the hell do you mean you'll get back to me?"

Lloyd proceeded to get up from his seat to leave the Renaissance Room.

"Hey, where're you going?"

"Just like I said, Mick. Give me a few hours and I'll tell you what it's worth." And Mickey, who remained at the table in a bewildered state, watched as Lloyd disappeared down the hallway.

Lloyd had actually returned to his room to retrieve his copy of the book that revealed many of Earth's unsolved mysteries. He settled into his leather recliner and opened the book to the introduction.

Two Midway Manor residents were credited with producing the book. One of the authors, John Bonano, had been a detective for more than twenty years prior to his arrival at the Manor. He had compiled all the information in the book, though initially he had used the Data Room computer to search for a particular piece of evidence regarding an unsolved crime that he had been obsessed with for many years.

He was so impressed with the information that was readily available, he began to research other events. Soon after, he got together with another resident, a former Earthbound writer named Kevin Stone. John continued to use the computer for research and compiled the information, which Kevin subsequently turned into readable prose. The director of the Manor had not only welcomed their diligent efforts, he had their work produced in book form for any residents who might enjoy the read.

After getting through the introduction, Lloyd then proceeded to read the book from cover to cover.

Chapter Fourteen
Bad day at Brightside

The day did not start out well.

The first thing that happened when Danny got to work was Ernie Wilson dropped dead. The aging editor, who worked in Ben Mitchell's division, was copyediting a manuscript when he suddenly slumped forward face down on his desk. There had been no sound, according to the other editors, and it may have been an hour or so before anyone noticed he wasn't moving.

Someone called an ambulance. Meantime, coworkers laid him out on the floor and covered him with brown wrapping paper from the mailroom. For some reason, it took more than an hour before anyone arrived to take the body away.

Several times, Mary Sullivan, who worked in the magazine room taking care of back issues and subscriptions, had to step over Mr. Wilson in the course of her business. She finally complained, rather insensitively, to Walter Ashburn that "Mr. Wilson is really in the way."

Following this unfortunate disruption, Danny had to deal with the stuttering Jack Henry, a cartoonists' agent who made the rounds weekly from one publishing company to another, representing a number of cartoonists. He would offer their cartoons rejected by other companies for a discounted rate, and often there would be a few gems in each batch.

Danny empathized with Jack's stuttering affliction, but it was difficult to converse with him because he was rather passionate in his attempt to peddle his clients' work and had a tendency to spit when he spoke. Danny had made the mistake on a number of occasions to get too close to Jack, only to be the unwitting recipient of his own personal misting system.

Danny ducked out for a quick lunch of a hot dog with onions at the corner umbrella stand. And then another quick stop at Charlie's for a couple of shooters to keep himself calm. He later regretted not having a few more.

The day grew worse.

When Danny returned from his abbreviated lunch, there was a man he didn't recognize sitting in his guest chair. He was just sitting there, staring out the window and holding a manila envelope in his hand.

"Can I help you?" Danny asked, hanging up his jacket and sitting at his desk.

"Yeah," the man said, handing Danny the envelope. "I need you to read this."

"An article?" Danny said as he pulled the manuscript from its sheath. He glanced at the title, "My Life at Creedmore."

"You wrote an article about someone in a mental institution?" Danny asked, recognizing the name.

"That's me," the man said, scrunching up his face. "I wrote about me in that place."

"When did you get released?" Danny asked, feeling just a tad uneasy.

"Last week."

"Well, okay then," Danny said, hoping his anxiety wasn't apparent. "We'll give it a look and get back to you in a few days."

"I want you to read it now," the man said, his eyes narrowing.

Danny swallowed hard, sizing the man up. He wasn't tall but he was solidly built, with broad shoulders and thick, muscular arms. *And there might be a knife,* Danny thought nervously. He picked up the phone and dialed O for Jeanie Switchboard. "Would you please have Harold come into my office," he told her.

"Are you gonna read it?" the man asked.

"I just don't have that kind of time," Danny said, relieved to see Harold and his huge hands standing in the doorway. "Just leave the manuscript with me and put your name and address on it." He handed the envelope and script back to the man. "And a phone where I can reach you."

"No phone," the man said, slowly printing his name and address on the envelope.

Danny didn't bother mentioning the required postage for returning a manuscript. The company would spring for this one. He took the article back from the man and put a hand on his shoulder, gently nudging him toward the door.

"Harold here will show you the way out. It's kinda tricky."

Danny got through the rest of the day with only minor annoyances and irritations. Ben Mitchell, the editor who headed up Brightside's other division of men's books, came into Danny's office huffing and puffing and wheezing after his amazing display of exertion—walking an unbelievable hundred or so feet from his section to Danny's.

Danny didn't know if Ben had a metabolism problem or an eating disorder, or both, but it was quite obvious that Ben was grossly overweight. He grunted after each sentence, ranting on to Danny about how Mr. Ashburn had shot down his latest cover mockup for *Man's Escape*.

"What the hell's wrong with this cover, Dan?" he asked. "I think it's great!"

"Well, Ben," Danny said with a forced innocence, trying to soften his imminent criticism as he studied Ben's proposed cover, "I think Walter's dissatisfaction may lie in the rather harsh, graphic illo."

"What's wrong with it?" Ben demanded to know. "It's just two guys in a knife fight with a chick looking on."

"The objection here, Ben, would probably be where you have one man ripping out the other guy's entrails. It's ... well ... pathological."

"That's realism, Dan!"

"No, Ben, that's disgusting."

Ben waddled off, grunting loudly, in search of another editor who might agree with him.

Danny sighed when he heard Allison's voice on the phone.

"I'm glad you called, Danny," she said. "I've been thinking about you all day. It's hard to concentrate on the work. I've also been feeling my dad's presence again, like he knows everything I do. I just can't shake the feeling."

"Okay, Spooky," Danny said playfully. "I don't want to seem insensitive, but you know what I think about that spirit world stuff."

"I mean it, Danny. It's not just something I think ... I *feel* him near me, like he's watching over me, protecting me."

"Listen, I'll watch over you. I'll protect you. And to show you how brave I am, I'll let you cook for me tonight instead of waiting for the weekend."

Allison laughed as Danny's levity eased her tenseness.

"You are a brave soul. Think you can find your way back to my place again?"

"No, but I'll get a taxi crab that can."

"A taxi *crab*? Okay, crabby, see you later."

Danny felt a joy in his heart as he thought about the evening ahead. He also felt a stirring in his loins when he remembered her soft, pliant body and how she moved in bed. Allison, he decided, was the best thing that's happened to him since little Ginny Sayers let him kiss her in the schoolyard in fourth grade.

It had taken an hour of kissing, hugging and intimate whispers of affection before Danny felt completely relaxed. Two wonderfully dry vodka martinis didn't hurt either.

Allison was an excellent cook who obviously used the very best ingredients. She had prepared a lasagna that Danny couldn't stop eating. And the Italian bread, which was warm, was obviously fresh.

"Did you make this from scratch?" Danny asked.

"Why, you don't like?"

"No, I love it, obviously. Maybe you didn't notice how I was shoveling it into my mouth. You'd give my mom competition, and up to now I'd considered Dorothy Wallace the best cook in the world. I just don't know how you did it so fast."

"Well, actually, I made it Sunday and put it in the freezer, so all I had to do was get some bread at the deli and then heat up everything."

Danny suddenly remembered plump Ben Mitchell huffing and puffing earlier that day and vowed right then that he would go on a diet tomorrow.

After dinner, Allison excused herself and disappeared into the bathroom. Danny began thumbing through her record collection, pleased that she had several Arlo Guthrie albums.

The scream cut through him like a knife.

Danny ran down the hall to the bathroom door.

"Are you all right?" he asked.

The door opened and Allison rushed out, her face pale with terror.

"There's a goddamn spider in my sink. It's as big as a pack of cigarettes!"

"Where's your bug spray?" Danny asked.

"It's all the way in the kitchen, under the sink. Why don't you just use my hair spray?"

"I wanna kill 'im, not groom 'im," Danny said, heading for the kitchen. He returned with the bug poison and sprayed the small spider, which shriveled up into a rigid dot, and flushed it down the toilet.

"My hero," Allison said, mashing her full body against Danny's and wrapping her arms around his waist. They moved to the bedroom and Allison didn't think about the spider, work or her father for the rest of the night.

Chapter Fifteen
Lloyd has an idea

Mickey glanced at his watch and immediately thought of his daughter. About ten minutes had gone by since Lloyd had left him alone in the Renaissance Room, promising to be back in two hours.

Mickey decided that even if his friend would return sooner, he still had time to spend at least an hour in the Data Room at the computer. "All those diaries I could have been reading," he said to himself. "What a fool I've been."

Since Lloyd's arrival a week ago, there had been a complete change in Mickey's attitude regarding the Data Room and all the information available there. Now, he found himself sitting in front of the computer like an old pro. *I owe this guy,* Mickey concluded, *I really owe him.*

Lloyd was already in the Renaissance Room when Mickey returned. "Well, are you ready for me to give you the bottom line on Jimmy Hoffa? And *now* do you know what it's worth to you if I tell?"

"To answer your second question first, I'd say millions, maybe more." But I already know the bottom line on Hoffa 'cause I just finished reading the entire book."

"Why you sonofagun, so that's what you were doing," Mickey snorted, not realizing Lloyd had much more to say.

"I have to tell you, every single chapter in the book was astonishing. During my whole career as a newspaperman back on Earth, I'd been a news junkie, always looking for a fix. I can't tell you what a magnificent feeling it is to read something that removes all speculation and just overwhelms you with the cold, hard truth. Oh yeah … and tell me, Mick, how is it that you failed to mention the chapter on UFOs?"

"Because you never gave me the chance to tell you anything more," Mickey said innocently.

"Well, my friend, we have ourselves something here. No … let me rephrase that. We have something here that's perfect for Danny and Allison. Are you following me?"

"No, not really. But you've got my attention."

"Good. What we need to do is get all this information about Judge Crater, Hoffa, Glenn Miller, the UFOs, the second Kennedy assassin, all of it, to the kids."

"Huh? What for?"

"Don't you see, Mick? The kids have the tools to put it all together and write a helluva book using all this incredible stuff. Everyone will want to read it. It'll sell like ice water in the desert. The kids'll be set for life."

"Kids? They're hardly kids."

"They're our kids, aren't they? It's the least we can do for them."

"I guess you're right."

"I know I'm right," Lloyd said, frowning. "But there are a couple of problems."

"Such as?"

"Well, first I'm concerned about the UFO thing. I know if I were still alive back on Earth, I'd have a problem with this knowledge. I think most people would have a problem accepting who's piloting these craft, and why. It actually might create a worldwide panic."

"Most people? Who wouldn't have a problem?"

"You ever hear about the Majestic Group, the MJ-12 project?"

"No."

"It truly exists, a government within the government. Their existence came to light after the Freedom of Information Act of 1966. These people have known since the nineteen-fifties what we now know, and they've been able to handle it."

"How did you learn all this?"

"In my business, I had to read a lot. Anyway, aside from that, I'm confident that Danny and Allison won't have any reservations at all about reporting this and the rest of it to the general population."

"Why?"

"Because the truth will set them free. Not just the kids, but everyone. They'll all be freed from living their lives under a veil of half-truths and speculation."

"Okay. This all makes good sense. So what's the other problem?"

"A minor detail … how do we get this information to the kids?" Lloyd asked, knowing Mickey wouldn't have the answer on the tip of his tongue.

"Did I hear you say a *minor* detail? How *would* we get this information to the kids? No, wait … let me guess first. Maybe we could just beam down to Manhattan à la Captain Kirk and Mister Spock and personally hand-deliver the goddamn book. Huh? How 'bout that?"

Lloyd laughed, "I sure as hell wish we could return to Earth for a visit. But you know as well as I do that going back isn't one of our options."

"So tell me … what options are there?"

"Well, last week when the director was giving me the basics on how to use the computer, he'd also mentioned something about there eventually being some sort of worldwide network of communication, a kind of electronic mail.

"Wait a minute!" Lloyd exclaimed, suddenly realizing they could query up almost anything on the Manor's computer system. "Let's get back to the Data Room. I'll explain when we get there."

"I'm lost," said Mickey, shaking his head. "I don't know what you're on, but you seem to be going full speed and I'm on seven-second delay."

In the Data Room, Lloyd quickly entered the word Query, followed by World Wide Web.

"This should give us a good idea of what the director was talking about," said Lloyd. "I've got a theory about what we might be able to do, but I want to get a few facts first."

The twin screens lit up with one streaming paragraph after another. Lloyd and Mickey read intently, trying to absorb the steady flow of information. They learned that in the 1960s, one Doug Engelbart prototyped an "oNLine System" (NLS) that did hypertext browsing, editing, e-mail, etc. He invented something called a mouse for this purpose.

Also in the '60s, Ted Nelson coined the word "hypertext" in "A File Structure for the Complex, the Changing, and the Indeterminate," 20th National Conference, New York, *Association for Computing Machinery*, 1965. And Andy van Dam and others built the Hypertext Editing System in 1967.

Another key link in the evolution of the coming World Wide Web will occur in 1980 when Tim Berners-Lee, while consulting for CERN, will write a notebook program, "Enquire-Within-Upon-Everything," which will allow links to be made between arbitrary nodes. Each node will have a title, a type, and a list of bidirectional typed links.

In 1990, Tim will write a global hypertext system and begin work on a hypertext GUI browser+editor using the NeXTStep development environment. He will call the program "WorldWideWeb." And the first Web server will begin in November of that year.

By 1993, there will be more than 200 HTTP servers in existence. And in October 1994, the World Wide Web Consortium will be founded.

Lloyd decided they'd learned enough. "Damn," he said, "it's just like I figured. None of this is going to happen until the nineties. We're talking fifteen to twenty years from now...."

"I'm still not following all of this," said Mickey.

"Okay then, I'll give it to you in two simple words—*blank journals*.

"The first step, Mick, is to make sure Danny and Allison are set up with a computer and able to receive electronic mail, or e-mail as they call it, by no later than January of 1996.

"Then we boil all the information in this mysteries-solved book down to the basic bottom-line answers and e-mail it to the kids in 1996."

"That means we have to stay here at Midway Manor for twenty years?"

"What's the problem? You know there could be worse places."

"Twenty years is a long time," Mickey said.

"Not for us, and not here. Why? You in a hurry to go somewhere?"

"Well, before, I just wanted to stay here and be close to my daughter and—"

"And you will be, for twenty years."

"Will you let me finish, for crissake. As I was saying, I'd eventually like to move on to Reunion Valley and see some of the people who left Earth before I did. Like my mom and dad ... and my brothers."

"And you will, but we've got an eternity for that."

"How do you know we'll be able to do this, this electronic mail thing?"

"I don't, but it's worth a try. What I do know is that as soon as The Authority determines what we're up to, we'll be shot off to the next destination faster than you can say Saint Peter. After that, I doubt we'll have any links with the kids again. I'd like to know that we at least tried to do something to guarantee their happiness and security."

"I'd like to say hi to my daughter in this—what'd they call it?—e-mail and tell her how much I love her," Mickey said, his eyes moistening.

"You can, Mick," Lloyd assured him. "First, we'll tell them all about Midway Manor and our experiences here, how much we love them, and then we'll tell them what to do with the data we'll send them. After we transmit the data, we'll explain how we must move on to the next wherever."

"So they suddenly hear from us twenty years after we, uh, die, and before they can get over that trauma, we tell them we're leaving again. Great."

"Mick, I know it's tough, but we've got to try this for the kids' sake. If you've got a better idea, I'm all ears."

"Wait a second, Lloyd, if we can get an answer from the computer on what's going to happen with computers and communication over the next twenty years, why can't we just ask it about Allison and Danny's future? If we know what's going to happen to them—and why—maybe we can alter or instigate events in their lives the way we've already done and help them avoid any serious problems."

"That's a fine and noble idea, but the Manor's computers have some kind of block on information regarding people and events that have yet to occur. We kinda lucked out when we found a loophole that somehow let's us influence events in the lives of Danny and Allison."

"I gotcha," said Mickey, nodding. "All right. Listen, I'll take care of extracting the important facts from the mysteries-solved book while you do whatever it is you have to do to set up the blank journals for January 1996."

"I'll see you at dinner," Lloyd said as he shut down the computer. "I'm going back to my room for a while and do some reading. If memory serves, I think there was another book there about the Manor's computers."

"There is," said Mickey. "I skimmed through it once but it was way over my head, so I never bothered trying to read it."

"I'll let you know if I find anything important."

Chapter Sixteen
Manipulating and monitoring

Lloyd and Mickey continued typing in Danny's and Allison's blank journals almost on a daily basis. They managed to maintain a distinct subtleness in what they wrote, allowing the couple as much freedom in their relationship as possible.

More importantly, though, the men did not want to call attention to their endeavors and find themselves in the director's office for breaching their privileges at the Manor. The major breach, as they continued with their preliminary plans for sending the unsolved-mysteries answers to the kids, would come years later.

The weeks passed. The two men watched Danny and Allison's relationship grow stronger. Lloyd had exhausted himself trying to convince Mickey not to interfere with Allison's difficulties at work. He was sure that any writing in empty-paged journals intended to evoke an act of revenge or punishment against Kate Ripley might backfire on the kids or themselves. "But that so-called managing editor makes unreasonable demands on my daughter," Mickey would mumble to himself on a daily basis. *Even when that witch isn't loud and aggressive, Allison can still catch a cold angry look in her eyes. I've got to do something about her.*

Mickey's decision to abide only in part to Lloyd's suggestion paid off. He had gone ahead anyway and written in Allison's journal that Kate, the woman who never wavered in her belief that she was better than anyone else, should be bestowed with a financial windfall and move on to greater endeavors.

Two weeks to the date of Mickey's decision to include this scenario in Allison's journal, he read about his daughter celebrating Kate's early retirement from the publishing business because she had recently become involved with a wealthy tycoon twice her age, and had unexpectedly quit her job.

"Gotcha," Mickey said under his breath, pleased that his daughter would not be putting up with Kate's irrational attitude anymore. And then, looking deeper into what he had just accomplished, he became conscious of something even more profound. Something that had always bothered him when he had been Earthbound.

I always wondered why certain hateful people like Kate would be so fortunate, he recalled. *But now I know most of them eventually get what's coming to them. Why, it'll be only a matter of time before that old multimillionaire drops her like a hot potato.*

Mickey knew that his carefully crafted words were intended solely to benefit Allison. That she would finally be spared, once and for all, from falling victim to Kate's wicked ways. And that, in his opinion, made his daughter the one who really came out the winner.

Lloyd, on the other hand, did not tamper with Danny's position at Brightside. He knew the company would be closing shop within the year and felt that his son was better off waiting it out before moving on.

There was never any discussion between Mickey and Lloyd about Danny's heavy drinking. Mickey was concerned about it but kept it to himself. Lloyd had already shared some stories about his own lack of control with alcohol and that he had been sober for more than twenty years, thanks in large part to the AA program. Mickey hoped that Danny would someday follow the same path to sobriety as Lloyd.

The jam sessions continued with Lloyd at the piano and Mickey on the guitar. Sometimes they got together when a resident moved on, or when someone new arrived. But more often than not they played just for the sheer pleasure of it.

The weeks flew by. Lloyd and Mickey would often spend an hour or so sharing the same computer. And then they would split up and use separate rooms for privacy to either do research for their upcoming future plans or to look up some old friends or other family members. They were able to do all this after Lloyd finished reading *Basic Guidelines for Using Midway Manor's Data Room Computers.*

Lloyd had retrieved journals on some of his old buddies at the newspaper. He even checked in on Susan from time to time, until she eventually moved in with a man. After reading in her journals that this man reminded her of Lloyd, he felt a twinge of guilt. *My God, the woman really loved me ... more than I realized.* But he reasoned his not knowing this was due to spending his last few months focused on the constant pain.

One time, Mickey called up the day of his own funeral and punched in the name of his ex-wife Margaret. He was aghast to discover that Margaret was the one who had snatched his daughter's gift from his wrist just minutes before the funeral director had closed the lid on his satin-lined coffin. *Why?* he wondered. *Why would this crazy woman take something Allison had given me?*

Lloyd would occasionally use the Data Room computer to check on his ex-wife, Dorothy. He still loved her very much and for the most part regretted leaving her and Danny, although Dorothy had not given him much of a choice. But he still felt they had both been better off without being directly subjected to his philandering ways.

In the spring of 1977, Lloyd found out through Dorothy's journal that she had been diagnosed with heart trouble. Her arteries were relatively clear if not squeaky clean, but her doctor had detected a dysfunctional heart valve, which would most certainly lead to an eventual heart attack.

To Lloyd's dismay, Dorothy waved off the doctor's warning as if he were telling her she'd had a broken fingernail. She decided to ignore the seriousness of her condition and the need for further testing. But Dorothy did see the importance of getting her affairs in order. She saw a lawyer and had an official will drawn up, and even arranged in advance for her own cremation.

Dorothy never mentioned her condition to her son Danny or to anyone other than her lawyer and the funeral home. Lloyd agonized over whether he should interfere, manipulating blank journals that would influence Dorothy to seek medical help to prevent a heart attack. But he was afraid any interference at this point might jeopardize his and Mickey's future plans to help Danny and Allison.

It turned out to be yet another decision he would later regret.

Chapter Seventeen
Death meets the deadline

It was a typically hot and humid July day in New York in 1977 when Murphy's Law went into overdrive. Danny had exactly two hours to wrap up the proofing and correcting of the October *Macho* bluelines and get them back to the printer. It was 2:00 PM and the messenger would be at Brightside no later than 4:00 that afternoon.

That's when Danny's world began to unravel.

He had called Allison right after he got back from his abbreviated lunch and confirmed that the movers had finished taking every piece of furniture from her apartment and put it aboard their van.

This turned out to be the last bit of good news he would hear for a long while. It had taken Danny nearly a year to convince Allison that it would be both emotionally and financially in their best interest for her to give up her apartment and move in with him.

Danny had agreed to let Allison replace some of his furniture with her Victorian antiques, though there were some items he just wouldn't give up.

The first bad news Danny got was Walter Ashburn summoning him to his office. Not the worst thing by itself, but what Walter had to impart to Danny was indeed a bombshell. He knew it was coming when he realized Ben Mitchell had also been called in at the same time, something Walter rarely did.

"There'll be a memo sent around later but I wanted you two to be the first to learn that we're shutting the place down. The confession and movie books have been sold, and we're simply ceasing publication of the men's books after the current issues you're both working on ... the October issues ... have been printed and distributed." He paused for a moment. "There will be generous severance."

Ben Mitchell and Danny stood there speechless, stunned by Walter's news.

"It's over, gentlemen. End of an era." He nodded toward his well-stocked bar. "Have a drink with me. Ben, give me about three fingers of that Wild Turkey. On the rocks."

Ben moved over to the bar and picked up a pair of tongs, dropping several cubes from the ice bucket into three highball glasses. He poured a generous amount of the bourbon into two of the glasses, then turned to Danny with a quizzical look. Danny managed to mumble, "I'll have the same, Ben."

Ralph Corona, the dilettante editorial director, and Larry Roberts, the art director, had joined them then, also deciding to have the same bourbon drink.

They all moved to a corner of Walter's office where there was a plush sofa and chairs available. They sat around and talked for a while, taking turns telling legendary stories of Brightside history.

"I remember my first day at Brightside," Danny said. "I had on a new, light-gray, summer-weight suit and a pigeon shit on me just before I entered the building."

"I think that's good luck," said Ben.

"Maybe," Danny said, "or maybe it meant bad luck that just took thirteen years to activate," referring to his tenure at Brightside.

"I've had good luck and bad luck in my career as a publisher," Walter offered. "But I'll tell you one thing, nobody gave me anything on a silver platter. I had nothing when I was younger. I rode the rails in boxcars when I was in my teens; I didn't even have a home."

Walter was feeling the one-hundred-one proof alcohol by now, which had loosened his lips. He spoke freely about his youth and how he had started the company from practically nothing.

Ben, conversely, said little. The bourbon had a tranquilizing effect on him, which was what a depressant should do.

"Anybody remember Stan Isaacs," asked Danny, "the older fella who used to work in the art department? You know, the layout artist."

They all nodded.

"Yes, well, every Christmas the stat house used to send over bottles of booze for most of the layout artists. They gave other artists boxes of cigars, which Stan always got. And being a nonsmoker, Stan always bitched about it.

"Well, one year Stan actually mentioned it to the stat house, figuring that the next Christmas he'd get a bottle of hooch.

"The next Christmas, Stan got absolutely nothing from the stat house. Poor bastard." They all laughed.

Danny's mind wandered while the stories went on. Losing one's job is a pretty traumatic experience, and Danny wondered how he would survive. He dreaded telling Allison.

"How about that little guy they once hired to do paste-ups," Larry Roberts said. "I think his name was Bobby White. The kid had no education to speak of and was a barely functional illiterate. I swear to God, he never spelled his own name the same way twice."

They all laughed again and Danny got up and went for a refill. When he returned, the subject of fond remembrances was the inimitable Gregory Patrick, a managing editor who had recently left Brightside after fifteen years to become politically active.

Greg had been directly responsible for re-energizing *For Guys Only*. The monthly magazine, which had enjoyed a circulation of nearly four hundred thousand during the early to mid-'60s, had begun to falter—until Greg took over the reins.

A Southern boy, Greg traveled north for his education, earning his BA in journalism from New York University. His first book about an up-and-coming but then little-known Democrat from New England won Greg critical acclaim, and a job as a reporter on a Boston newspaper. Like most of the editors at Brightside, Greg, through a series of unexplainable events, wound up as an editor of a men's adventure magazine.

"He was a helluva damn fine editor," said Walter, recalling someone who had been responsible for putting money in his pocket.

"And a pretty funny guy," said Ralph. "He made me laugh."

Greg was a forty-something intellectual with a very dry sense of humor and a knack for digging out the irony in a situation. About five-eight or nine, with thinning salt-and-pepper hair and a middle-aged paunch, Greg had an eye for younger women and a taste for older whiskey. His mind obviously performed at a speed far exceeding that of the average Brightside staffer, which caused him to speak in a way that left most sentences unfinished. But somehow, he still managed to communicate quite well.

"I remember the day he came in wearing a very expensive red silk tie that stood out against his light blue buttoned-down shirt," said Danny. "Unfortunately, it was the very same tie that Walter was wearing that day. Remember that, Walter? You had called him in to discuss cover proposals and there you and Greg stood, face to face, belly to belly, tie to tie.

"'Glad to see you're doing so well, Greg,' you had said somewhat sarcastically. I remember that Greg came back to his desk, ripped off the tie and stuffed it in a drawer. He never wore it again."

The five men laughed heartily at that, all of them by now on their second or third drinks.

"What about Carolyn and her pets?" said Ben. "She was something else."

"Yeah," Danny said. I remember Carolyn quite well. "She was a single gal, not unattractive, but she had this thing where she had to save all the less fortunate animals in the world."

"Remember when she threatened to quit if we didn't cut out a chapter from a book condensation that depicted bears being killed?" Ben asked.

"Which was rather difficult," said Ralph, "since the whole book was about grizzlies gone amok."

"She actually had two apartments in the same building in the Village," said Danny. "She had thirteen cats in the one where she actually lived, and then she had a separate apartment for eleven dogs. She just couldn't resist taking strays home."

"She told me once how the super thought she had four cats," said Ben, "and that was already against lease rules. She had to buy litter in fifty-pound sacks, and one time the sack split open and litter spilled all over the stairway. The super had a fit."

"No one's mentioned that kid, Martin what's his name," said Ralph.

"Beck, Marty Beck," said Danny. "I'll bet you're referring to the cheese incident. That's when one of the illustrators came in with a huge, three-pound hunk of imported cheese and offered to share it with everyone. He'd come into our bullpen and slapped the cheese down on one of the desks, asking if anyone had a knife.

"Well, this kid Marty Beck opens his bottom drawer and takes out a white towel all bunched up. He opens the towel and gingerly lifts out this absolutely humongous butcher knife. I mean, you could slice up half of the East Side with this fucker."

Everybody laughed harder than usual, obviously trying to blot out the sense of dread most of them felt deep within themselves. Nobody wanted to think of what would happen next. Walter, of course, would never have to worry about money, but he was losing a publishing company he had built from scratch, a company he had put his life into for almost forty years.

"Danny, there's an urgent phone call for you." It was Brenda, Walter's secretary. "You can take it at my desk."

Danny excused himself and went into the anteroom just outside Walter's office. "Dan Wallace speaking," he said into the phone.

"Mister Wallace, this is Doctors Hospital in Westfield, New Jersey." Danny's heart sank. His mother lived near Westfield.

"Yes," he said, his voice cracking.

"I'm sorry to say that your mother has suffered a heart attack and is in our intensive care unit."

"H-How is she?" Danny asked.

"She's not too good, Mr. Wallace. Is it possible for you to come here right now?"

"Yes ... yes, of course," said Danny. "I'm on my way."

Danny briefed Brenda who was standing in the doorway and asked her to tell Harold to take over. He raced back to his office and called his apartment, explaining what happened to Allison. "I'll call you later from the hospital," he told her. Allison was concerned that Danny might need her for moral support and offered to go with him, but Danny explained there was no time. He pointedly did not mention his imminent layoff. *Plenty of time for that nugget of negative news,* he thought.

Danny had trouble getting a cabbie willing to go all the way to Jersey. He finally convinced one driver with the promise of a $50 tip above whatever the fare wound up being. By now, Danny was partially anesthetized by the bourbon, but the news of his mother had cleared his head quickly. As the cab sped across the George Washington Bridge, Danny began to go back over his life, already feeling guilty for not calling his mom more often.

I haven't been a very good son, he thought. *If Mom goes, I'll have no more family!* The realization hit him hard. *Dad, why did you die? I need you here with me right now. You were hardly there for me when you were alive. Damn you.*

Danny never heard the strains of "Stardust" playing on the cab's radio. Quietly, hunched up in the darkness of the taxi's back seat, he wept softly.

Danny arrived at the hospital two hours and twenty-three minutes later and went directly to Intensive Care.

He was too late. Dorothy Elizabeth Wallace, age sixty-seven, had stopped breathing due to congestive heart failure.

Chapter Eighteen
Danny moves on

Danny and Allison walked around the small, white-shingled house that had belonged to his mother. In his hands was the blue marble box containing Dorothy Wallace's ashes. He stopped to study the tall lilac bushes his mother had planted when she first bought the house. The spring blooms had faded, but Danny could almost smell the wonderful fragrance from memory. They had been a favorite in the family for years, probably stemming from the wall of lilacs surrounding his paternal grandmother's house in Illinois.

Nearby was the familiar rose bush Danny had given his mother the year before. It was in full bloom, with more roses than he thought possible. Allison leaned forward and inhaled deeply, almost swooning from the fragrant aroma of the purplish red flowers.

Danny conjured up an image of his mother, filling his mind with the face of the woman who had brought him into the world. An attractive woman, even beautiful in her youth, she had the bluest of blue eyes. You could look into them and see the gentleness, the kindness that radiated from within. But if you looked hard enough, you could also see the rough life she had at an early age. Danny remembered her stories of her childhood and how she had been forced to quit school at fourteen and wait tables to support both herself and her sister. She had educated herself, reading everything she could get her hands on. Fortunately, she had been born with an extremely acute native intelligence. She was at times quite worldly, yet retained a certain childlike innocence that stayed with her even into her sixties.

Danny opened the box and began scattering his mother's ashes over the rose bush and the soil beneath it. They moved back to the lilacs and Danny tossed out the remainder of her ashes. It was what Dorothy Wallace had wanted.

Danny spoke for the first time since they had left the house and gone into the yard. "My mother was the warmest, kindest, most generous woman I have ever known," he said, tears welling up in his eyes. "And she was always there for me, through the worst of times and the best of times. She was so unselfish and so giving."

"I'm sorry I didn't get to really know her," said Allison. "I only met her once and she seemed to be a truly wonderful person."

"Yes, she was," said Danny, "and I was pathetic as a son." Danny could no longer hold back and he wept profusely. "I could have visited her more often, and I certainly could have called her more frequently. I've just been too busy being selfish and self-centered. Maybe if I'd been there for her, this might not have happened."

"That's ridiculous," said Allison, taking his hand and squeezing it. "That's actually egotistical. You can't be responsible for or affect what happens to someone else."

"What do you mean?"

"Don't you get it, Danny? You're not in the picture here. Her heart attack had to do with genes, *her* family background, *her* eating habits, *her* lifestyle. Perhaps you could have called her more often, and gone to see her more than you did, and I'm sure that would have pleased her. But for God's sake, don't blame yourself for her death."

Danny nodded, trying to squeeze his eyes dry with his fingers. He felt drained, and a sadness filled his stomach, much like the feeling of homesickness he had when he went away to Navy boot camp at seventeen. He had felt that same homesickness a year or so after his parents had divorced. His mother had eventually put him in a boarding home out on Long Island while she worked as a waitress. He was only about eight years old and for a solid year he felt that emptiness, that loneliness, that feeling of abandonment.

That lonely little boy had stayed with Danny into adulthood, remaining inside him, influencing the way he responded to people, to circumstances, to life in general.

Danny had tried psychotherapy, which helped him to recognize his inner child. He later realized that this little boy was part of why he drank too much. But Danny also knew from reading the literature that ongoing research suggested a genetic link with alcoholism's root cause. Intellectually, he knew he would have to get sober sooner or later. But he was not ready in his heart. In less than two years, he had lost his father, his mother and soon his job, all of these right at the top of the stress-level charts.

Danny said goodbye to his mother and locked up the house. It was legally his now, but he knew he would have to put it on the market. As far as he was concerned, it was too far away from Manhattan for a practical commute.

They drove back to the city in Allison's car. While Allison negotiated the nerve-rattling traffic, Danny gazed out the window, reviewing his life to date. He remembered the drunkenness, the abandonment, the boarding home, the less-than-satisfying Navy experience.

He had spent three-and-a-half years aboard three different destroyers, much of it at sea. He had gone through several shakedown cruises in the Guantánamo Bay area, visited a number of European countries, passed through the Suez Canal, seen Ethiopia and Pakistan, and through all of it he had felt something was missing.

He had always had a flair for writing, probably due to his dad's influence, though he had shown a talent for drawing and painting in high school. But when he left the Navy, his first civilian job was weighing vegetables and stacking cans in a grocery store.

Danny smiled when he remembered how his Uncle Edward had raised hell with his father when he found out he was working in a supermarket. His dad responded by getting Danny a job in the mailroom of a large, privately owned publishing company. Within a few short months, Danny had secured a job in the production department, wrapping and sending metal plates to the printer. Danny also started college at night.

In less than a year, Danny had been promoted to the editorial department. And for the next few years, Danny worked as assistant to the production editor of a large-circulation men's magazine and went to school at night. By that time, Danny was writing and selling fiction and nonfiction articles to a number of men's magazines.

Which is when Brightside became part of his life.

"Thinking about Mom?" Allison asked.

Allison's voice brought Danny back to the present. It was then that he realized they were already in Manhattan.

"Sorry, I guess I was going over my whole life."

"That's understandable," said Allison softly. Then, trying to lighten things up, she said, "Are you all done now, or do you want me to drive around for a while longer?"

Danny laughed. "No, let's find a parking space and get upstairs. I've got a job interview in the morning."

As Allison began the hunt for an available parking space, which in Manhattan is closely akin to searching for the Holy Grail, they both became aware of the guitar-piano version of "Stardust" playing on the radio. This time, though, there was a woman singing the lyrics.

They looked at each other then and Allison smiled.

"That's another version" she said excitedly. "That's another guitar-piano version of 'Stardust,' with a woman doing the vocals. Danny, our dads, and your mom, are here!"

"Maybe so. I like this version." Despite his skepticism, Danny found himself wondering if there was even a remote chance that Allison was right.

Perfect Publications was far from it. The receptionist was busy chatting on the phone with a friend when Danny entered the small suite of offices. She seemed annoyed when Danny introduced himself and informed her that he had a 9:30 AM appointment with the publisher, Seymour Greenberg.

Danny waited in the small lobby, sitting in one of only two chairs. Ten minutes later, the receptionist told him to go in through the door and make a left. "Mister Greenberg's office is straight back," the receptionist said, cracking her gum.

Seymour Greenberg was unlike any publisher Danny had ever seen. A tall, broad-shouldered man with a football player's thick neck, Seymour wore his dark shirt open at the collar and several of the top buttons undone. His shiny gold chains stood out against the mass of dark curly chest hair that matched what was on his head. Danny's first impression was that the man was a gangster.

As it turned out, Danny wasn't far off.

"Scott tells me you can do it all," Seymour said. The Scott he referred to was Scott Nielsen, an art director Danny had worked with in the past. They had been drinking buddies back in the early Brightside days. He had run into him in a pub recently and Scott had said they were looking for an editor and that he would arrange the meeting with Seymour for this morning. But Danny already was feeling bad vibes about Seymour and his little company.

Conversely, Seymour was immediately impressed with Danny and, without ceremony, offered him the job at thirty-five thousand a year. And despite Danny's reservations about the place, Danny accepted.

The magazine, *Strut*, was strictly a stroke book, with a heavy emphasis on photos of women in various stages of undress, including the by now almost obligatory gynecological shots. The articles were short and for the most part badly written, without much substance. But it was a job and there were still a number of tasks that would keep Danny busy.

After about a week, Seymour started coming into Danny's office and yelling. He was a loud, mean-spirited man who seemed to revel in his own power by demeaning those around him. What he hollered about was either miniscule or misdirected.

"Why don't we have a back-page ad for this issue?" he once screamed at Danny.

"I don't know, Seymour," Danny had replied, trying to stay calm. "I think you need to check with the advertising department. I'm not—"

"I don't wanna hear it," Seymour had interrupted. "Just make sure it don't happen again."

Danny was appalled by Seymour's grammar, but even more upset by his abuse. He knew he would not be able to take this kind of treatment for very much longer. It would be just a matter of time before he had to move on, but he also knew he had to find something else first while he was still working. Danny had long ago figured out that people who hire people always seem to be more impressed with a person if he or she is currently employed. It's like if you're out of work and need a job, you're damaged goods; there must be something wrong with you.

During the second month of his tenure there, Danny learned the truth about Seymour. The man had been dating a Mafia don's daughter and had borrowed money from her. Later, when she asked him to pay it back, he turned her down, saying he didn't have it. She asked him for it several more times, and each time Seymour cried poverty.

The woman got angry and told her father, the Mafia don, who promptly put out a hit on Seymour. But Seymour had the survival ratio of a feline. Through the grapevine, he heard about the contract out on his life and so he married the girl. Problem solved.

Danny heard other stories about Seymour and the cronies he surrounded himself with, which only helped to supercharge Danny's search for another position.

Then one Monday evening, when Danny arrived home and checked his mail, he discovered to his utter horror that his paycheck from Perfect Publications had bounced.

It was a nightmare.

Danny had sent out personal checks to creditors all over town, based on that paycheck. When he got to work the next morning, he learned that everyone's paycheck had bounced.

Seymour's right-hand man, Tony Frizzoli, assured all of Perfect's employees, all fifteen of them, that cash would be brought into the office that afternoon, and not to worry.

Sure enough, a not-so-friendly individual arrived at the office a little after 3:00 with a suitcase full of money in small bills. Everyone was paid and released to do their banking.

Later, in a bar three blocks from the office, Danny and Scott agreed that they would not return to Perfect Publications. They drank to it over and over again, and both vowed to stay in touch.

Danny arrived back at the apartment in a less-than-sober state, much to Allison's chagrin. She was beginning to worry about Danny's excessive drinking and said so the next morning, despite Danny's apparent hangover.

Danny managed to stop drinking for a while, long enough to land a job with a startup publication that would become the American edition of one of Europe's top-selling men's magazines.

A partnership had been set up with a publishing group in Rome, and the American publisher had permission to use color separations, articles, illustrations, and any other material the Italian magazine produced. This, in turn, would be reciprocated by the American publishing group with any new material generated in New York.

The art director would be Scott Nielsen, Danny's longtime drinking buddy.

Chapter Nineteen
Surprise visits

Dorothy Wallace arrived at Midway Manor at precisely 9:30 PM on the last day of July in 1977. Her blue eyes sparkled as she walked through the Renaissance Room and directly up to the man seated at the piano. Lloyd Wallace looked up and his lower jaw dropped significantly.

"Dorothy," he yelled loudly, "it's you!"

Lloyd stood up and took his former wife into his arms. They hugged each other tightly.

"How are you, Lloyd?" Dorothy asked when they finally broke apart.

"Pretty much dead. Otherwise fine, I guess." He paused, not sure what he should say to the woman he truly loved. He felt bad she had to leave their son, but he really was very happy to see her again.

"It's good to see you, Lloyd." She paused, taking a long look at him. "I have to say, though, you're looking pretty good for a dead man."

"And you, sweet lady, are as beautiful as ever."

"Too bad we had to meet again in a place like this."

"Actually, it's kind of nice here. You don't have to worry about anything. And I can play the piano all I want."

"What about the women?" she asked, glancing around the room. "You still have that wandering eye?"

"I can honestly say that's all behind me now. That fire is out."

Dorothy smiled then, realizing the absurdity of the question she had just asked. "You went to a lot of trouble to quit a bad habit."

"I'll say."

Lloyd suddenly became aware that Mickey was standing nearby, holding his guitar by the neck.

"Dorothy, I want you to meet my friend Mickey Parks. Mick, this is my former wife Dorothy."

Mick extended his hand. "Danny's mother?" he said.

"Yes, I am, uh, was," Dorothy said, pausing for a moment to acclimate herself to her new state of existence as well as her surroundings. "I guess I'm still his mother, in a manner of speaking. I'm pleased to meet you, Mister Parks. I guess you know about Danny from Lloyd."

"We've shared some information about our past lives, who we left behind. My daughter was … is … Allison. Allison Parks. I believe you met her once."

"Oh, my. Well, isn't that a coincidence. Yes, once. Briefly. She seemed like such a nice young lady. A good match for my son, I thought. I liked her right from the start."

Mickey grew excited, realizing that here was someone who had seen Allison recently, been with her, talked with her. "Dorothy, it's such a pleasure to meet you."

Dorothy could sense Mickey's excitement and bonded with him instantly. As a parent, she knew the intense feelings he was experiencing. What was still hard for her to get used to was that these feelings still prevailed even after death.

"Yes. I guess it was about four months ago. Danny brought Allison out to see me and they stayed for dinner. We had a nice visit, although it could have been longer."

Mickey grinned broadly. "How did she look? Is her hair still long? Is she still slim?"

"She was gorgeous," said Dorothy. "You should be real proud of her."

"I am. I am," said Mickey, fighting back tears.

The three suddenly became aware of the attendant, Paul, standing rigidly nearby.

"I think they want to show you to your quarters, Dorothy," said Lloyd. "You don't know it yet, but if memory serves, you'll probably fall asleep to the wonderful fragrance of fresh lilacs and be very refreshed tomorrow morning. Why don't we all have breakfast in the dining room, say about nine? We'll come by your room and pick you up."

Dorothy smiled at both men, thankful she didn't have to begin this new journey alone.

"See you in the morning," she said as she began following the attendant.

When Dorothy had left the room, Lloyd pulled Mickey aside and cautioned him to watch what he said tomorrow. "I don't think it would be a good idea to tell Dorothy what we're doing," he said furtively.

"Why not?" Mickey asked, puzzled by Lloyd's secretiveness.

"Because we've got to hang around here for quite a while before we can get that information to Danny and Allison, and the more people who know about it, the less chance we have of keeping it a secret. Didn't you ever hear the term, 'Loose lips sink ships'?"

"I guess you're right, Lloyd. Mum's the word. But did I hear you right?" Mickey asked, quickly changing the subject. "When you told Dorothy about the lilacs … what the hell did you mean when you said 'if memory serves'? Why, you must be falling asleep before the scent floats through your room, you lucky son-of-a-gun. And I guess you never had insomnia when you were back on Earth, either. Am I right?"

"You're right. I never did have any trouble sleeping at all. Not there or here," Lloyd said, laughing. "Well, this is good news for all you insomniacs, and I'm very glad the Manor was able to come up with a solution to the problem."

"Not exactly," Mickey said. "Don't you remember me telling you that I'd always sneezed at least a dozen times right after that scent floated though my room?"

"Yes."

"Well, I'm still sneezing every night, so there's still a bit of a problem."

Lloyd was silent for a moment, sorry that the Manor couldn't have also come up with a way to alleviate Mickey's apparent allergy. But he remained preoccupied with Dorothy's arrival. "Say, Mick, how 'bout we call it an evening. I need to check at the front desk to find out what room Dorothy's in. I'll catch up with you in the morning."

Lloyd and Mickey arrived at Dorothy's room at precisely 9:00 AM.

"Good morning," she said as she opened her door and peeked out cautiously, unable to break old habits.

"Well, good morning to you," Lloyd said.

"How's your appetite?" Mickey asked.

"Actually, I'm surprisingly hungry. Why is that? We don't need food anymore, do we?"

"We may not *need* food," said Lloyd, taking Dorothy's arm and guiding her down the hall, "but The Authority has been kind enough to let us retain our appetites and the ability to enjoy food, among other amenities."

Dorothy was puzzled. "Who's The Authority?"

"Management. The Authority runs the place," said Mickey.

"Well … not only does it run Midway Manor, but The Authority runs *all* the destinations in the afterworld," Lloyd added.

"Will I get to meet with this Authority?" Dorothy asked.

"I don't think so. Mick and I have wondered if *anyone* ever gets to meet The Authority." Lloyd lingered for a moment, thinking to himself whether the plans that he and Mickey were working on would negate the statement he had just made.

"Oh," said Dorothy, not sure she had been enlightened on the subject at all.

"But you'll meet with the director, Joseph Patrick. Nice fellow. He'll probably give you the grand tour of the Manor sometime after breakfast. Right, Mick?"

"Yeah. Right after breakfast. Come on … let's go in."

"This buffet is terrific," said Lloyd. We can eat all we want and never worry about our weight or anything."

"… or heartburn," Mickey joked.

"Let's go see what they have," said Lloyd as they entered the large dining room.

"Oh, dear," lamented Dorothy. "This is so much food."

"Just take what you want," Mickey advised her.

The trio filled their plates and sat themselves at a nearby table.

"Well, Lloyd," Dorothy said between bites, "you were so right about my getting a good night's sleep. Why, I slept like a baby. And, if you remembered, I've always loved fresh lilacs. I would've liked to have stayed up all night enjoying the scent, but I fell asleep. Then this morning," Dorothy continued, "when I was enjoying a nice hot soak in the tub before I dressed, I realized that the pain I've always had in my left knee was completely gone.

"Not only that, the cataract in my right eye seems to have disappeared and the haze has lifted. I see better than I ever have. And I no longer have any hearing problems. I feel wonderful."

Lloyd smiled and wiped his mouth with a linen napkin before speaking. "I'm glad to hear it. But I'm not surprised."

Dorothy's blue eyes suddenly filled with tears. "I need to know that Danny is okay before I move on. The poor darling didn't know anything at all about my heart condition. I just couldn't tell him and have him worrying about me—"

"Danny will get through this," Lloyd interrupted. "I know it'll be tough for a while, but he'll be all right. I promise."

Mickey grabbed the coffeepot. "Anyone care for a refill?" he asked, trying to head off Dorothy from asking Lloyd the inevitable question of how he could make a promise that Danny would be okay.

"How can you be so sure, Lloyd?" Dorothy asked, dabbing at her eyes with her napkin. "He's lost both his parents in the space of a year. He's got to be pretty despondent, don't you think?"

Lloyd, of course, agreed. Having been to the Data Room earlier that morning, he knew from Danny's last journal that his mother had passed away prior to his arrival at the hospital in New Jersey. He also discovered that Danny was about to lose his job. Lloyd explained about the Manor's computers and how he and Mickey have been monitoring Danny and Allison through journals. When he shared with Dorothy what he had read in Danny's last journal, she became even more distressed.

"Oh, my dear boy," she cried.

Later, after Dorothy calmed down, she reflected on Lloyd's concern for Danny. But she still couldn't quite understand why he was at Midway Manor after more than a year. She sensed instinctively that something was going on, that Lloyd, and maybe Mickey Parks, too, were up to something involving Danny and Allison. But not knowing anything about computers, and vague about this business of journals, she decided to keep her suspicions to herself, at least for the time being.

Several hours after breakfast, Dorothy found herself sitting in front of a computer in the Data Room with the director of Midway Manor, Joseph Patrick, who was just finishing his basic set of instructions. "It's that simple. Do you have any questions?" he asked.

"No," Dorothy said softly, not feeling comfortable at all with the process of retrieving information on her son, and anxious to find Lloyd. "I want to thank you so much for showing me around. It's a very lovely place here." She sighed and then referred to what they had talked about earlier in the director's office. "As I said before, I only plan to stay here a few days, long enough to determine that my son is all right. But I'm really looking forward to seeing my sister Naomi at … what did you call it? Reunion Canyon.…"

"Valley. Reunion *Valley*. Just let me know when you want to leave and I'll make all the arrangements."

"Yes, I certainly will."

The director escorted Dorothy down to the main floor before they went their separate ways. Once again, Dorothy found Lloyd at the piano. "Hey, how'd it go on the tour?" he asked, surprised that the sight of her still made his heart sing.

"I found it a bit confusing," she answered, hoping he would offer to call up journals with her.

Lloyd was perceptive. "Well, we could go to the Data Room together. How do you feel about that?"

"Yes. I'd like that. Thank you," she said, smiling. "For now … I'd like to listen to you and Mr. Parks play a little bit."

Halfway through the first stanza, Dorothy, one arm resting on Lloyd's piano, began to sing the words to "Stardust." Both men smiled their approval and Dorothy continued with her dulcet tones, much to the delight of the Manor residents in the room.

During Dorothy's short visit to Midway Manor, she and Lloyd stayed pretty close. Lloyd spent time each day in the Data Room with Dorothy, showing her how to use the computer and how to print out a journal. Dorothy listened and watched intently and eventually learned the basics, but she was by no means comfortable with any of it.

Dorothy and Lloyd also indulged in long conversations about their earlier life together, keeping the negative aspects of the past to a minimum. They walked the halls of the Manor, and even ventured outdoors to stroll through the fragrant, colorful gardens. The couple concentrated on the more joyous times they did have together, and contemplated the future that might have been.

They spoke at length about Danny and his editorial career. Lloyd also shared what he knew about Mickey's daughter, Allison, and the promising relationship she had with Danny. And they considered the prospects of a grandchild. Mickey occasionally joined them, but for the most part kept his respectful distance.

Dorothy spent time each day with Lloyd at the computer until the words projected on the side-by-side wall screen had revealed Danny's visit to her modest home in New Jersey. It was on that day when Danny, with Allison at his side, had scattered Dorothy's ashes over the burgeoning roses and her favorite lilac bush. Dorothy broke into tears and Lloyd held her in his arms, trying earnestly to contain his own heartache.

Since Dorothy's arrival, however, she had always sensed that something was going on between Lloyd and Mickey. And her concern had intensified because Lloyd had always insisted on spending additional time in the Data Room alone with his buddy. On August 9, Dorothy confronted Lloyd and Mickey as they left the computer room.

"Hello, again," she said, standing directly outside the door as the two men emerged. "I wanted to let you know that Mr. Patrick is arranging for my trip to Reunion Canyon ... for tomorrow. Perhaps the two of you would like to accompany me on this journey?" she asked, her instincts telling her this offer would more than likely be turned down. She waited patiently for their response.

Lloyd carefully considered Dorothy's question and knew that he had two choices. He could try to pacify her with some trumped-up fairy tale, or he could tell her the truth. Lloyd decided to take the honorable route and lay it all out for her.

"You see, Dorothy, not only are Mickey and I monitoring Allison's and Danny's journals, but we're also writing into their blank journals and influencing events yet to come. We believe it was actually what we wrote in their blank journals that made the two of them hook up in the first place. Oh, and I believe it's Reunion *Valley*, not Canyon."

Lloyd went on to tell Dorothy of his plans to send Danny and Allison the unsolved mysteries revelations, some of which Dorothy had read. "The goal here is for the kids to write a book using the information we send. With the money they should earn from the book sales, they ought to be secure for life," he said enthusiastically.

Dorothy's reaction was mixed. She certainly embraced the idea of helping Danny and Allison become financially independent. But her biggest problem was justifying in her own mind the morality of intervention from the other side. She also had her doubts that the plan would even work.

But Dorothy decided that whatever happened, the intervention would not have a negative effect on Danny and Allison. Worst case scenario, Lloyd and Mickey wouldn't be able to get the material to the kids. And so Dorothy spent the rest of the day enjoying the company of both men, talking, dining together, and often singing along with the two of them as they played their music.

That night, after Dorothy had said her goodbyes, she retired to her room. In the wee hours of the morning of August 10, 1977, a fascinating beam of amber light drew her to it, engulfing her in its warm glow, and Dorothy suddenly found herself standing in the most beautiful, lush green valley she had ever seen. The smiling face of her sister Naomi, arms outstretched, welcomed her to an eternity of peaceful bliss and joyous serenity.

Six days later, on August 16, rumor spread throughout the Manor that Elvis Presley was in the building. Lloyd and Mickey had just finished eating dinner when they heard the news.

"Well, there's the backup guitar you were looking for, Mick," said Lloyd. "And now we got ourselves a male singer."

"We'll be a trio instead of a duo," Mick added as the two hurried toward the Renaissance Room.

But Elvis had apparently gone directly to the Data Room, read the journals he was looking for, and quickly arranged for his departure to Reunion Valley to be reunited with his beloved mother. There was plenty of speculation for months afterward as to whose journals Elvis selected, but the Manor's privacy rule kept that secret intact. Lloyd and Mickey were disappointed that they had missed the King, but they soon reconciled to the fact that Elvis had indeed left the building.

Chapter Twenty
Danny goes to Rome

The first thing Danny noticed about his new office at The Jonas Publishing Group was the long, brown leather couch. Its presence immediately conjured up two images in his head—afternoon naps and evening assignations.

The second thing Danny noted was the view from the window and the panoply of Manhattan skyscrapers. And if he looked out to his left, he could easily see the elaborate facade of Grand Central Station.

It was by far the largest office he'd had in his career to date, and the most comfortable. A smaller room next to it sat empty, except for one lone light box apparently used to look at color transparencies.

Danny had arrived at the Park Avenue publishing company well before 9:00 that morning, anxious to begin his new job. He had walked briskly across the building's marble lobby to the bank of elevators and was quickly whisked up to the twentieth floor.

The sultry brunette receptionist gave Danny a big smile when he passed through the glass entry doors and identified himself. She hit a button and said something into the phone and moments later a young blond woman opened the inner office door and asked Danny to please follow her. She took him directly to his office.

"Go ahead and settle in," the blonde said. "Mr. Nielsen will be in shortly and he'll show you around." She turned and left, and Danny couldn't help but stare at the way her well-rounded buttocks moved under her cotton dress.

Danny took off his coat and looked behind the door, hoping to find a clothes hanger. An unadorned hook glared out at him. He made a mental note to bring a hanger from home.

"Hey, buddy, how goes it?" Scott Nielsen, the art director and Danny's faithful drinking companion, stood in the doorway. The man who had gotten him this job towered over Danny at nearly six-six. Slim, with curly silver and black hair and a mustache, he drew women to him like a human magnet.

"Good so far," Danny answered. "I like my office."

"Well, that's a start. Did you get to meet the blonde, Arlene?"

"If you mean the gal who showed me to my office, yeah. Nice caboose."

"That ain't all that's nice," said Scott, looking down at Danny with one eyebrow raised lasciviously.

"Are you doing her?"

"For the past two months."

"What about Ellen? And Melissa?"

"Yeah, I see them from time to time. And also Brenda. Beautiful Brenda."

"Scott, they're gonna leave your parts to medical science when you check out." Danny rolled his eyes. "I don't know how you do it. You drink with both hands and your liver's probably pickled by now. How do you even get it up?"

"Never had that problem," bragged Scott.

"What about jealousy? I also can't figure why one of them doesn't shoot your ass."

Scott laughed. "I've been lucky, I guess. Listen, before I forget, we've got a ten-fifteen with the big guy in his office."

Danny knew that in New York, there were an inordinate number of publishers in the men's field who were considered con men. Most of them just nickel-and-dimed a writer to death. They forgot to pay part of or the entire fee they agreed on, or they somehow overlooked a royalty due. Or they lost material and later mysteriously found it. Or they just flat didn't pay the writer or artist for his work. And sometimes, when they were challenged, they would get defensive and nasty about it.

But not Warren Jonas, a publisher unofficially known as "the gentle con man." Warren was capable of fleecing his own mother, but his demeanor remained that of a gentleman. This made it difficult not to like the man.

Warren Jonas appeared to be in his early fifties, about six feet tall, with rounded shoulders, thinning gray hair and a bit of a paunch. He wore steel-rimmed glasses, which he constantly took off and misplaced. His publishing empire consisted of several mediocre slick men's magazines and a line of paperbacks. Of the latter, the historical romance titles were the most lucrative.

Warren's office would make an empty warehouse look small in comparison. When Danny and Scott came in and stood in the middle of the room, Warren moved around from behind the huge desk and greeted Danny warmly. "Good to have you with us," he said, smiling broadly. "Lemme tell you something right from the start. This magazine, *Ciao*, is gonna knock *Playboy* and *Penthouse* right outta the box.

"To do that, we're gonna need big-name writers for the columns and articles we generate here. We have access to a few famous bylines generated in Rome, but we need our own all-star lineup. Can you pull that off, Danny boy?"

Danny nodded, slightly intimidated by Warren Jonas' somewhat aggressive manner. "I'll get in touch with some of the better agents in town, and I have my own sources." Danny tried to sound matter-of-fact, as if he got big names to write for him all the time. But in truth, Danny felt a little frightened, a bit insecure. He knew this wasn't a men's adventure magazine or just another stroke book. He sensed, perhaps, that he might be on the verge of playing in the big leagues.

Danny kept his self-doubts to himself. As Warren droned on about the future and what he had planned to do to promote the magazine among the wholesalers around the country, Danny thought about Allison and how he wished she were right there with him. He briefly thought about his dad and his mom, which brought back that familiar ache in his gut. And then he thought about how much he needed a stiff drink.

Later, after several hours on the phone with literary agents, Danny went to lunch with Scott and had that stiff drink. He had several, in fact, as did Scott, and that enabled both men to get through the rest of the day.

The days became weeks as work progressed on the first issue of *Ciao*. Danny managed to land a few prominent bylines through several of the literary agents he called, and even Samantha Hodges delivered a couple of well-known writers. The first issue began to shape up as a blockbuster, with a never-before-published piece by Henry Miller, an interview with Marcello Mastroianni, and articles on women terrorists, California's open-sex spa, and cosmetic sex surgery for men.

Danny and Scott worked diligently with their Italian collaborators to add visual punch to the lineup, adding an infusion of erotic cheesecake using color separations from Rome, and other Italy-generated features such as Picasso's "forbidden" erotic drawings and photos of nude actresses.

The publisher of the original *Ciao* in Rome, Sophia Torino, and her entourage arrived at Kennedy International Airport via Alitalia Flight AZ 579 at 1:30 PM, April 11, 1978. Included in the group was Piero Moretti, *Ciao*'s editorial director, and Frank Bianco, the Italian magazine's art director. Both men spoke English, though Frank's fluency proved less than adequate.

Piero, a relatively squat but distinguished-looking gray-haired man in his fifties, wide of girth, displayed a hair-trigger sense of humor. He and Danny were simpatico as soon as they met.

Frank, a much younger man, handsome, with dark-brown hair and eyes, effected an almost effeminate manner. He was as quiet as Piero was loud.

Sophia, an exquisitely slender blond woman in her thirties, exchanged pleasantries with Danny, obviously quite adept in conversing in both languages. However, while in New York she stayed fairly close to Warren Jonas.

Danny had no trouble making himself understood to Piero, though sometimes Piero admitted that when Danny got into his typical New York City mode and spoke too fast, it would give him a severe headache. And Danny, for the most part, was able to understand Piero. Conversely, communication between Danny and Frank remained quite limited and needed ongoing assistance from Piero.

Within an hour of arriving at the New York office, Piero, Frank and Danny, along with Scott Nielsen, his assistant Tom Hammer, and Warren all crammed into the small room with the light box. Scott had asked them to consider a batch of thirty-five millimeter slides he had placed on the light box for possible first-cover treatment.

The problem was that except for Danny, all of the men were smokers. Within five minutes, the poorly ventilated room had become thick with smoke and it became increasingly difficult to breathe.

When Sophia came back to join them, she gasped and started to cough. "Is suicide you gentlemen are trying to commit, no?" she finally managed to say without choking.

Warren decided to solve the problem by declaring a moratorium on smoking while in the light-box room.

Danny hardly saw Allison during this time, working late and on the weekends as well as hoisting a few with Scott. The pressure on Danny was enormous and alcohol seemed to be the only way he could cope with it.

To add annoyance to an already hard-pressed staff, Warren's penny-pinching assistant publisher, Roselyn Shwartzman, sent numerous memos advising *Ciao* personnel to turn off their air conditioners when they went to lunch or left for a meeting, and run them on low when they *were* being used. She also advised staffers to remember to turn lights off when they left their office, and on sunny days try to work without them.

There were other problems. European humor, either in text or in the form of cartoons, did not travel well. American humor is largely based on irony, whereas Italian humor is more "slapstick" in nature. There was also a constant problem with translators when it came to fiction. But over time a lot of the minor kinks were ironed out and the birth pains eased.

Two weeks before Danny and company were scheduled to print the first issue, MPs showed up at the door. They were there to escort Scott's art and paste-up assistant, a young black man named Maurice Bennett, to the stockade. It seems that Maurice had overlooked a requirement that he show up for two weeks' active reserve duty. While stunned staff members looked on in disbelief, the Marines led Maurice away in handcuffs.

After several issues of *Ciao* had been produced, it was decided that Danny and Scott should travel to Rome and spend a week there at their counterparts' villa, going over the vast inventory of color separations and editorial material that would be at their disposal.

On August 20, 1978, Danny and Scott boarded Alitalia Flight AZ 614 at Kennedy International Airport. During their overnight transcontinental flight, the two managed to drink the 747 dry of white-wine splits.

Upon arrival in Rome, Danny and Scott were taken by chauffeured limousine to their hotel, an offbeat hostel frequented by Europeans but not usually visited by the typical American tourist. After unpacking, Danny and Scott went directly to the hotel bar and continued their nonstop drinking marathon.

Danny experienced his first blackout that night, awakening at 4:00 in the morning, fully dressed in a three-piece suit, completely oblivious as to how he got there. At about 7:00, Scott entered Danny's room and advised him that the limo would be there around 9:00 to take them to the villa.

"I've got a monster of a hangover," said Danny, finding it painful to even speak.

"No kidding," said Scott. "You certainly drank enough. I looked up at one point and you were gone. I checked the men's room, and even the ladies' room, and you were nowhere to be found. That's when I came up here and found you lying in state, as it were. Geez, Dan, you really tied one on."

"Yeah, well, I could use a little hair of the dog right now."

"No problem," said Scott, producing a bottle of the local white wine. "This ought to fix you right up." He filled two water glasses with the wine and handed one to Danny, who drank it right down.

"What's the problem, Alli," Marlene asked.

"I'm okay," Allison replied, pretending to concentrate on submersing a doughnut into her coffee cup.

"Yeah, right. You drive all the way the hell out here to Jersey to show me a sourpuss, and then you tell me you're okay."

"I am. I just miss Danny."

"Honey, we go way back and I know when something's bothering you." Marlene pushed away from the dining room table and went over to her friend. When Allison looked up, Marlene cupped her chin.

"Danny's drinking again, isn't he?"

Allison nodded, tears spilling down her cheeks.

"I knew it!" Marlene said, pulling Allison up out of the chair and hugging her tightly.

"I'm really worried about him," Allison confessed, gently breaking free of Marlene's grip and walking into the living room. "Now he's in Rome and God knows what's goin' on with him." She sat down on the sofa.

"Girlfriend, you've got to confront Danny," Marlene said, following her. "When he gets back, you have to tell him it's either you or the booze."

"I don't know—"

"Damn it, Alli! If you don't do this now, you'll regret it for the rest of your life."

"Oh, Danny's probably working his butt off right now. I bet he doesn't even have time to drink."

For the rest of the week, Danny and Scott worked through the day at the villa, viewing and amassing a great deal of potential material for the American edition of *Ciao*.

In the mornings, before going to the villa, Danny and Scott would have the limo driver stop at a cafe where they would have a little breakfast. This included a couple of shots of vodka to clear the cobwebs and get their blood flowing. At night, the two men enjoyed excellent Italian cuisine at a number of fine restaurants, courtesy of the Italians. And they drank. Heavily.

Accompanying Danny and Scott on a daily basis were two young female translators, Rosa and Kristina. Both women were dark-haired and attractive, and Scott had no trouble sleeping with Kristina on their second night in Rome. Danny's interpreter, Rosa, however, was somewhat reserved. She kidded and lightly flirted with Danny, and even had a drink with him, but for the most part she conducted herself in a professional manner.

Danny certainly had urges, and the alcohol magnified them, but he continually thought of Allison back in New York and the very special link they had with each other. Their relationship was apparently strong enough to keep Danny zipped up and he managed to avoid being unfaithful while in Rome. He didn't know it then, but that resolve would be tested once more when he returned to Manhattan.

Allison stood waiting at the gate after Danny and Scott got through customs. She ran into Danny's outstretched arms and they kissed passionately, holding each other tightly. Neither wanted to let the other go. After a while, Scott cleared his throat loudly and muttered something about getting a room.

Allison drove back to Manhattan and dropped Scott off at his apartment. When they got home, Danny went immediately into the kitchen and removed a bottle of vodka from the cabinet, relieved that it was relatively untouched.

"Care to join me in a martini," he asked, setting down two glasses.

"I suppose," Allison said, sitting down on the sofa, her lack of enthusiasm genuine. The last thing she wanted to do was encourage Danny to drink.

Danny walked into the living room and tried to pick Bratly up, but the calico had developed an attitude after Danny had been away for so long. She remained aloof for an hour or so, but before long she was rubbing up against Danny's leg and meowing her acceptance of his return.

"She really missed you," said Allison. "And so did I."

"I don't see you rubbing up against my leg," Danny said teasingly.

Allison patted the spot next to her on the Victorian sofa. "C'mon and sit down next to me and I'll rub anything you want."

Danny eased himself down on the couch, placed his half-empty martini glass on the coffee table, and took Allison in his arms. She snuggled in close to him. As they so often did when they were alone together, they talked.

"I don't know what it is about you, Danny, but you do something to me. I have a constant urge to tell you my innermost thoughts, to share my most private feelings with you."

"Maybe you didn't notice," said Danny, "but I, too, have a habit of spilling my guts out when I'm with you. I guess that's part of what love is all about."

"I guess." Allison paused, debating with herself whether she should confront Danny about his drinking.

"You know, honey," she said finally, pushing her hair away from her eyes the way she always did, "I've noticed how tense you've been with this *Ciao* magazine thing."

"Yeah, there's a lotta pressure up there." He downed the rest of the martini.

"And … and it's causing you to drink way more than you should."

"Who the hell made you my judge and jury?" Danny snapped. *I love this woman but I don't need her trying to run my life.*

"Honey, I'm not telling you what you should or should not do," Allison said, as if reading his mind. "I'm just worried about you. I don't want you to get sick." She was quiet a moment. "I want you to stick around for the good part."

"Just what I need, a mother my own age."

"Danny, come on. Don't get nasty. It's not your nature."

Danny mumbled an okay as he got up to fix himself another martini. Allison bit her tongue, suppressing an urge to scream to Danny that his nonstop, out-of-control drinking was slowly killing him.

Danny returned to the sofa with another drink. He took a couple of sips and then put the glass down on the coffee table, pulling Allison close again. He wrapped his arms around her and promised he would try to cut down, that he's just been under a lot of pressure.

Allison had heard it all. The excuses, the convoluted reasons, the empty promises. *I love this man with all my heart. I want to believe him. Can I believe him?* Allison relented, deciding to take Danny's word. He was moving his hands over her body, touching her intimately, and she found herself caught up in the passion of the moment.

Later, in bed, they made love. For a fraction of a moment, the image of Rosa the translator flashed in Danny's head. But when Allison moaned softly, he focused on her and quickened his movements until she cried out in orgasmic relief. Danny reached his own climax moments later. They soon fell into a deep, satisfying sleep, holding each other tightly. She and Danny had, Allison decided, communicated in mind, body and spirit.

The months passed quickly as Danny and Scott produced issue after issue of *Ciao*. Because of the collaboration with the Italians and the logistics, production time was tight and the stress factor continued to increase. Danny was now lacing half-empty cans of Coke with vodka and drinking them at his desk.

One Friday afternoon, Scott asked Danny to meet him at one of the local pubs. "Brenda will be there," he told Danny. "She'd like to say hello. I'm buying."

Never one to pass up a free drink, Danny readily agreed to meet him at Costello's around 5:30. Later, when he got to Costello's, Scott and Brenda and another attractive woman, a redhead, were already sitting in a booth in the back. They waved Danny over when he walked in and Danny sat down next to the redhead.

"This is Brenda's friend, Lillian," Scott said, grinning broadly.

"A pleasure," Danny said, shaking Lillian's hand.

The four sat there and drank several rounds of drinks, with Scott constantly reminding everyone that he was picking up the tab.

Meantime, Allison arrived at Danny's office thinking she would surprise Danny and maybe have dinner out. When she was told that Danny had gone over to Costello's, she returned to her car and headed over to the bar, long familiar with this favorite hangout of the city's literati.

Danny to this day doesn't recall how it actually started, but before he even realized what was happening, Lillian had unzipped his fly and slipped her hand inside his pants.

Danny knew she was already high and had gone over the line. He also knew that by not stopping her—despite having no intentions of sleeping with her—he, too, had gone over the line.

When Allison came in and walked over to the booth, the first thing she saw was the redhead's hand snaked inside Danny's pants and moving up and down. She looked at Danny whose eyes were half-closed and reacted spontaneously.

"You cheating sonofabitch prick bastard!" she said, fighting back the tears. She turned to leave, then added, "I'll be gone before you get home!"

Chapter Twenty-one
A sudden change of plans

Mickey had barely finished pouring himself a second cup of coffee when Lloyd bolted from his chair. "Gotta go," he said with a forced smile.

Every morning for the past several months, Lloyd had deliberately selected a skimpy breakfast consisting of nothing more than one fried egg and a small glass of orange juice. He set up this regimen so that he wouldn't waste any time getting to the Data Room computer. Mickey had eventually stopped asking the same old question, "What's the rush?"

Lloyd's robotic response had been repeatedly short and simple. "I was just checking to make sure Danny's okay," he would say, not wanting Mickey to know how worried he'd become about his son's drinking. Lloyd had been carefully studying Danny's daily journals over the past months and he could see that his son's consumption of alcohol had in fact escalated.

The heavy drinking during Danny's trip to Rome when he had his first bona fide blackout was the turning point, in Lloyd's mind. And remembering his own out-of-control drinking days, he knew it was more than likely just a matter of time before the drinking would give rise to some sort of catastrophe. That morning, Lloyd's uneasiness became a reality.

As he read the events in Danny's journal that had taken place the previous day, he winced at the words describing an alcohol-induced sexual act with someone named Lillian. Indeed, the account of the incident brought back memories of his own past and he began to relive the series of compulsive transgressions that had pushed him further and further away from Dorothy and his son. Lloyd also remembered the feelings of guilt and shame that had gnawed away at his insides during his years on Earth.

He warily continued reading Danny's diary, not ever expecting to find out that Allison had not only witnessed the act, but she had opted to abruptly move out of their West Side apartment as well.

"Oh, my God," he cried. "This can't be happening." Lloyd read the words once again on the side-by-side screen, hoping his mind was just playing a trick on him. "Damn it, Danny," he mumbled to himself after reading it a second time from beginning to end. Lloyd struck the print key and then quickly shut down the computer. *I've got to find Mickey before he reads Allison's journal,* he decided, hurrying off to the main floor.

Mickey, who had apparently stopped by the Renaissance Room after drinking his second cup of coffee alone, was chatting with a few residents when Lloyd unexpectedly showed up. "Hey, buddy, come on over," Mickey shouted. But when Lloyd didn't respond to his verbal invitation, Mickey excused himself and headed over toward his friend. That's when he noticed Lloyd's face was as red as a New York City fire hydrant. "Are you okay?" he asked.

"Not really," Lloyd answered. "How 'bout we take a walk outside in the gardens so we can have some privacy. We need to talk."

Mickey looked directly into his friend's eyes and could see that Lloyd was fighting back tears. "Yeah … sure, let's go." At the very moment they stepped outside, Mickey spoke up again. "Okay, now … talk to me. What's going on with Danny?" he asked, assuming something in Danny's journal had upset him.

Lloyd looked down and took a deep breath. "It's over, Mick. Our mission here at Midway Manor is over."

"What? What's happened to Danny?" he asked again, thinking the worst.

"It's not just Danny. It's the kids …"

Mickey grabbed Lloyd's arm, barely able to fight the dread that was now consuming him. "The kids? Oh, my God. Tell me what's happened."

"They've split up. Yeah … Danny and Allison aren't living together anymore."

Stardust Dads

"What? They split up? That's it? You mean they're okay ... they're not hurt or anything. Oh, thank God." Mickey released his grip on Lloyd's arm, trying to catch his breath at the same time. "Why the hell didn't you just tell me that right away? Damn ... I thought they were hurt in a car accident or something. Oh, thank God they're okay."

"Listen to me," Lloyd interrupted. "No ... there wasn't a car accident or anything like that. But the situation is serious ... and I'm sorry to have to tell you this. You see ... an incident took place," he said carefully, "an incident that got Allison quite upset."

"Allison? An incident? What incident? No, never mind. I'll find out for myself," Mickey said angrily as he turned and headed toward the main entrance.

"Wait." Lloyd called out as Mickey rushed away, "There's more. We need to talk about this. Please, Mick."

Mickey could not comply with his friend's plea and quickened his pace. At that moment, getting to the Data Room to read his daughter's journal was the highest priority in his mind. But when he rushed through the door at the front entrance, Mickey bumped right into the director, Joseph Patrick.

"Whoa there, Mr. Parks," Mr. Patrick said, clutching Mickey's arm to catch his own balance. "Mr. Parks, is something wrong?" he asked when he released his hold.

Mickey looked up at Mr. Patrick without answering his question. He was too choked up to speak.

"Mr. Parks," the director said softly, "why don't we step into my office?"

"I can't," Mickey blurted, his voice trembling. "I have to get to the Data Room."

Mickey was about to rush away when Lloyd bolted through the front entrance. Lloyd stopped short by just a few feet. And the trio stood before one another.

"This is perfect," the director said. "Mr. Wallace ... Mr. Parks ... excuse me for interrupting your morning, but please follow me to my office."

Lloyd and Mickey looked at each other. They were both wordless, hesitant, but instinctively they felt they could do nothing but abide by the director's sudden and unusual request. They followed him into his large office.

"Please have a seat," Mr. Patrick said, motioning to the chairs in front of his desk. "I've been deficient in not speaking with you sooner."

"But … I can explain," Mickey blurted out.

Lloyd turned in his seat to give Mickey a look that pleaded for his silence and then quickly decided to verbally stifle him. "No. If you wouldn't mind, Mick, I'd like to speak first."

"Sorry, fellows," Mr. Patrick said, smiling. "Like I said, I've taken much too long to speak with you about this matter and I cannot put it off any longer."

Mickey and Lloyd remained silent while their eyes followed the director's every move, though all he did was nothing more than slowly turn away to take a seat at his desk. He appeared to be carefully preparing to find the right words and as the seconds passed, Mickey's heart pounded faster while Lloyd's mind raced.

I feel like the jury has just reached a verdict, Mickey thought. *And I'm not ready to leave here. Especially not now.*

The director looked over at the duo and smiled again.

I wonder just how long it's been that he's known about us tampering with the kids' journals, Lloyd deliberated in his mind.

"Gentlemen, I'm sorry for the delay in speaking to you, but I do want both of you to know how much you're appreciated around here." He paused, allowing his words to take effect. "In no way would I even suggest that you stay here any longer than you care to, but all of us—and I speak for the majority of the residents—enjoy the music you so graciously play for us. Now, I know you both will eventually move on. It's just a matter of time before you'll want to be with loved ones who had left Earth earlier and have chosen other destinations. But for as long as you remain at Midway Manor, your music will be warmly welcomed."

Lloyd and Mickey both listened attentively to the director's words, waiting for the other shoe to drop. After he had personally thanked them for their daily musical sessions in the Renaissance Room, he said, "Oh, yes … and there is something else …"

Mickey gripped the arms of his chair. Lloyd sat up straight and cleared his throat, prepared to defend his friend and take full responsibility for their tampering with Danny's and Allison's journals.

"I'm sure that by now you're both familiar with the books we have on the shelves in each Midway Manor room. In particular, I refer you to the book, *Earth's Unsolved Mysteries Revealed*."

Mickey and Lloyd leaned forward. *Here it comes,* Lloyd thought, clenching his teeth.

"This book was compiled by former Midway residents John Bonano and Kevin Stone," the director continued. "Well, what I'd like to do, with your permission, of course, is to have you tape-record some of your songs so that the residents will always have the opportunity to enjoy your music, even after you've left the Manor. Like the book, we would have the cassette tapes on hand in each resident's room. We would, naturally, give you clear attribution. Would you both be agreeable to recording some of your songs?" he asked.

The duo sat in silence for a few moments, trying to overcome what had been their needless anxiety. When Mickey and Lloyd absorbed the fact that the journal tampering and their upcoming plans to provide Danny and Allison with the answers from the book of unsolved mysteries was still a secret, they finally responded, almost in unison. They agreed to record some of their songs and then thanked the director for his kind words. And not wanting to spend another minute in the director's office, they jumped up from their chairs, shook hands with Mr. Patrick and quickly left his office together.

"That was *not* what I expected," Mickey said as he headed toward the Data Room, with Lloyd following at his side.

"We're in the clear for now," Lloyd said. "And I'm thinking that maybe we haven't needed to be all that subtle in what we've been writing into the kids' journals. And … if I'm right about this, I think we can fix things up between Danny and Allison. Unless, of course, you don't want them to get back together again."

Mickey and Lloyd spent the rest of the day sharing the same computer. Lloyd called up dozens of Danny's journals to prove beyond a shadow of a doubt that his son, with the exception of this one time, had always been faithful to Allison. He methodically explained to Mickey, who was completely misinformed on the subject of alcoholism, how this one-time incident was alcohol-induced.

Mickey was once again convinced that Danny was truly devoted to Allison. He then agreed to Lloyd's proposal to manipulate Danny's journal regarding his alcoholism. They would try to somehow set up a roadblock to contain his runaway drinking. He knew that Allison's love and support would undoubtedly make a difference in Danny's recovery.

Lloyd comforted Mickey while he read Allison's daily diary from the day before, how she had witnessed the incident, grabbed a few items from their apartment and driven off, not knowing where she was going. Mickey was somewhat relieved that Allison's good friend Marlene had finally arrived home in time to receive her phone call, to let her talk things out.

Mickey cringed when he read that his daughter had told Marlene she thought Danny had probably been fooling around with other women for months. And all the time telling her he had been working evenings and weekends. He knew he had to get Allison to see that Danny had not planned any of what had taken place. He had to somehow get her to realize that this had been a spontaneous act of sexual aggression on the part of Brenda's friend Lillian. That because of Danny's alcoholic haze, he allowed himself to go over the line.

Besides getting Allison to see the light, to see that Danny really did love her and that her place was with him, the Midway dads still had the major obstacle to overcome—Danny's drinking. And Lloyd decided he had the solution.

"We'll get Danny to join Alcoholics Anonymous," he told Mickey. "We'll just type it into a blank journal. He's vulnerable right now. He's still saturated with alcohol, he's hurting, and he's lost Allison. He's suffering what AA calls hitting one's personal bottom.

"For some people, the bottom means skid row, but that's the extreme case. For many, the bottom can be losing a job, or losing someone you love, or, as Thoreau once wrote, simply 'leading a life of quiet desperation.' I think in Danny's case, Allison really is the number one priority in his life. And now he's lost her."

"I understand," Mickey said, "but I don't think he's going to go anywhere until he's found Allison and brought her back into his life."

"You're probably right, but I doubt that your daughter's going to be willing to go back to him. She'll have to be ... wait, I know ..."

Lloyd called up Danny's blank journal for the next day and went all out when he began typing. Mickey read the words as they appeared on the side-by-side screen on the wall. Lloyd was very direct in what he typed. He was determined to have his son get his life back, and that included getting Allison to return. His first order of business was to induce Danny to make a positive move regarding his alcoholic drinking.

"Do you think that you've gotten a little carried away?" Mickey asked when Lloyd had finally finished typing.

"Not at all," he answered as he called up Allison's blank journal. "Go for it, Mick. These kids need us."

Chapter Twenty-two
Clean, sober and committed

Danny sat horrified moments after Allison stormed out of Costello's, transfixed by the event that had just taken place. Lillian quickly withdrew her hand from Danny's crotch and he zipped up his fly.

Scott and Brenda sat there, still not quite sure what had just transpired. Danny mumbled an apology as he slid out from the booth and stood up. "I've got to track her down and straighten this out before it gets worse." He carefully avoided looking at Lillian. "See you guys later."

There was no sign of Allison when Danny got outside. He flagged down a cab and headed for the apartment.

Bratly's breath-holding meowing told him Allison was not there. After checking her closet and determining that one of her suitcases was gone, he scoured the apartment in the hope that she had left a note telling him where she'd be. But there was nothing except a half-empty box of tissues on the kitchen counter, with a pile of discarded tissues next to it. Apparently Bratly, in her own feline frustration over Allison's abrupt departure, had pawed the tissues out of the box one by one.

Danny felt that familiar homesick feeling in the pit of his stomach, a feeling of fear, anxiety, dread and loss all rolled into one. He went into the kitchen, took a bottle of vodka out of the cabinet and began to drink at the pain....

The tears streamed down Allison's cheeks as she drove through the midtown traffic, almost obscuring her vision. She barely avoided slamming into the trunk of the car ahead of her as it braked for a traffic light.

That bastard, she thought. *He's probably been cheating on me for months. Here he's telling me he's working late and all the time he's doing it with someone else. There probably have been others. I wonder how many.* She suddenly found herself driving over the Queensboro Bridge.

On Queens Boulevard, Allison impulsively pulled into the parking lot of a diner. *Maybe some coffee will help clear my head,* she thought. She found a booth in the rear of the diner and sat down, telling the waitress she wanted a cup of coffee and a Danish.

Allison's emotions were flying. She felt betrayed, hurt, angry. She choked back the tears, trying to get a grip on herself as the waitress set the coffee and pastry down on the table.

"Can I get you anything else, hon?" the waitress asked.

Allison shook her head. *How about a man who's honorable, who won't cheat on you behind your back?* she thought. The anger welled up inside her again. The idea of taking a gun and killing Danny passed fleetingly through her head. *God, what am I thinking?*

She suddenly remembered that Marlene had moved to Queens several months ago. She rummaged around in her purse until she found her address book. Sixty-second Street in Woodside. Marlene said it was just down the street from the el, the number seven line that went out to the old World's Fair grounds and Shea Stadium where the Mets play.

Allison walked over to the phone booth in the front of the diner and called Marlene's number. When she got Marlene's answering machine, she hung up without leaving a message. She went back to her booth and ordered another cup of coffee.

What did I do wrong? she thought. *We had a good life together. I had nothing before I met Danny.* Allison thought back to her childhood and the mother who never had an approving word for her. She adored her father who doted on her, but her mother made her life miserable.

She remembered the time when it was Mother's Day and she had no money to buy a present. She had picked some flowers from a yard down the block after getting permission from the neighbor, and brought them to her mother. But instead of appreciation, her mother had thrown the flowers in the garbage and criticized her for stealing them.

"What a horrid little girl. I'm writing this down in the book," she had said to Allison. She was always writing in her book about the alleged bad things that Allison did. And Allison recalled how much it hurt, the same hurt she was feeling because of Danny's betrayal.

When Allison called Marlene again an hour later, Marlene answered. "That rat bastard," was her girlfriend's reaction when Allison recounted the day's earlier events. "You're going to stay with me. Get over here as soon as you can."

Allison left the diner then and got into her car. *Thank God I have this car to get away from all this,* she thought. *But damn, I thought I'd be using it to get away from a neurotic mother, not from the man I love.*

Danny drank himself to sleep. When he awoke after 9:00 AM, he briefly panicked over the prospect of being so late for work. He got up off the stiff Victorian couch, still dressed in yesterday's clothes, and tried to recount all that had happened in the last twenty-four hours. He winced when he realized how much his head hurt. He staggered into the bathroom and relieved himself, feeling the anxiety welling up inside him. Experiencing a sudden wave of nausea, he leaned over the toilet and deliberately put his finger down his throat. He gagged as the dry heaves wracked his body. He finally brought up the bile, the yellow liquid from his stomach, and he felt better. He had been through this before.

He stumbled into the kitchen looking for the vodka and discovered he had drunk all but maybe one ounce. He lifted the bottle to his lips and drank the clear liquid straight down. It burned for a moment but he knew it would eventually help. "How am I gonna get through the day at work the way I feel?" he asked himself.

Bratly rubbed up against his leg, scolding him for not paying any attention to her. Danny picked her up and carried her over to the couch and sat down, stroking the back of the cat's neck as he tried to unscramble the cobwebs of thought in his head. He replayed the previous day's events, and as he did so he realized that it was Saturday and there would be no work.

"Thank God," he muttered to himself.

A light bulb went off in his head. *Marlene! Of course. That's where Allison went, to Marlene's place.* He reached over to the end table and extracted the address book from the top drawer. He vaguely remembered Allison mentioning that Marlene had moved back into the city and was now living in Queens. He thumbed through the small black book until he found Marlene's name. Her old address and phone number were crossed out and a new number in red ink was written below it.

Danny picked up the phone and dialed the new number. Marlene answered.

"Hey, Marlene. It's me, Danny."

"She doesn't want to talk to you."

"Listen, you've got to let me speak to her ..."

Click. There was a dial tone. Marlene had obviously hung up.

Danny put the receiver down and leaned forward, holding his head in his hands. *What the hell am I going to do? I love her so much. I can't bloody well live without her.* He wept softly ... for Allison ... for his mother ... for his father ... for the mess his life had become.

Danny sat on the couch for a very long time, alternately weeping and trying to figure out what he should do next. And then, ever so slowly, he began to see the light. It was like a revelation, as if someone from above had imparted a divine inspiration. It was so simple.

He would get sober.

It was a miracle. Everything was crystal clear. He opened a phone book and looked up the number for Alcoholics Anonymous. AA had gotten his dad sober, so why wouldn't it work for him? He dialed the number and the voice on the other end gave him a list of meetings in his immediate area. There was a meeting at 3:00 that afternoon at the church around the corner.

The next thing Danny did was to call the local florist and order a dozen roses, which he ordered sent to Allison in care of Marlene Wills at her Woodside address. The note he dictated over the phone read: "Dearest Allison, you are the heart and soul of my life, my only true love. I cannot bear to live without you. Love, Danny."

It was 3:10 that Saturday afternoon when the downstairs buzzer rang. "Flowers for Ms. Parks," the voice said, and Marlene buzzed the vestibule door open. Allison sat in Marlene's living room and cried as she read the note. Teardrops moistened the rosebuds as Allison carefully lifted them out of their boxed prison and placed them one by one into a vase filled with fresh water.

"Oh, Marlene," she said, sobbing, "I can't help it. I love Danny so much. What am I going to do?"

"That's a choice you have to make, sweetie. I'm crazy about Pete Hines, but I know the son of a bitch is screwing around."

"You know that for a fact?"

"Well, I can't prove it, and I haven't really tried. It's just little things, like the time I smelled another woman's perfume when I got close to him. And I swear there was lipstick on his underwear once, although he claims it was red ink from when he was marking up a blueprint. So who works in his underpants?

"And a number of times when I was hot to trot and wanted some loving, he gives me this song and dance about working too hard and not getting enough sleep and that his libido was suffering from malnutrition or something. He's a lying bastard, but he's fun to be around, and when he's in the groove, he's a tiger in bed. So I put up with his extracurricular activities and use him for sex, but I'll never allow myself to get serious or marry him."

"I'm going to call him back," Allison said, walking over to the phone. "I'll confront him, ask him directly if he's fooled around with this bitch before, or with any other women. I have to know." She dialed her number. The phone rang and her voice answered. "This is Allison—Danny and I aren't here right now. Please leave a brief message and we'll return your call as soon as we can."

"Where are you *now*, Danny?" Allison said into the phone, an accusing tone in her voice.

Danny sat in a chair in the back of the room, listening intently as the speaker recounted her long bout with alcohol. The room was thick with the haze of cigarette smoke. Most of the men and women sitting or standing in the audience held a coffee cup in their hands. Danny looked around at the various people, noticing an intense seriousness on each onlooker's face.

The speaker finished and received a round of applause. Someone else got up and asked everyone to join him in reciting the Serenity Prayer. Danny felt uneasy, not ready to get involved in anything that remotely resembled religion. He certainly believed in a Higher Power, as they referred to God in the AA vernacular. But organized religion was not for him.

"God grant me the serenity to accept the things I cannot change, the courage to change the things I can, and the wisdom to know the difference." Everyone in the room spoke the words in unison, clearly and with enthusiasm and conviction. Danny felt comfortable being among them, safe in a way. He knew he would be here for the next meeting.

Danny went back to the apartment and saw the light on the answering machine. He listened to the message and promptly called Marlene's number.

Allison answered the phone.

"You called me?" said Danny.

"Where have you been," she said icily. "Did you go back to Costello's and have that bitch finish you off?"

"Honey, believe me, that wasn't exactly what it looked like."

"Oh, I'm sorry. How stupid of me to assume that just because some skinny bitch has her hand wrapped around your dick, she's jerking you off. Obviously, she was demonstrating some sort of new massage technique."

"Allison, for crissake, listen to me. I was drunk and *she* came on to *me*. I know I crossed over the line, but it wasn't planned and I'm deeply sorry I let it happen. I didn't have intercourse with her, and I wouldn't have even if you hadn't come by."

"What about the other times?"

"What other times?"

"You know, when you were supposed to be working late."

"I *was* working late when I said I was."

"And there were no other women?"

"Absolutely not. Never."

"Can you prove that?"

"How can I prove it? If I did something, I could probably prove that. That's a tangible. But no one can prove they *didn't* do something."

Allison was silent for a few moments, trying to digest what Danny was saying. "So where have you been today?" she finally asked.

"I went to an AA meeting. I'm going to stop drinking."

Another long pause. "You did? You mean that?"

"Of course I mean it," Danny said, sensing that Allison was finally coming around. "I love you with all my heart ... and ... and I want you to be my wife." Danny wasn't sure he said what he said. He hadn't planned on saying anything like that because up to that point he hadn't felt ready for such a serious commitment. But the thought of losing Allison was too much for him. If sobriety and marriage were what it took to keep Allison, then as far as Danny was concerned, that was the way he was going.

Something in the way Danny said it clicked with Allison. She believed him. She believed he had not cheated on her with other women, that Costello's was an isolated incident and that alcohol had indeed played a major part.

"I'll be home in the morning, Danny," Allison finally said. I'm going to stay here with Marlene tonight and visit with her while I have the chance. I'll see you tomorrow. Good night."

Danny said good night, thankful for Allison's understanding. He knew the days and weeks ahead would be difficult, but he was determined to see it through.

Naturally, Danny had no idea of how much help he had already received from others behind the scenes, or how much more he would get....

Chapter Twenty-three
New job, new vows

It took another two years before Danny could state without challenge that he had been sober for a full year.

Allison returned to the apartment the day after she left. A Sunday. The moment she walked through the door, Danny pulled her into his arms and attempted to kiss her. Allison pulled back, her guard up, hesitant to surrender to Danny's selfish alcoholic demands.

But it had been more than thirty-six hours since Danny had swallowed that last drop of vodka, and Allison was instantly aware of it. Like so many alcoholics before him, Danny had tried to conceal his drinking by using breath mints and sprays. But no matter how many breath mints he devoured—after years of drinking heavily—the booze routinely seeped from his pores. So when Allison didn't detect the familiar odor usually emanating from Danny's body, she concluded that his statement that he had stopped drinking was truthful.

Danny was reluctant to loosen his grip on Allison. He tried to press his mouth on hers and she squirmed in his arms.

"We have to talk, Danny," she said, breathless from the exertion of fighting Danny off.

But Danny was resolute, unwilling to let her go. He held on to her tightly and covered her mouth with his, until finally she gave in to Danny's aggressiveness and her own physical yearnings, and the two made love for a long time.

Later, they talked about what had happened, with both of them doing a lot of mutual inner reflection. It was Allison who had decided they should wait a while before getting married. She had often thought about having a child with Danny, but she still felt insecure about whether or not Danny could remain sober. In her mind, there was no way she was going to bring a child into this world with an active alcoholic father.

Danny continued to go to AA meetings, at first every day, and then later he cut back to several times a week. He stayed away from bars and parties, which made Scott feel as if he had lost a friend.

But the stress at The Jonas Publishing Group grew worse. Sales were weak and the investors were getting antsy. They wanted to see a better return on their money, and Warren's solution was to heat up the magazine, make it raunchier. Danny disagreed, as did his Italian counterparts, and together they waged an ongoing, day-to-day battle with Warren.

Eventually, Danny succumbed to the pressure and began to have a couple of quick shooters after work. He picked up his first martini after about eight months of being dry, and when reefer madness didn't set in, when he realized he could have a few and not get tanked, it made it easier to pick up the next drink.

In no time, Danny was back on the alcoholic merry-go-round. Which, of course, scared Allison half to death. She confronted him over and over again, until finally she threatened to walk out on him, this time for good.

"Danny, I don't think I can deal with your drinking anymore," Allison said one morning as Danny got ready for work.

"I can't do this now," he said, buttoning his shirt. "I'm already late for work."

"You'd better find time, Danny, because I've had it." Allison stood in the bedroom doorway, one hand holding onto the door jamb, the other on her hip.

"We'll discuss it tonight, okay?"

"We'll discuss it right now, or I won't be here when you get home tonight."

"All right," Danny said exasperatingly, sitting down on the side of the bed and giving Allison his full attention. "Go ahead."

"It's really quite simple. You stop drinking right now, or I'm walking out for good."

"Okay, I'll cut back—"

"No! No cutting back. None of that bullshit. No more drinking. Period."

"What about your smoking? It's hurting both of us. When are you gonna give that up?"

"Danny," she said softly, "I realize I've got my own personal demons to deal with, and I will, eventually. But this isn't about me or cigarettes. It's about you and your destructive alcoholism."

"And smoking a known carcinogen is not destructive?"

"Danny, I mean what I say."

"All right."

"I mean it, Danny. No last drink. No nothing. The booze is over … or we're over. You've got to decide. It's either me or the bottle."

For whatever reason, Danny finally heard her and believed her, and he stopped drinking, again. On February 19, 1980, Danny celebrated one full year of solid sobriety. One month later, he gave Warren two weeks' notice.

In mid-April 1980, Danny went to work for a small publishing company located on Eighth Avenue. The publisher was a congenial fellow who had transplanted himself and his family from Montreal several years earlier.

Sam Saltzman had cut his editorial teeth on the Canadian equivalent of the *National Enquirer* tabloid. Following ten years of muckraking journalism, Sam moved to New York with his wife Sheila and their two sons, buying out the publisher of several erotic magazines. Within two years, he had added a line of romance magazines, several crossword puzzle books, and a hot-selling magazine, *CrimeBusters*. Danny was hired to take over the editorial reins of the latter.

After three years in a relatively stress-free work environment, Danny had not only remained sober but had become somewhat attached to the Saltzman family. He was finally working in a company where management showed him both respect and appreciation. Oh, to be sure, there would always be the acceptable stress of never-ending deadlines, and minor disagreements in editorial policy, but these distractions were nothing compared to the nerve-jangling episodes Danny had experienced over the length of his career.

And, of course, due to the nepotism factor, Danny had to work alongside the two sons, David and Ethan, and thus experienced a degree of office politics in which he clearly could never quite come out a winner. Blood beats talent every time.

The money could have been better, even when Sam moved him into the position of editorial director, responsible for the entire editorial output of Vancouver Publications. Nevertheless, Danny was content. He felt relatively secure, and he looked forward to going to work.

Sam was an easygoing individual, well-liked by everyone in the industry. Tall, with a full beard and a somewhat generous midsection, he enjoyed moderate success as a publisher and took special pleasure in coming up with innovative ideas for new publications. But Sam had a wonderful sense of humor and would rather tell a joke than work. And he loved Danny.

Sheila Saltzman delighted everyone around her. The publisher's diminutive wife, an attractive brunette with a somewhat Rubenesque figure, had a bubbly personality that proved to be infectious. She laughed easily and often, and showed extreme insightfulness. If she sensed you were in a down mood, she brought you up. Unlike Sam, Sheila didn't tell jokes—she simply spoke and carried herself in a positive, upbeat manner. Her smile brightened every room she entered.

One mid-April morning in 1986, Sam called Danny to his office. "What do you think of the idea of a magazine devoted to the paranormal, specifically to life after death?" he asked, his eyes wide open in eager anticipation of Danny's reaction.

"You know I don't buy into any of that supernatural stuff," Danny replied.

"Yeah, I know," said Sam, disappointed at Danny's less-than-enthusiastic response. "But why don't you just open your mind for a moment and consider that there's an enormous amount of interest in the subject among the general public."

"Well, first of all, I thought the magazine *Fate* pretty much covered that topic, although I'm not at all sure it's still being published. Anyway, there's never been any evidence to prove the existence of an afterlife, or reincarnation, or ghosts, or any of that crap."

"You're not hearing me. There is interest out there and I've got an idea for a new kind of magazine that would touch on all those subjects. And it would be a helluva lot better than *Fate*. Or did you forget that we're in the magazine publishing business?"

"No, I didn't forget," Danny said, grinning, "but don't try to convince me that I'll be coming back as your grandson's hamster."

Sam laughed, appreciating Danny's wit. "I'd like you to do some extensive research and, if you'll pardon the expression, some soul-searching legwork and come up with format ideas and titles for the name of the magazine." He paused for a moment. "Take all the time you need ... and get back to me on Monday."

"Sam," said Danny, feigning seriousness, "did you ever think about your initials?"

"Whaddya mean?"

"Your initials, SS ... kind of ironic for a Jew, eh?"

Sam laughed hard this time. "Get the hell outta my office and do some work or something."

That evening, after work, Danny met Allison at their favorite Chinese restaurant. Over dinner, Danny told her about Sam's magazine idea and she got very excited.

"I'd be glad to help with the research. You know how I feel about my dad and how he's been looking after me all these years. And maybe we can solve the mystery of the song 'Stardust,' the guitar-piano version I heard the night we first met. You remember ... coming back to the city the day we sprinkled your mother's ashes? On the car radio. Only that version had a woman singing. You heard it, too. I went to all those music stores and ... nothing ... no one ever heard of it."

"Yeah, well you know how I feel about that shit," said Danny, insensitively.

"You're in for some big surprises one of these days, Mister Daniel Wallace. And by the way, when am I going to be Mrs. Wallace?"

Allison had a distinctly unique and sometimes annoying habit of taking a conversation and making an oblique left turn with it, causing it to head in a totally different direction.

"Any time you want, sweetheart," said Danny. "Just say when and where."

"I was thinking of Vegas."

"Las Vegas?"

"Why, there's another kind of Vegas? Of course Las Vegas. Complete with Elvis. I've always wanted to visit there and I think it'll be a real kick."

Danny nodded, knowing Allison wasn't kidding.

Danny and Allison boarded a direct flight to Las Vegas the second week of August 1986. It was late afternoon and the plane bulged to capacity, with many of the passengers getting a head start on their Vegas vacation, drinking and carrying on and generally raising hell.

"I feel like we're on a school bus for adults," Danny whispered to Allison.

Allison giggled. "Yeah, but wait'll we get to school. You ain't seen nothin' yet."

"I'm a little uncomfortable with the booze, you know."

For a brief moment, Allison felt a twinge of dread, recalling Danny's bout with the bottle and how easy it would be for him to pick up a drink again. But Danny sensed her uneasiness and quickly dispelled any feelings of insecurity.

"Don't worry, I have good sobriety and there's no way I'd get back on that alcoholic carousel."

It was nearly 10:30 at night when they approached the city of Las Vegas. Danny and Allison stared out the window at the spidery network of lights on the ground.

"Look at the lights!" Allison squealed. "There must be hundreds of thousands. I never realized how big this town was. And we get to spend a whole week here!"

"It didn't used to be," Danny said, remembering the stories his mother had told him.

"Didn't used to be what?"

"Big. Mom used to fly out to LA to visit her sister Naomi who lived in Santa Monica, in the Pacific Palisades. She'd stay for a couple of weeks or so and they'd drive to Vegas on the weekends. She said it was once just an itty-bitty town in the middle of the desert. That was before they started expanding on the Strip."

"So what are all those lights?"

"Well, there's the Strip. But mostly it's communities and street lights and shopping centers. For whatever reasons, people started moving there in droves. I think I read somewhere that it's becoming the fastest-growing city in the country."

They landed at McCarran Airport at about 11:00 PM, picked up their luggage and took a taxi to their motel downtown. Allison had made arrangements to rent a motel room on Fremont Street because the weekly rate ran far below the rates charged by the major hotels downtown and on the Strip. And she figured they would be close to the action downtown, which was more old Las Vegas than the Strip—and where Dorothy Wallace and her sister Naomi used to go for many years.

The first thing they noticed when they got out of the cab was the heat. It was getting close to midnight and the temperature still hovered at a hundred and three.

The second thing they noticed was the seedy area surrounding their motel.

"Frankly," said Danny, "I think I'd feel safer walking around in the South Bronx."

"Just think about all the money we're saving," reassured Allison.

"Yeah. That is, if we live through this."

"Very funny, Wallace."

"I'm sorry," Danny said, laughing. "Just trying to lighten things up." He looked around the motel room, checking the beds, the dresser, the bathroom.

"At least the room is clean," he finally commented.

"The wedding's scheduled for tomorrow," Allison reminded Danny, "so let's hit the street and do some serious gambling."

Danny agreed. They left the motel room and walked up the street to the El Cortez, with Danny constantly looking over his shoulder. They played various slot machines, ate fabulous club sandwiches at 2:00 in the morning, and wound up back at the motel around 3:00.

When they walked into the room, the first thing Danny spotted was a bug on the wall the size of a man's wallet. Allison screamed. A blood-curdling scream, in the best Hollywood tradition. Danny turned immediately around and walked straight to the office.

"*Cucaracha,*" the Mexican manager on duty stated matter-of-factly. "They clean palm trees yesterday. Probably came from one of them. I send someone to take care of it for you."

"Never mind," said Danny. "Just give us another room, one without bugs big enough to take dancing."

Later, in the new room, Danny and Allison lay in bed, eyes wide open, scanning the darkness for imagined bugs.

"Are you awake?" Allison asked.

"Of course."

"What are you thinking about?"

"About how we paid a lot of money to fly all the way out here to encounter a cockroach that probably could eat half of Brooklyn."

"You're not thinking about us getting married tomorrow?"

"Well, of course, that, too."

"I'm excited, Danny. I don't think you know how much I love you."

"You're my life, sweetheart." Danny rolled over and kissed her tenderly. "We shoulda done this years ago."

Allison sighed. A happy sigh. She had never been happier.

On August 10, 1986, Danny and Allison said their I do's inside a small wedding chapel on Main Street in downtown Las Vegas, complete with Elvis himself ... almost. The guy dressed up as Elvis had a beer belly, a bald spot and a sideburn half peeling off. And Danny swore later that the guy farted at least three times during the ceremony. But Allison loved every minute of it.

They spent the rest of their weeklong honeymoon playing roulette, blackjack and various video poker and slot machines, and lost more money than they needed to.

They also didn't get much sleep.

But Allison was a relatively happy woman, and that made Danny a happy man. Which made two gentlemen at Midway Manor also very happy.

Mickey and Lloyd were, in fact, ecstatic, running around the Manor, up and down hallways, in and out of rooms, sharing the wedding news with anyone who would listen. At the buffet that evening, the Manor did its part by providing a three-tier wedding cake—complete with a miniature Elvis playing his guitar, and a plastic couple on top who looked remarkably like Danny and Allison. The celebration continued long after dinner, with residents singing and dancing in the Renaissance Room as if they were still back on Earth.

But in life, happiness is fleeting. Margaret Parks was far from receptive to the news of her daughter's marriage to Danny. When Allison had called and told her, her mother had grunted and said something like, "It's about time." Whatever her reasons, Margaret simply could not bring herself to even pretend that she shared Allison's happiness. *Was it envy? Or something else?* Allison wondered.

When Allison finally hung up, her tears had quickly turned to anger. She vowed, as she had done so many times before, never to call her mother again and subject herself to the pain and anguish the woman inflicted upon her whenever she had the opportunity.

Danny plowed headlong into the project Sam Saltzman had assigned him. It took up a lot of his time, a commodity he did not have in large supply. The day-to-day editorial workload had grown heavy enough, not to mention the correspondence and meetings with writers. Danny also wrote at least one article a month for magazines other than Vancouver's. And he would almost salivate when he thought about starting the novel he had been threatening to write for years.

Samantha Hodges took some of the burden off Danny by providing writers who contributed many workable article ideas. And the writers themselves were talented and reliable, who met deadlines and conducted themselves in a professional manner.

Still, Danny felt obligated to use other writers who were not from Samantha's stable, and this turned out to be more time-consuming than he had expected. Allison, who still worked full time for *Home and Hearth*, proved to be a big help on Sam's paranormal project. But to Danny's dismay, the more she got into the research, the more firmly she believed that her dad was somewhere in the wings, watching over her and somehow influencing her life as well as Danny's.

With Danny at the helm, Sam got the okay from his distributor to publish the first issue of *Psychic Eye*. The print run of one hundred thousand quickly sold out and Sam was ecstatic. He wrote Danny a bonus check, which normally would have been cause for celebration in the Wallace household.

Unfortunately, Bratly became very ill. The little calico vomited several times a day and began to lose weight rapidly. Allison and Danny took her to the vet and tests were run, determining that the cat's thyroid was not functioning properly and that this affected the heart and kidneys. She had become dehydrated, and the medicine used to anesthetize Bratly during the tests had made her condition worse. On the vet's advice, they left Bratly there so that they could hydrate her, feed her intravenously, and administer oxygen.

The doctor called at 9:00 that night. Bratly had died.

Danny and Allison were devastated. The vet was not sure exactly how Bratly had died, whether her heart or her kidneys had failed. It was irrelevant. The little calico was gone.

It took a long time for the two to get over Bratly's death. It may or may not have been coincidence, but shortly thereafter Danny and Allison began having some medical problems of their own. Allison's blood pressure had become slightly elevated and the doctor had put her on medication. Conversely, Danny's blood pressure had miraculously remained normal. But the doctor was concerned over his elevated level of bad cholesterol and insisted that Danny begin taking medication to better control it.

Danny and Allison tried to conceive a child for a while. After several years of Danny being sober, Allison decided to stop using any birth-control measures. But for some reason, their efforts went unfulfilled. Eventually, they both agreed it was too late in life to have a baby and they stopped trying.

They both continued on in their jobs, with Danny still searching for the meaning of life. It became something of a running gag with those in the industry who were close to Danny. A public relations friend, Marcia Grimwood, sent him a note one day, claiming it was the answer to his eternal question:

> *Buy low, sell high*
> *Fish gotta swim, birds gotta fly*
> *Make your bed and in it lie*
> *They'll all get theirs by and by*

The Burma Shave-type limerick put a smile on Danny's face for the rest of that day, but of course the question regarding the purpose of life remained elusive. To be sure, Danny grew wiser with age and experience. He learned that good things happened from time to time, and usually came about leisurely. But bad things almost always happened quickly. He also came to the conclusion that the essence of happiness could be boiled down to three things: having an interesting job or hobby; having someone to love; and having a goal, something to look forward to.

In the meantime, the years passed for Danny and Allison. Sam had purchased a personal computer for the office and his son Ethan used it to juggle sales figures and other business stats.

Ethan and David, both of Sam's sons, had informed Danny on many occasions that computers were here to stay and that one day they would revolutionize the publishing industry. "Get with the program, Dan," Ethan would say. "Learn all you can or you won't survive."

Danny had shrugged off the young man's advice as nonsense. He felt perfectly happy with his beat-up old Royal upright and wasn't about to change his ways. In fact, though he refused to admit it even to himself, he harbored a fear of the electronic machines.

In 1993, Danny changed his mind. Even *he* could see the "handwriting on the computer screen." He read as much as he could about computers, and he sat with Ethan and became familiar with his computer—which had now been upgraded several times.

Allison, however, had already key-stroked miles ahead of Danny when it came to the electronic devices. She also had been trying to convince Danny what the future held in store for them regarding computers. "They're going to change our lives!" she said emphatically to Danny.

She had no idea just how prophetic that statement was.

Chapter Twenty-four
The plot thickens

As the years flew by for Mickey and Lloyd, the daily routine at the grand Manor of Midway continued to include their joint visits to the Data Room, keeping a close watch on Danny and Allison, enjoying the fabulous dining room buffets, and engaging in alternating lively or soothing string-and-ivory jamborees. They also took advantage of several new amenities recently added to the Manor, such as the indoor heated swimming pool, the outdoor tennis courts, and—much to Mickey's delight—the ten-lane bowling alley. When the men were not together, however, Mickey continued to spend much of his spare time just shooting the breeze with the other residents.

Lloyd, on the other hand, favored going off on his own to continue his in-depth study of the Manor's computer options, while also spending quality time to thoroughly scrutinize his copy of the volume on *Destinations in the Afterworld.* He considered the opportunities of life-after-life covered in its chapters to be not only surprisingly numerous, but riveting.

The destination called Reunion Valley was the most compelling. And now, Dorothy, the love of his life, had been added to his growing list of family and friends whom he yearned to see again. The list, for sure, would eventually be handed over to the director, who was responsible for making the final arrangements at the Valley get-together. This would definitely be Lloyd's next destiny, but certainly not his last.

"God, I miss you," he said softly to himself, thinking of Dorothy's short visit at Midway. He leaned back in his leather recliner, wondering where she was now after she had completed the rendezvous with her sister Naomi. The choices were many. So many, in fact, that after all this time, Lloyd himself had not been able to come to any decisions about his own future beyond Midway and Reunion Valley.

His thoughts of Dorothy reminded him of the time when he had come across a computer file called "Locating Family and Friends in The Afterworld." His delight was deflated by the fact that this particular file, as were so many others that he had discovered during his diligent research efforts, had required a password. And Lloyd was never able to find a way to access any of them.

Another file that Lloyd remembered he couldn't access was simply called, "Family Photographs." But he was sure that this was how the director, Joseph Patrick, had so quickly gotten his hands on the photograph of himself and his son, the one that had been available for him the day after he first arrived. "Not so magical, after all," he had said to himself after locating the file, though still appreciative of the Manor's kind gesture and the extraordinary capabilities of their computer system.

Access was also denied on one file called "The Future," and another file named "Reincarnation." The words would pop up on the computer screen in bold red lettering: *Access denied. Password required. This file is unavailable for resident computer users.*

Lloyd, who did so on many different occasions, had consulted the Manor's dictionary to look up the word reincarnation. The definition included an explanation that many had first appeared before The Council with pleas to return, but a very select few were ever granted permission by The Authority. It most clearly referred to those who would thus be reborn in another human form back on Earth.

After reading that definition, Lloyd recalled flipping back the pages to look up the word "haunting." He not only wanted to satisfy his own curiosity, he also needed to be absolutely certain this wasn't one of any possible options of his ever returning to Earth. Though now, after all the time he had spent at the Manor, he knew in his heart that this indeed was the better of the two worlds.

The definition of haunting, according to the Manor's dictionary, revealed how certain souls who had adamantly refused to follow through with their journey along any of the light paths were actually trapped between the many lights of destination and Earth. Consequently, these lost souls often returned to Earth to wander aimlessly.

Which put Lloyd's curiosity to rest and for the most part explained the many haunting incidents reported over the years.

But despite the Manor's dictionary and its definitions, there indeed was a legitimate option listed in the book of destinations that permitted—on rare occasions—certain residents of the hereafter to actually contact loved ones on Earth. Again, however, a very select few were granted permission by The Authority to go back, and the approval was always based on extraordinarily exceptional reasons.

The fact that The Authority had the final say in a range of situations confirmed Lloyd's suspicion that what he and Mickey planned to do with the Data Room's computer and its electronic mail capabilities was strictly against the rules. But both he and Mickey were determined to follow through with their plans that they had set in place for the beginning of January 1996.

Lloyd had also discovered there were two very special, heart-warming destinations. The first was dedicated to children of all ages who had arrived in the afterworld. A place simply described as "where all angels dwelled, with love and laughter and joy and song. A place without tears or sorrow or pain."

The other heart-warming destination was called "The Garden of Animal Spirits," a place where one could visit with their pets, or where anyone who just loved spending some time with God's lower animal species could hang out. This included all breeds of cats and dogs, of every age. There were also birds and reptiles, ferrets and fish, to name just a few categories. And they all shared their own lush private world in perfect harmony.

Through all the research that Lloyd had completed to date, he did not feel any of the destinations offered the diversity that he had thrived on during his life on Earth, with the exception of one: "The City of Lights."

Later that evening, Lloyd and Mickey lingered longer than usual in the dining room to ramble on about their stay at the Manor. They were just months away from their target date.

"You know," Lloyd said, wiping the corner of his mouth with one of the Manor's now-familiar linen napkins, "it won't be long now. In fact, the big day is just around the corner for us and I tell you … I'm ready for it."

He placed the napkin on the far side of the plate. "By the way, I took care of all the old journals we'd printed out."

"Took care of them?" Mickey wasn't sure he understood Lloyd.

"You know, the blank journals we tampered with. What we used to keep track of our, uh, manipulations. I took care of them … discarded them … incinerated them … vaporized 'em. Whatever happens to them when you put them into that slot in the Data Room. You know, the library on the third floor. Mr. Patrick showed us. Crissakes, Mick, don't you pay attention when people tell you things?"

"Hey, what's all the testiness about?"

"I'm sorry. I guess I'm just tense about what's comin' up."

"That's okay, buddy. I'm feeling a little uptight myself."

Lloyd cleared his throat. "I can honestly say I'll really miss this truly fine establishment and all the good people here. And, oh yeah … I guess I'm gonna miss you, too," he added, trying to get a rise out of his friend.

"Well, you play a pretty good piano, I'll say that," Mickey replied, trying to even the score. He had been feeling quite at ease with the objective that he, too, would soon be leaving the Manor. And this was due to the fact that Danny was in Allison's life, to love and protect her as well as he himself could have. "But seriously, what we've done for Danny and Allison over the last twenty years is more important than us two old goats."

Lloyd laughed and then straightened out his silk tie for effect, knowing he didn't look a single day older in all that time. "Old goats? Speak for yourself. And it's not *quite* twenty years."

Mickey ignored Lloyd's remarks and continued. "You know, I took a liking to your son right from the start. And after reading all those journals, I know for sure what a fine young man he really is … and how *good* he's been for my Allison."

"But … he's not a *young* man anymore," Lloyd said, getting a kick out of editing everything Mickey said. "He's what now … fifty-five?"

Lloyd paused. "Damn … I just realized … Danny's just a few years away from the age I was when the doctor hit me with the news that I had cancer."

"Hey, what kind of talk is that? We've taken good care of the kids all this time. Besides, Danny's got a whole lotta livin' to do. And so does Allison." Mickey looked directly into Lloyd's eyes. "Would you mind staying on track here and let me finish what I was trying to tell you?"

"Sorry. Go ahead."

"Thank you. Now, you can believe me or not," Mickey said, "but I even remember when you and I shared our first breakfast together. You told me only two things about Danny. That he was an adult … and real smart. But I could see in your face how proud you really were. And what I wanted to say before you interrupted me is that, well, I'm real proud of him, too.

"And another thing. I still feel we made the right decision when the two of them went off to Las Vegas to get married. You know what I'm saying …" Mickey's voice trailed off. He looked carefully around the room to be sure no one could pick up on what he was going to say next.

"We could've … you know … done our thing in the blank journals and maybe we might have been able to have 'em hit the big one. But I'm glad we've waited. You know … giving the kids the answers to the unsolved mysteries so that they'd have the stuff to write their very own book. But be honest with me. Do you really think we can send all that information to them with the Manor's computer?"

"I told you some time ago. Don't you remember? I found the program that will enable us to send electronic mail, e-mail. All we need is the kids' computer address; you know, exactly where to send everything. And we'll get that info from their journals once they've purchased a computer and gotten themselves hooked up to the—what do they call it—the World Wide Web."

"What if they never get a computer?" Mickey said, playing devil's advocate.

"Listen, everything we've written in their blank journals has come to fruition. Everything. Why would this be any different?"

"Well, all right, so they get a computer and we're able to send the material. And I know they can write the thing," said Mickey. "But what kind of guarantee is there that anybody will publish it?"

"Well, you know, it's all a crapshoot. All we can do is give them the raw material so they can write it. But the kids are pros and they can run with it. You know that."

"All right. Suppose they do write this book solving all of the world's mysteries. And they get someone to publish it. What then? How're they gonna explain where they got their material? I mean, someone, the FBI, the government, the goddamn CIA even—somebody's gonna start asking a lot of questions."

"That's not really a problem. Sure, in certain instances in capital crimes, they could legally be made to reveal their sources or go to jail. But most of these cases go way back, like Earhart and Hoffa and Glenn Miller. When they read what actually happened, they'll check it out and the proof will be there.

"As far as UFOs, well, the aliens'll take care of that."

Lloyd was starting to get annoyed. "Are you finished being a royal pain in the butt?" he asked Mickey.

"I'm sorry. I guess I'm getting a case of buyer's remorse or something. I know we've had a plan and it's a good one, but I'm getting a little nervous. What if they suspect something? What if they—"

"What if they what?" Lloyd interrupted him. "If they suspected something, we would've already heard about it, believe me."

"And when they do find out?"

"They *will* find out, and when they do, we're outta here. We just have to be careful and get the information to Danny and Allison *before* they get wise to us."

"And we do that how?"

"Wait a minute," Lloyd said, feeling exasperated. He reached over, picked up the pitcher of ice water and refilled his glass. After drinking half of it, he blotted his lips with the linen napkin and again addressed Mickey.

"We write a note to the kids telling them all about Midway Manor. We explain that after they receive this note, there will follow a series of facts that will reveal the truth behind many of Earth's celebrated but unsolved mysteries. And just to make sure they understand why we're doing all this, we'll suggest how they should take this startling material and use it as the basis for a book."

"And after that? Will they be able to reply to us?"

"I honestly don't know. Maybe. We'll have to play it by ear." Lloyd finished drinking the ice water, then added, "You know, I have one concern about the plan myself. What if the kids don't believe the computer mail is from us? What if they think it's some kind of prank?"

Mickey didn't hesitate in his answer. "My daughter is intuitive, psychic even. She'll know it's the real thing. Listen, Lloyd, it sounds like it all might work. If it does, it'll be our legacy to Danny and Allison. It gives me goose bumps thinking about it ... wait a minute, how can I be dead and have goose bumps?"

"According to the Manor's dictionary, you're not dead, you're—aw, let's not go through that again."

Mickey laughed richly then, feeling a true bond with Lloyd. "Let's go play some music, partner."

Chapter Twenty-five
Computer Christmas

It started snowing Christmas Eve morning in Manhattan. The year was 1995 and the snow had begun lightly, with small flakes and not much of a wind. It was the kind of snow children dream of, and the kind some adults pray for so that everything shuts down and they don't have to go to work.

By evening, the accumulation had reached about three inches, enough to slow down traffic but not nearly enough to cripple the city. As was typical of the night before Christmas, crowds of people were out and about, frantically scurrying up and down the snow-covered sidewalks and in and out of stores. It was the eleventh hour for the procrastinators of the world. They darted here and there, bulging shopping bags stretching their arms like lead weights as they searched madly for one more last-minute gift.

Danny Wallace walked among them. Not that he had procrastinated. The present for Allison that he clutched tightly to his chest, using his coat to shield it from the wetness, was the kind that couldn't be brought into the apartment until the very last minute.

Traditionally, he and Allison always opened their presents to each other on Christmas Eve. They did this because they both would rather sleep in on Christmas morning. Danny remembered their first Christmas living together. They both had been as excited as young children, eager to see the other's reaction to their gifts. It was all they could do to sleep through the night, the anticipation building up to a point where they both arose at 5:00 AM. The upshot was that later, after they had opened their presents, they remained exhausted for the rest of the day.

Danny hurried down the block, looking for a taxi. Suddenly, he spotted a Yellow Cab that had pulled over to discharge a passenger. A *true Miracle on Thirty-fourth Street,* Danny thought. With Allison's gift clutched protectively to his chest using one hand, and the other gripping an overly full shopping bag, Danny couldn't signal the cabbie and had to yell as loudly as he could.

"Taxi!" he shouted, sloshing toward it through the wet snow.

When Danny heard the shrill whistle and spotted movement out of the corner of his eye, he realized someone else was trying to get to the cab first. He began running then, mindful of how easily it would be to lose his footing and fall. Adrenalin pumped through his veins as the anxiety level reached the critical point.

Danny put the shopping bag down and grabbed the taxi's door handle as the passenger got out of the vehicle. A moment later, the other cab-seeker arrived, red-faced and panting heavily.

"I saw it first, you know," the beefy stranger said, grabbing the edge of the cab door.

"I got here first," said Danny, placing the shopping bag and the other gift carefully onto the back seat of the cab. He stood up then, face to face with the stranger, thinking of Allison waiting for him back at the apartment. *No way I'm giving up this cab,* he vowed. He prepared to do battle, realizing he hadn't actually physically fought anybody since high school.

The man was persistent but not belligerent. He calmly explained how he had been shopping for his little girl and that she was all alone and he needed to get back to her as soon as possible.

"I ain't got all day, fellas," the cab driver growled impatiently. "You guys keep jabbering all you like 'cause I'm gonna start the meter running." He proceeded to push the flag down.

"Look," Danny said, "it's Christmas Eve. Peace on Earth, good will toward men. I've got someone waiting for me at home, too. Why don't we both share the cab?"

"That's a super idea, and I appreciate your Christmas spirit. I'm at twenty-one East Eighty-first."

"Great. We'll head there first," Danny said, repeating the address to the cab driver as they slid into the back seat....

When Danny walked through the door, Allison barely gave him time to put his packages down, greeting him with a very long, deeply passionate kiss. Over the years, a lot of things had changed for them both. Their primary interests, for one, had progressed from collecting material things to stocking up on the latest "hot" vitamins. The aches and pains of simply growing older had slowed them down just a bit, but one thing had remained constant—their passion for each other.

As Danny took off his coat and hung it up in the hall closet, he glanced at the tree. There were a number of wrapped gifts at the base, with one very large box standing out.

"I have to give you your present right now," said Danny, reaching for the loosely wrapped gift he had placed on the hall chair.

"Oh no," said Allison, "I want you to open yours first."

"Meow …"

Allison looked at Danny and he laughed.

"What the hell is that?" she asked, grinning broadly.

"Guess the present opened you first," Danny said, tearing away the paper from the cardboard pet carrier and opening the top flaps. The little calico kitten's tiny head emerged, peering cautiously around.

Allison let out a small gasp and then erupted in a flood of tears. "Oh, Danny, she's so beautiful. I love her." She carefully lifted the orange, black-and-white ball of fur out from the box and clasped her close under her neck.

Danny walked over to the tree and knelt down beside the large wrapped box. "Is this one for me?" Danny asked.

Allison went into the living room and sat down on the sofa, still cuddling the now-purring kitten. "Yes. Go ahead and open it."

Danny stripped the paper away quickly and saw that it was a computer, which he had suspected. "I love it," he said, "but I thought we were going to buy this together."

"Don't worry, I researched everything thoroughly. It's got a built-in modem and it's supposed to be very fast. Open the other box."

Danny tore the paper off the second box and read that it was a printer. "This is really great, honey. I can't wait till we get hooked up to the Web. Everybody's talking about how they e-mail their friends and relatives and save on their long-distance phone bills."

"Take it easy, hot shot," said Allison. "I've taken care of it. We even got a rebate for signing up with an Internet service provider for the next three years."

"And how much is that gonna cost us?"

"Don't worry, it's less than our phone bill. Do you want to get it set up now?"

"Well ... no ... I'm kinda beat. I'd rather start fresh in the morning. Let's open the rest of our presents, have dinner and then get to bed."

"Okay by me. I wanted to give you your last present tonight, in the bedroom...."

"Hand me the flashlight, will you, honey," said Danny, trying to make sense of all the wires and cables behind the computer. "I think I just about have it."

Danny pushed in one more jack and then straightened up. "Done!" he said proudly. "Mechanical ability" were not words usually included in his portfolio.

"Hurray!" said Allison, putting aside the guidelines for the PC hardware setup and reaching for the next batch of instructions for installing the software. "I'm going to turn it on." The computer hummed to life and the screen lit up.

It took more than two hours to follow the step-by-step prompts for installing the software and completing the onscreen applications for the computer programs, the rebates, and the printer. At one point, the new kitten ran and hid behind a box under the Christmas tree, frightened by Danny and Allison yelling at each other.

When Allison was finally ready to access the Web, Danny put his arms around her and whispered, "I love you. Sorry I got so tense over all this." Allison melted against him, never able to stay angry for long.

"Are you thinking what I'm thinking?" she teased.

"Yeah," said Danny. "Let's access the Web, baby."

They both waited patiently, listening to the strange noises it made as they came online. Allison giggled. "It sounds like we're contacting another planet."

Once again, to their frustration, there was a set of instructions to follow and an online application to complete. Which included their member identification and their chosen e-mail address.

"*Now* go to e-mail," Danny said, his patience exhausted.

Allison complied. "Who you gonna e-mail?" she asked.

Danny grinned sheepishly. "I dunno. I have to think about that."

Stardust Dads

Suddenly, a voice from the computer said, "You've got mail," and the same words appeared on the screen. Allison clicked open the receive-messages box and there were two messages. The first was a welcome letter from their Internet service provider, and the second message was for purchasing computer paper.

"Great," said Danny. "It's a goddamn advertisement."

When Danny got home Friday evening, December 29, Allison was already planted in front of the computer. He recognized the honeyed tones of Billie Holiday singing "I Love My Man" on the radio. Danny put down his attaché case, hung up his coat and kissed her on top of the head. "What're you doing, my little computer addict?" Danny asked playfully as he made his way to the kitchen.

"I'm e-mailing my cousin Diane in Connecticut."

"Give her my love," said Danny, spooning the kitten food onto a dish. He put the dish down on the kitchen tile and watched the kitten lap hungrily at it.

"What are we going to name the kitten?" he asked.

"I told you I like the name Ashley. Is that okay with you?"

"Ashley it is." Danny came back into the living room and plopped down on the sofa. "I'm glad it's Friday and we have a long weekend. How come when there's a holiday and it's a four-day week, the week seems to drag on forever?"

"Does this typing bother you?" Allison asked sarcastically.

"Sorry. I'll be quiet and just sit here in the dark."

Allison got up from the computer, went over to the sofa and snuggled up close to Danny. "Poor baby," she said. "I didn't mean to neglect you." She kissed him then, softly, careful not to use her tongue, which would have instantly activated the passion machine.

"You know, Danny, I've had some strange feelings today."

"What kind of feelings?" he asked, having perfected the meaning of her double messages and tactfully moving his hand away from its initial target.

"I'm not sure. They got stronger after I got home. Sometimes, these feelings I get make me crazy because they're so difficult to understand. But I sense that something very significant is about to happen and it involves my father."

"You've seemed kind of tense lately, and I know this undercurrent of tension has to do with your psychic ability. Do you feel like something bad is going to happen?"

"No, not really. But it will be monumental, whatever it is."

Danny picked up on the music now coming from the radio. Dinah Washington's voice was unmistakable as she sang "What a Difference a Day Makes."

Allison burst into tears.

"What the hell's wrong?" asked Danny.

"That song," said Allison, reaching for the tissue box. "That's the first record my dad ever gave me. It was a forty-five. Danny, I think my father's trying to tell me something."

Chapter Twenty-six
You've got mail

"How you feeling this morning?" Lloyd asked Mickey as they sat down to breakfast.

"Nervous, of course. I can't believe today's the day. I don't think I ever got this edgy when I was alive."

"You *are* alive. You're just ... oh, never mind, I give up. You're deader than a doornail."

"You're a little short-fused again this morning, old buddy."

"You're right," said Lloyd, buttering his croissant carefully. "I guess it began when we read in Danny's journal that they got the computer, got on the Web and signed up for e-mail. In a little while, we're going to go up to the Data Room and change the lives of our kids forever ... hopefully for the better. We've waited a long time for this, and done a lot of homework. I just hope it pays off for them."

"Well, you're the one who's always telling me to think positive," Mickey said after drinking the last of his orange juice.

"Do you have the UM notes?" Lloyd asked.

"What's UM?"

"Unsolved mysteries. C'mon, Mick, get with the program."

"I'm ready whenever you are, wise guy."

"Hey, listen, why don't we head over to the Renaissance Room and get one more session in before we go to the Data Room. I have a feeling we'll soon be leaving here very quickly."

"I'm up for that. Lead the way, McDuff."

After beating a path to the Renaissance Room, Mickey picked up his guitar and began adjusting the strings to make sure it was tuned properly. Lloyd sat down in front of the Steinway as he had so many times before during their years at Midway. And as was their custom, they started in with the familiar "Stardust," this time with both men singing as they played.

Close to an hour later, the two wrapped up the session with the popular strains of "What a Difference a Day Makes."

Later, in the Data Room, Lloyd checked the door to make sure it had automatically locked behind them. He then sat down and booted up the computer while Mickey pulled up a chair alongside him.

Lloyd called up the e-mail program and entered the kids' e-mail address in the appropriate space. He began the message:

Dear Allison and Danny, you both will no doubt find it virtually impossible to believe that this communication is coming to you from your fathers. You will quite obviously assume it is a gag or a hoax and at first will not take it seriously. But for your own sakes, I implore you both to keep an open mind and know that anything is possible on Earth and in Heaven.

Where we are isn't Heaven, but it's pretty close to it. We are in a place called Midway Manor and it is, by anyone's standards, the most fabulous place you could imagine. We have been here a very long time. Allison, your dad has been here since his passing in 1973. Danny, this is your father and I've been here since 1976. We became fast friends right away and have been playing music together the whole time.

The reason for this communication is to send you a list of answers to many of Earth's unsolved mysteries. What we are advising you to do with this information is to use it as a basis for writing a book, which we believe will become an instant bestseller. This of course will result in your never having to worry about money again.

But first I'd like to tell you more about Midway Manor. I should also mention, Danny, that your mother was here and we had some very long talks. She's gone on to Reunion Valley, which I'll also tell you about later.

Allison, Mickey wants to say a few words, too, so I'll give him the keyboard for a few minutes.

Hi, honey, this is your dad. I love you, baby. We've been watching over you two for a lot of years and we're proud of you both. If there's any way you can reply to this message and confirm that you got it, please do it now.

He looked at Lloyd and nodded. Lloyd clicked on the Send button. They both uttered a sigh of relief when the words "Message sent" instantly appeared on the screen.

Allison screamed as she sat in front of her computer screen. "Danny! My God! It's my dad ... your dad!"

"What're you talking about?" Danny looked over Allison's shoulder and read some of the words on the screen. "Nah. It's gotta be some kind of sick joke or something."

"Wait!" Allison cried as Danny began to walk away. "You need to read the whole thing. It's real, damn it!" Allison trembled, a scared feeling coursing through her body. She silently admonished herself. *How can you be frightened? It's your own father.*

"Come on, sweetie, do you hear yourself? It can't possibly be real. Get rid of it now," he insisted, "or the white coats will be coming to pick you up." Then Danny circled back toward Allison, planting a kiss on the top of her head in an effort to take back his impulsive harsh words.

In disbelief, Danny watched as Allison composed herself and clicked on Reply. She began typing:

Dear Dads, we got your message and we'd sure like to believe it's you. The whole concept is indeed difficult to conceive, but I've had sort of a premonition about this for some time. Still, if you don't mind, I'd like some verification. Tell me, Dad, if you really are my father, what was the name of the song and who sang it on the first record you ever gave me?

Allison clicked on Send and seconds later "Message sent" appeared.

"Oh, what the hell," Danny said after reading her reply. He nudged Allison over and typed in his own message:

Dear Dad, if you are my dad, tell me what Uncle Edward did the day of Grandma Wallace's funeral that got you so upset. If you can answer this, maybe I'm a believer. Love, Danny.

Danny clicked on Send and again "Message sent" appeared on the screen.

Danny got up and went into the kitchen, still not convinced he had been contacted by his late father. *How the hell could this be?* he wondered. *The whole concept of my dad contacting me from beyond the grave is something right out of HBO's Tales From the Crypt. I should have my head examined for even considering the possibility. Still …*

He suddenly realized the screech he heard was Allison. "Danny! They're back!" she yelled. "Come quick!"

Danny ran back into the living room and read over Allison's shoulder:

Dear Loved Ones, Mickey says to tell Allison that the very first record he gave her was on Christmas morning when she was about fourteen. It was a forty-five and the song was "What a Difference a Day Makes," sung by the inimitable Dinah Washington.

As for Uncle Edward, Danny, he pretended he'd overslept at the hotel on the morning of my mother's funeral and I was indeed momentarily upset until he came prancing out of his hotel room dressed to the nines, along with that ridiculous hat and monster cigar. Can we proceed now?

Allison began crying again and Danny was visibly shaken. This wasn't the movies. It wasn't television. This was real. Their fathers were somehow communicating with them from beyond, from some unlikely place with the alliterative name of Midway Manor. And by computer, no less.

As Allison continued her uncontrollable crying, Danny grabbed a chair and placed it next to Allison's. "It's okay, babe," he said softly, stroking Allison's arm. "Everything's okay. But we need to answer their e-mail."

Dear Dad and Mr. Parks, this is Danny. Midway Manor? It all sounds a little too fantastic for reality. I feel like I've just been given a part in a Twilight Zone episode. How can all this happen? Love, Danny.

Lloyd replied shortly thereafter, going on and on for pages with details of the Manor, their experiences there, the visit by Danny's mother, and the fact that their clandestine activities were totally against the rules. He admitted how they could be stopped from what they were doing at any time and their communication to Danny and Allison cut off for eternity.

Danny, if something does happen and we lose our link with you, and we have to leave here, please know that if there's any way we can contact you again, we will.

Lloyd was careful to explain that nothing would actually happen to them in the form of a punishment, that they simply would be banished from Midway and sent on to another destination. He ended the transmission saying that the next e-mail they received would reveal the second Kennedy assassin, disclose the true origin of UFOs and who was piloting them, and answer once and for all what actually happened to union boss Jimmy Hoffa. These revelations would be followed by dozens and dozens more, all of which Danny and Allison should use in the manner they had advised earlier.

Danny acknowledged his father's e-mail, promising he would study whatever information Lloyd sent and certainly give the book idea serious consideration.

Lloyd's fingers poised over the keyboard as he got ready to type while Mickey read from his notes detailing the revelations of Earth's unsolved mysteries. The first one involved the second shooter in the John F. Kennedy assassination in 1963. As Lloyd began to type, a series of knocks on the door interrupted them. Lloyd and Mickey froze, stunned momentarily by the intrusion. The knocking grew louder, the lights dimmed and the computer went dead, cutting Lloyd off in mid-sentence. Their worst fears had been realized. The Authority had shut them down.

Lloyd opened the door and stood face to face with the Manor's director, Joseph Patrick. "I'm sorry, gentlemen, but I think you know why I'm here."

Danny and Allison stayed glued to the computer screen, almost holding their breath, waiting for the next communication from Midway.

And then the words "You've got mail" resounded like a bomb exploding. The two stared at the screen and began to read:

On the morning of November 22nd, 1963, Lee Harvey Oswald and his Russian-born friend—

The message was cut off in mid-sentence. Danny clicked on reply and started typing furiously:

Dad, what happened? Where are you? Your last message was incomplete. Please tell us you're okay.

Danny hit Send.
Silence. Five minutes passed, a period that seemed more like five hours, when a message popped up on the computer screen. The screen was filled with wordage, codes and symbols, most of which Danny couldn't understand. But the gist of the message was obvious: MAIL UNDELIVERABLE.

Allison screamed again in anguish. "They're gone! We've lost our dads again! My God, they're gone!"

Danny pulled Allison out of the chair and held her tightly....

Chapter Twenty-seven
A novel idea

As the director escorted Mickey and Lloyd down the hall, Mr. Patrick explained how this should never have gone as far as it did. "It was our fault, a rare oversight on the part of the Manor. There should have been a block on the e-mail program, a password situation as we have with other sensitive sites."

"What happens to us now, Mr. Patrick?" Lloyd asked, pretty sure of the answer.

"Well, I think you know the rules here by now. You'll both have to move on, of course. The destination is your choice, but you'll be leaving some time during the night."

"Can we, uh, move on together?" asked Mickey.

"Well, not in unison, if that's what you mean. The transition is kind of complicated. You wouldn't understand it even if I tried to explain the process. But you both certainly can go to the same destination."

Later, before they parted to go to their individual rooms, Lloyd asked Mickey, "Will I see you in Reunion Valley?"

"Absolutely, Lloyd old buddy. Besides Mom and Dad, all my brothers should be there. My sister Terry's the only one still living, so she won't be there. And you?"

"Well, Dorothy will be there, of course. And my brother Edward. And my folks. I'll be happy to see them all."

They hugged then, slapping each other on the back. "It's been one hell of a ride, really, Mick. I'm sorry we didn't get that information through to the kids, but I think we've helped them a lot anyway."

"You're right, Lloyd. We certainly gave it our best shot. By the way, that last bit of typing you did …" He paused, giving Lloyd the widest grin he could muster. "I hit the Send button before they pulled the plug."

Lloyd grinned back. "No shit."

Allison didn't go to work for a week. She called her publisher and lied about coming down with the flu. She hardly ate, preferring to sit in their bedroom and stare out the window for hours at a time.

During the day, she gazed intently at the sky, yearning to find some trace of the Manor that might lie beyond the cotton-white clouds. In the evening, she studied the stars, searching for a sign of her twice-lost dad. Even Ashley, their new kitten, sensed something different about Allison. She would cautiously creep into the bedroom and hesitate before jumping up onto her lap. And when Allison finally did acknowledge Ashley's presence, gently stroking her back, Allison's eyes remained focused on the sky.

Danny anxiously checked the computer for e-mail messages every day, refusing to admit what he already knew at gut level—that there would be nothing. He did everything he could to cheer Allison up, short of hiring a three-ring circus.

"How 'bout we go out to dinner tonight, sweetheart," Danny offered one Friday evening. I'll take you to that fancy steak place you've been wanting to try. The hell with the cost."

"No, thank you," Allison replied. "I'm not very hungry."

"You haven't been hungry for more than a week."

"I know."

"You've got to eat. You've got to keep your strength up."

"I know."

"Honey, listen to me. I'm sorry about your dad ... my dad. It's awful that we've lost them twice. But maybe—"

"Maybe what?" Allison interrupted angrily.

"That's good."

"What's good?"

"Your anger. That's healthy. It shows you may be coming out of your depressive state. Let it loose."

"Fuck you!"

"That's a little too angry."

"Fuck you!"

Allison softened then. "I'm sorry, Danny. Please ... leave me alone right now."

Danny gave up and left the apartment. He walked the streets for a long time, trying to figure out what to do next. When he spotted a small florist on Eighty-third Street that was—miraculously—still open, he went in and ordered a large bouquet of flowers for Allison. He excitedly dictated the address, confirming that the flowers would be delivered within the hour.

He walked around for another hour or so and then anxiously returned to the apartment. Sure enough, the flowers had been delivered and Allison had mellowed out. Unfortunately, it didn't take long for Danny to realize that the anger had dissipated but the depression lingered.

"Are you all right?" Danny asked, taking her in his arms.

"I'm okay," she said. "Just sad. Thank you for the beautiful flowers. They're lovely."

"Would you like to go dancing?" He knew how much she loved to dance, and she usually had to drag him to clubs.

"No. Not really." She pushed him away, walked over to the window and peered out.

"But you love dancing."

"I'm just not up for it, Danny. Please understand. I can't bear the thought that I've lost my dad again. I ... I almost ..."

"Almost what? Don't do that to me, Allison."

"I almost want to take a razor blade and ... get it over with."

"Woman, that's insane talk." Danny's heart pounded in his ears. Her talk about suicide frightened him.

"Maybe I'll be able to meet up with my dad then."

Danny took her back in his arms and held her tightly.

"Darling, I didn't enjoy losing my dad again, either. But don't worry me with this kind of talk. Losing you would kill me, too. Promise me you won't do anything so goddamn foolish."

"I promise," Allison said, her voice barely a whisper.

The next day, Danny offered to use every last penny of their savings and take her to Paris, or anywhere else in the world she wanted to go. But Allison turned him down, remaining in a state of deep depression.

"I've got an idea," Danny said the next morning as they sat drinking their coffee. "Why don't you rearrange the whole place? Move the furniture around any way you like."

This was an unprecedented, last-ditch attempt on Danny's part to shake Allison loose from her depressed state. Allison's very favorite thing in life, going back to when she was a kid helping her dad rearrange the antiques in his store, was to come up with new ways to situate furniture in a room.

For the first time in days, Allison smiled broadly.

"But ... but you hate me to move anything. You get upset when I move a lamp more than three inches."

"Yeah, I know. But I've changed my mind."

"Really?" Allison's eyes sparkled in excitement. "Well, I always thought that the chair over by the window would look a lot better in the bedroom, and ... "

Danny nodded as Allison went on excitedly, sharing her redecorating ideas. And she was okay for a few days, implementing what she had described to Danny. But after she returned to work, Danny could see that her exuberance had waned, that life for her had once again become meaningless. When she came home in the evening, her despondency would be smeared all over her face.

Allison's depression had worn Danny down to a dangerous level. Coupled with his own heartache over losing his father a second time, that nagging insanity, that need to fix himself with a drink, was back.

One night, Danny stopped at a local bar and ordered a very dry martini, straight up with an olive. He sat and stared at the chilled martini glass for a very long time. He thought about Allison and his heart ached for her, knowing how much emotional pain she was going through. He thought about his dad and how much he still missed him.

For a brief moment he felt anger, anger that his father had once again been taken from him. But then the anger subsided and gave way to an unusual calm as he raised the martini glass in a silent toast. *Wherever you are, Dad, I love you very much. And thank you and Mickey both for trying to help, even if you didn't succeed in your mission.*

He put the glass back on the bar before he could take a sip, trying to shake the new feeling that he had let his dad down. *Wait a second! It's not my fault they didn't get that information to me. How am I supposed to write a book without the facts?*

Danny reached for the martini glass again, feeling sorry for himself. He almost missed hearing "Stardust" playing on the jukebox.

My God, Allison was right! They're with us! With stunning clarity, Danny realized his dad, and Allison's dad, and his mom, on whatever level, still existed. *And the meaning of life? It may lie in the simple fact that life is not finite after all.*

And that's when the inspiration hit Danny, as if the dads had tapped into his head directly. *Sonofabitch! I'll write a book anyway! I'll write a novel about Midway Manor!*

He left the bar then, leaving the martini still in its pristine state.

Danny notified Sam that he was taking his two weeks' vacation as soon as he could wrap up some loose ends and leave the place in working order. He confided in Sam that he planned to start the novel he had often talked about, leaving the part about Midway Manor out of the conversation.

"You're gonna write a book in two weeks?" Sam asked, feigning seriousness.

"No, but I'm going to get a good jump on it."

"So what's it about?"

"You'll have to buy a copy to find out."

Sam laughed good-naturedly and wished Danny good luck with his venture.

Allison at first left him alone when he started writing the book. Danny key-stroked for hours that first day, initially pecking out a sketchy outline of the novel. He pored over the e-mail from the dads, trying to visualize Midway Manor and its residents.

After a few days, Allison grew curious. Standing in the doorway to his den, she peeked at him as he typed away earnestly. She watched for a little while longer, her curiosity building, and then walked over to the desk and started reading what Danny had written so far.

"Wait a minute," she said, more animated than she had been since the brief redecorating stint. "You need to start out with a scene where they're alive. I don't think …"

It turned into a joint effort after that. They took turns writing chapter after chapter on the computer, with Allison doing most of the Midway Manor material and Danny concentrating on what he knew best—what it was like to be an editor for men's adventure magazines during the '70s. What it was like to live in New York and be in love.

For Danny and Allison, the whole project proved to be an uplifting experience. When Danny wrote a chapter, he would turn it over to Allison for critiquing, editing and proofing. And when Allison finished a chapter, Danny would do the honors.

Not that it was all harmony and honey.

From time to time they would disagree about something—loudly and often passionately—but as professionals they would work it out and eventually meet each other halfway. And the collaboration had taken care of Allison's depression for good.

They finished the book in six months. The next step was finding an agent. Danny called Samantha, who promptly explained—in her own unique, convoluted way—that though she had written a number of romance books that had been published, she herself did not have the appropriate contacts in the book business.

Additional weeks passed while Danny and Allison fought over the drafting of a one-page letter seeking representation by an agent. Among other things, the so-called query letter would have to include a single paragraph about the book that would pique the agent's interest. Which wasn't easy to do. There was no simple way to explain the book's premise in a few short sentences. Plus, they had to convince an agent of the viability of an alternative to Heaven in the afterworld, and make it sound believable. And potentially appealing and compelling for readers. The query letter would also have to include a brief description of Danny and Allison's writing credentials.

Finally, after writing, rewriting, honing and re-honing, the letter was ready to submit to agents.

"We need to write a synopsis," Allison told Danny.

"Done," Danny said.

Weeks later, after further battles over various verbs and adjectives, the query letter—along with a concise, two-page outline of the novel from beginning to end—found its way into the mailboxes of dozens of literary agents.

Several months passed as the rejection slips piled up.

Eventually, an intuitive agent, who herself had lost both parents at an early age, saw the potential in Danny and Allison's story and signed a contract with them. Astonishingly, in a matter of weeks, a publisher was found.

Midway Manor reached book stores across the country a year later.

People started reading it, and they related to it. They envisioned their late parents or grandparents relaxing in the Renaissance Room, enjoying themselves in the Manor's dining room, or monitoring loved ones in the Data Room. They told their friends and relatives about the book, and they in turn bought and read it. They started talking about it on TV, on late-night talk shows, and in a very short time *Midway Manor* became one of the hottest reads in the country.

And there was talk of a movie option.

Chapter Twenty-eight
Looking for the Truth

"Keep going …" Lynn Holloway pleaded.

Her husband looked up over his reading glasses and smiled.

"Please, John … don't stop now."

John Holloway thumbed through the last pages of the novel he'd been reading to her all afternoon. "We've got … let's see … nineteen … twenty … twenty-two pages to go. Twenty-two pages," he repeated, getting up from his chair and sliding it away from her hospital bed.

"You're a tease," Lynn answered in a barely audible whisper.

"Aw, just give me a minute to stretch my legs." John leaned over to straighten her pillow, and then kissed his wife. Her cheek felt cold and he lingered by her face, hoping the warmth of his breath would comfort her in some way. He hated that she was dying and fervently wished there was even a noodle of truth in the novel he was reading about the so-called afterworld. If only he could be certain that his wife, the love of his life, was destined for something beautiful after she left him. It would make these final hours with her easier to bear.

He even tried to convince himself that spending the entire afternoon reading aloud a novel about a destination in the afterworld named Midway Manor was not a waste of precious time. Certainly the concept was a far cry from Heaven. Or was it?

John moved his chair back next to her bed, trying to ignore the antiseptic hospital smells and block out the loud voices from somewhere down the hallway. Shuddering at the distant sound of a bedpan hitting the floor, he opened the book to the first page of the last chapter and began reading aloud. Lynn closed her eyes, trying once again to visualize herself in this other world, an alternate world that had already become a reality in her mind.

Reading the rest of the story did not take much time at all and when John finished, he closed the book with a deliberate thump, as if to drown out the hospital noise. "Done," he declared, glancing at the picture of the middle-aged couple on the back cover. He remembered the authors' names, Danny and Allison Wallace.

He wondered what kind of a relationship a man and woman would need to be able to collaborate on a whole book, then immediately decided it had to be a very close, intimate one. He imagined momentarily his son Carson and Carson's wife Kathleen and how they might write a book together. He almost laughed out loud. *No way,* he told himself. *Carson's a good enough writer, but the marriage ... there's always some crisis going on. Why, a day doesn't go by—*

"What a wonderful place Midway Manor is," Lynn rasped, interrupting John's thoughts.

John smiled, assured by his wife's comment that she had been charmed by the story. He decided to play along. "Yes, Midway Manor has a lot to offer, but I'd prefer heading right for that other place ... uh ... Reunion Valley. You know ... the place where you can meet up with old friends and family. You know who I mean." John hesitated a moment as his head flooded with familiar names and faces. *And they're all dead and buried and gone for good,* he thought to himself before he continued. "God, what I wouldn't give to see my father and mother again." His voice cracked as he considered the possibility, becoming fully conscious of how much their sudden deaths, of losing both parents at the same time back in 1976, had left him with an unyielding heavy heart.

"It would be nice to see your parents again. And mine, too. But, John ... I can't do that. I *must* go to Midway Manor. At least there I'd have access to a computer and be able to read all about what you and Carson are up to." Lynn paused, trying to muster the strength to continue. "I'd feel closer to you both." During the past few weeks, Lynn had asked John to promise her that he would keep a close watch on their son Carson after she had passed. She needed to know her husband would be there for their son, and like so, their son would be there for his wife Kathleen and *their* son Brian. "Yes, I've decided. I'm definitely going to Midway Manor to make sure everyone's okay," she repeated.

"Yes, all right," he answered, patting the top of her hand, trying hard not to sound patronizing.

But Lynn jerked her hand away. "I'm serious, John. I've made up my mind."

"Okay ... okay, sweetheart, whatever you want," he said gently this time, not wanting to upset her any further.

When it was time for John to leave the hospital, he grabbed the book from the bedside table and carried it off with him. On his drive home, he began a dialogue with himself. "This is just somebody's fantasy about the hereafter. It's drivel. Midway Manor. Reunion Valley. These places don't exist."

"You fool! Of course they exist. You just read about it," Lynn's voice countered in his mind.

John clutched the steering wheel with his left hand as he reached over with the other to pick up the book. *Trash. Who gives a damn about the hereafter? When Lynn goes, my life will be over.* The blast of a horn from an oncoming car startled John, causing him to overreact. The car went into a spin and swerved off the road....

Carson Dolan Holloway sat in front of his computer, fighting back the tears as he tried to suppress the memory of burying his father only a few hours earlier. He pushed aside the fact that his dad's fatal car accident was unfair and utterly ill-timed, and how his mother, who remained so gravely ill, had been unable to leave Parkview Memorial Hospital to attend her husband's funeral.

Carson's fingers flew over the keyboard as he finished up his editorial for the January issue of the *Tennessee Senior Citizen*. His editorial was about food. *Food, the staff of life. What irony,* he thought. *My father's dead and I'm writing about what keeps you alive.* The Wilson supermarket chain was putting on its mammoth annual food show at the civic center that weekend and he and his wife Kathleen needed to take advantage of the opportunity to hand out hundreds of free copies of their paper. Wilson Foods had taken out a full-page ad with them, a paying ad, with the understanding that Carson would include copy on food in the current issue of the monthly tabloid.

Despite the funeral, despite his grief over his dad's unexpected death, despite being expected to show up at the daily newspaper's printing facility with thirty-two camera-ready pages at 7:00 tomorrow morning, Carson knew he would meet the deadline for this issue. He knew this because he knew how to write, and because the mechanicals for everything else, including halftones, were pasted down and ready for the paper's pre-press crew to shoot and hang plates.

"Could you come up to my office, Carson?" The voice on the intercom belonged to Carson's wife, Kathleen. It was not really a question but more like a summons.

"Yeah … in a minute," Carson yelled back into the intercom. He finished typing the last sentence, ran the text through spell check and then printed out the double-spaced, four-page editorial so that Kathleen could read it and give him her okay. When it came to the editorial side of the paper, he and Kathleen had no problems. She bowed to his much more extensive editorial experience and writing abilities. She did, however, insist on reading his editorials before they were published. On occasion, she would suggest he eliminate a sentence, or rework a section. And Carson would usually comply. He knew he sometimes let his emotions cloud his good judgment and would write something that would leave the paper open to a lawsuit or, worse yet, cause an advertiser to pull their ad.

But when it came to the business side of the business, Kathleen and Carson fit together like two jigsaw pieces—each from a different puzzle. If Carson had his way, the monthly tabloid for seniors would print thousands more copies each month than it did. Conversely, Kathleen was always looking for ways to trim the print run and lower their overhead.

There also were other issues on which they did not agree, and sometimes they would engage in heated arguments that would quickly become passionately ugly. Carson remembered one incident in which Kathleen hurled a typewriter at him. He managed to avoid personal injury by dodging the heavy machine, but a handyman had to be called in to repair the rather large hole in her office wall.

"Are you comin' or not?" Kathleen yelled over the intercom again, her New York accent more obvious this time.

"Right there," Carson yelled back. He grabbed the pages from the printer and left his office, climbing the narrow, steep rear stairway to the second floor. He walked down the hallway to Kathleen's office and tossed the editorial on her desk.

"That wraps this issue up," he said, sounding both proud and relieved at the same time.

Kathleen got up and came around to the front of the desk. "I need a hug," she said, and Carson complied. She was a perfect fit, snuggling in against him and holding him tightly. Carson hugged her back, aware that her soft, ample breasts and well-proportioned body of forty-five years still excited him. Despite having been married for twenty-three years now, the sex was still as vibrant and passionate as it was when they had first met.

For a brief moment, Carson fantasized picking her up, carrying her up to the apartment on the third floor and making love to her in their king-size four-poster. But there was too much to do. As usual, there just wasn't enough time in the day to get everything accomplished. It's what frustrated Carson the most, and there were a lot of things that frustrated, annoyed or angered Carson. Like people not taking responsibility for what they do. Or lacking common courtesy and consideration of others. The world had changed drastically in Carson's fifty-year life, and he wasn't too happy about it.

"Are you gonna have time to go to the hospital tonight?" Kathleen asked. "I know you have a deadline …"

"Of course," Carson replied, deciding it was a stupid question. "I told you this wraps it up. And even if I did have more work, I'm still gonna visit my mother. She's dying, for chrissakes." Carson pulled away from Kathleen, his anger taking over.

"Calm down, Carson. I was just making sure." Kathleen knew Carson's anger was simply a mask for the fear he was really feeling, the fear of losing his mother, a fear that had intensified by the sudden, shocking loss of his father. She walked back behind her desk and sat down, shuffling through some papers.

"By the way," Kathleen said, trying to temper Carson's ruffled demeanor. "You know that girl who called about the ad sales job? The one we agreed to hire?"

"Yeah," said Carson, less ruffled now. "I remember her. She sounds like she can really do well for us, although we haven't actually met her in person."

"Well, forget about her. She just called and informed me she was under house arrest. She asked me if I have a problem with that." Kathleen laughed.

"She what?" Carson laughed, too. "Good grief, there's not much of a gene pool to work from here, is there?" They both laughed harder, trying to dispel their disappointment. Good sales account reps, people who sold advertising space in the paper, were hard to come by. They also were a strange breed. Finding them and then keeping tabs on them was a full-time job in itself. In the two years that they had published the *Tennessee Senior Citizen*, they had gone through several dozen sales people, and Kathleen and Carson figured there weren't any surprises left. But of course surprises were what the future was all about....

Lynn Holloway was sitting up in bed when Carson, Kathleen and their son Brian arrived at the hospital. Brian, twenty-two, had been imported from New York to help his parents with the paper's distribution. They had offered Brian and his nineteen-year-old girlfriend, Blair, room and board in exchange for distributing the monthly publication. He had nothing to lose by relocating since his work in home construction was seasonal and he was idle more than he was busy. Brian was crazy about his grandmother and became grief-stricken when he learned she was not expected to live much longer.

Brian had driven to the hospital in his own car and had met them in the lobby. He explained to Carson that he'd left Blair at home to feed the cats and tidy up their room.

"How ya feelin', Mom?" Carson asked, taking his mother's hand in his and kissing her on the forehead.

"I'm okay," Lynn Holloway said unconvincingly. She pressed the button on the gadget she held in her left hand, delivering another shot of morphine from the bottle hanging alongside her bed. "Midway ... Midway Manor ..." she whispered.

"What?" Carson asked, not understanding what his mother was talking about.

"It's the book your dad had read to her, *Midway Manor*," said Kathleen. "It's a novel about some place in the hereafter. Fiction."

"No, it's true," rasped Lynn, trying hard to make her voice louder. "There really is a Midway Manor. And a place called Reunion Valley. Your father ..." Her voice trailed off and she drifted into a drug-induced sleep.

"Grandma," Brian called, leaning over the bed. "Grandma ... is she?"

"No, Brian," said Carson. "She's just resting. We'd better go now. I'll talk to the doctor."

The three left the room and walked down the hallway to the nurses' station.

"Is Doctor Talbot available?" Carson asked the charge nurse.

"I'm afraid you just missed him. He's making his rounds on another floor." She paused, looking down the hallway. "You just came from Mrs. Holloway's room, didn't you?"

"Yes, she's my mother," explained Carson. "We were concerned about her condition. Is she—?"

"Don't worry," the nurse cut him short. "Mrs. Holloway's resting comfortably. We're watching her closely. I don't think you have anything to worry about for now. I'll have Doctor Talbot call you later at home if you like. It's not necessary to stay here tonight."

"I'd appreciate that. Here's my business card. The paper's number will ring at home. He can call anytime." Carson reflected for a moment. "Are you sure we shouldn't stick around here?"

"I'm sure, Mister Holloway. Go home and get some sleep."

In the car, Carson questioned Kathleen about the book, *Midway Manor*. "What's all this about Mom's preoccupation with ... what did she call it ... Midway Manor? It sounds like she's confusing fiction with reality."

"Well, just humor her. How can it hurt? If she wants to believe Dad's residing at a Midway Manor, or in a Reunion Valley, let her believe it. Maybe it helps to ease the pain of his passing."

"I don't know how healthy that is."

"Christ, Carson. If it comforts her, then it's healthy."

Carson didn't answer, concentrating instead on his efforts to pull into their driveway that ran down alongside the seventy-year-old building and into a parking area at the rear of the house. He avoided parking in the detached, dilapidated, doorless garage that appeared to be on the verge of collapsing come the next windy day.

Entering through the rear door of the building, Carson went into his office.

"You go on up and I'll be along shortly," he said. "I wanna check the boards one more time, just to make sure."

"All right," Kathleen said, climbing the narrow stairway. "Try not to be too long."

Carson turned on the bright, overhead fluorescent lights and began going over the thirty-two pages of the paper. The pages, called mechanicals, were laid out on slanted wooden tables specially built to Carson's specifications. Sure enough, one of the headlines had the wrong punctuation and Carson quickly booted up the computer and laser printer. Fortunately, he had left the wax machine on, just in case he had to make a last-minute change. Otherwise, he would have been there forever waiting for the block of wax to dissolve.

As Carson typed out a corrected headline, his thoughts went back to his mom and the curious obsession she seemed to have with the book called *Midway Manor*. To his own amazement, he began to wonder if there was anything to it. *Maybe I should read the book and see what all the fuss is about.*

In the morning, Carson packed up the mechanical boards and delivered them to the printer, which belonged to Evansville's daily newspaper, the *Mountain Record*. As he usually did, he brought a box of freshly baked doughnuts for the pressroom crew. It was a generous gesture that kept Carson in favor with the pressroom boys, and a good public relations ploy that smoothed the way for Carson to get constructive response when he pointed out printing glitches during the press run.

On the way home, Carson stopped at the local drug store and bought a paperback copy of *Midway Manor*. He read more than half of the book before driving back to the hospital to see how his mom was doing, and then finished it in the early morning hours.

Fiction, of course, Carson thought. *But there's something about it, I don't know ...*

As the weekend neared, Lynn Holloway's condition worsened. Kathleen and Carson visited her each evening, sometimes with Brian and Blair, sometimes alone. Most of the time, Lynn slept. On the rare occasion when she was awake, she mumbled over and over again about Midway Manor.

While Brian and Blair were out finishing up the distribution of the paper, Kathleen and Carson prepared for the food show at the civic center. On Friday morning, they loaded the car with bundles of various back issues of the paper, including one bundle of the latest issue.

They decorated the back wall of their assigned booth with front covers of previous issues. Traci, the paper's secretary, stayed at the office and answered the phone. She was a tall, slender, striking blonde with an ever-present smile that heartened Carson even when he was feeling blue.

Carson knew that Traci lived with another young woman, and that the two were obviously lovers. But it didn't stop him from fantasizing about being in bed with Traci, her long legs wrapped around his waist as he thrust inside her. He also would visualize Traci and her lesbian live-in locked in naked embrace, their tongues busily exploring each other's bodies.

Sexual fantasies sustained Carson's active libido, which he would eventually satisfy either with Kathleen or by himself. The idea of cheating on his wife, though he had thought about it briefly from time to time, was never considered an option by Carson. He believed in the sanctity of the marriage vows, and he was sure Kathleen shared the same convictions.

When Kathleen and Carson got back home following the first night of the food show, Traci greeted them anxiously. As soon as Kathleen saw her face, she knew something was wrong.

"Doctor Talbot called and he wants you to call him at the hospital," said Traci, choosing her words carefully.

"It's Mom," said Carson, rushing to the rear stairway.

"Where're you going?" asked Kathleen. "The doctor wants us to call."

"I'm going to the hospital. The hell with the phone."

"Wait, I'm coming with you …"

Dr. Stephen Talbot was waiting for them when they arrived at the hospital, his reserved, austere manner intact. It was the way he carried himself at all times. Even when he found something amusing, he would do his best to contain his smile and hide the twinkle in his eye. This time, his somber face appeared more wooden than ever.

"Folks, I'm afraid your mother's gone. She passed on a couple of hours ago. She died quietly and peacefully."

"Did she say anything before she died?" Carson asked.

"Only what she'd been saying these last few days ... the *Midway Manor* thing."

And that's when Carson realized he had to go back to New York, to Manhattan, to look up the authors of *Midway Manor*, Danny and Allison Wallace. He wasn't sure why, but somehow he knew intuitively that his mother's ramblings were more meaningful than he had originally thought.

Chapter Twenty-nine
A field of flowers

"Where the hell is everybody?"

After awakening every day for the last twenty-three Earth years in the same bed at Midway Manor, Mickey Parks felt it rather odd to find himself on this January morning standing alone in a field of wildflowers. He stood there in silence, trying to adjust to his new surroundings. Amidst a cornucopia of countless colors and overpowering fragrances, he wondered why his lifelong allergies weren't acting up ... why he hadn't sneezed.

But aside from the surrounding spectacle being a threat to his allergies, he realized that both his vision and audible range were immeasurably acute. He could see the details of all the blooms, even at a distance from where he stood. And he was astounded to hear the whirr of a butterfly's wings as it fluttered from one flower to another.

"Where the hell is everybody?" he asked himself again.

Mickey Park's sudden departure from Midway Manor had apparently taken place sometime during the night. While he was asleep, his spirit had miraculously journeyed to Reunion Valley. Not that he'd planned to move on so abruptly, but after being caught red-handed using the Manor's computers illegally, he and Lloyd no longer had a choice.

"Where the hell is everybody?" Mickey asked for a third time. He looked down, keenly aware that he had no body. He was fully intact but without any physical form. "And where the hell am *I*?" he cried.

"Mick ... Mick, is that you?" the friendly voice called out.

"Hello," Mickey answered. "Who's there?"

"It's me, old buddy. Where are you? I can hear you loud and clear, but I can't see anything but these damn flowers."

"Lloyd, is that you? Well, you're not the only one who can't see me 'cause I can't see myself either! Where are you anyway?"

"Now take it easy, Mick. Don't go panicking on me."

"Panic ... me? What's to panic about? The only thing that's gone right this morning is that I haven't—" Mickey's words were cut off in mid-sentence as he sneezed six consecutive times.

"Do it again, Mick," Lloyd said.

"Do what?"

"Sneeze. When you were sneezing, I swear I saw you. Tell me, are you standing alongside a sunflower the size of a dinner plate?"

Mickey looked around to make sure there weren't any other platter-sized sunflowers near him besides the one Lloyd was referring to. "Yeah, I am ... but I can't just sneeze at will."

"So how 'bout you fake a few for me?"

"Yeah. Okay. Ah-h choo." Mickey repeated his version of a faked sneeze several more times before asking, "Can you see me now?"

"I sure can. Turn around, Mick. I'm right behind you."

Mickey turned around. Lloyd was no longer invisible. And neither was Mickey. The physical forms they had both maintained for the last twenty years during their tenure together at Midway Manor had reappeared. Mickey in his fifty-eight-year-old version, and Lloyd the same vibrant sixty-three-year-old model. The two men hugged one another, slapping each other on the back, reassuring themselves that their earthly torsos had once again returned.

"I guess our spirits arrived before we did," Lloyd joked.

"Yeah. But where are we?" Mickey asked. "Is this place Reunion Valley or what?"

"I don't know," Lloyd said, surveying the immediate area. "My guess is that we're in the right place but somehow our spirits were beamed off target."

"Maybe," said Mickey. "But I noticed you somehow lost your silk tie and jacket in the process."

Lloyd, a handsome man by anyone's standards, was still well-dressed, wearing a light-blue broadcloth shirt with open buttoned-down collar, golden-orange cardigan and wrinkle-free slacks. He also wore beige, soft-top Italian tennis shoes.

"Yeah, but I'm not sure who's in charge of wardrobe around here," Lloyd said. "These are pretty much the kinds of clothes I wore when I dressed casually on Earth back in the seventies. And hell ... it's 1996 back there. How about you? You're wearing the same short-sleeved white shirt and khaki pants you did at Midway Manor. And you still have that watch on."

Mickey didn't answer, thinking for a brief moment about the watch his beloved daughter Allison had once given him, and the replica with which Midway had so generously replaced it. He raised his hand to his mouth, preparing to cover up another episode of multiple sneezes. "I need to get away from here," he said when the outburst was over. "These weeds are killing me."

"Then let's go," Lloyd said, heading away from the sun. "I think this is the way to the valley."

Mickey began to tag along without questioning Lloyd's instinct to travel west. And aware that his heightened senses of sight and sound had returned to normal, he wondered if he had imagined it all. "By any chance," he asked guardedly, "did you notice anything strange when you first got here? See or hear anything odd?"

"You mean my being able to hear the hum of a butterfly's wings? Or the ladybug crunching on a leaf? Wasn't that something? It's gone now. And my vision is back to what it had been."

Mickey absorbed the words, glad to know that they had both momentarily experienced this oddity. Without Lloyd's admission, though, he would never have believed that he hadn't been hallucinating.

As the two continued walking briskly through the field, they couldn't help but notice the vibrant beauty of the wildflowers, each one touting not only perfection but also an obvious uniqueness. There were thousands of varieties. Some that would normally grow exclusively in specific areas back on Earth such as forests or fields, or in deserts, or jungles, or swamps, or on mountainsides, or along the seashore. The bright sunlight here, obviously, did not affect the ones that usually thrived only in dimly lit forests. All the flowers were in full bloom, all the time.

"I've never had much of a green thumb myself," Lloyd commented, "but whoever's been tending to this field is the gardener of all time."

Mickey agreed, in spite of his allergies continuing to act up. And as he hurried by some of the flowers that he'd recognized, he called out their names. "Violets. Jack-in-the-Pulpits. Asters. Bluebells. Wild roses. Buttercups …"

There were hundreds that he didn't know by name or had ever seen. Like the Rafflesia arnoldi, the largest flower in the world, which one would have found back on Earth in Indonesia, its petals measuring up to one-and-a-half feet long and an inch thick. Or the smallest flower called the duckweed.

"Hold up, Mick. Look!" Lloyd yelled out. He pointed past the end of the flowering field to a lush green lawn as smooth as a carpet of felt. And on the lawn in the distance, he could see a gathering. "Could they be our families?"

Mickey tried to make out facial features but they were too far away. He fought back the tears. "I can't tell," he answered with a lump in his throat, conjuring up the familiar faces of his parents and brothers whom he hadn't seen in more than twenty years. "Let's get down there."

The two quickened their steps to join the group. As soon as they reached the end of the flowering field, a figure moved away from the crowd and began to walk toward Mickey and Lloyd. Even at the considerable distance that still separated them from the stranger, the two Midway Manor refugees could discern that the figure was a heavyset woman dressed in a long-flowing white ensemble.

After several yards, the woman stopped and raised her hand, waving for Lloyd and Mickey to continue their approach.

"Welcome to Reunion Valley," she said when the two men stopped in front of her. "I'm Marcy Madeline Bates, your administrative guide."

Mickey smiled shyly, remaining behind Lloyd who returned her greeting.

"Please come and join the others," she said warmly, giving each of them direct eye contact. Both men sensed a mystical aura about her. "They've also just arrived here," she continued. "We were expecting you and wanted to wait until we could all go on to the Pavilion together for further introductions."

Mickey, Lloyd and the group then followed Marcy into a large auditorium located on the ground floor of the multi-storied, domed building. Mickey immediately took note of the music playing in the background. It sounded familiar but he couldn't place it at the moment. He nudged Lloyd, asking him if he heard the music, too. Lloyd nodded but didn't speak, as if mesmerized by his surroundings.

As the men and women took their seats positioned in a semi-circle, Marcy moved to the opened center of the circle. She waited until everyone was seated before reaching into her pocket to retrieve a small clicker.

"Once again," she said to everyone in the room, "I'd like to welcome all of you to Reunion Valley. I know that for some of you, this is your first destination in the afterworld. For others, it is not. But before we discuss the many options available to every one of you during your visit here, it would be nice if we went around the room and had each of you introduce yourself. John, why don't you start?"

John Holloway looked around the room, making sure she meant him, and then stood up from his seat. He was a tall, slender man in his seventies, with thinning gray hair and a slight osteopathic hunch to his shoulders. "Hi, my name is John Holloway. This is my first destination. I'm here to meet with my parents ... I haven't seen them in over twenty years." John stifled an urge to cry.

Marcy Madeline intervened. "It's all right, John. Everyone in this room understands the depths of your feelings."

John looked directly at Marcy and smiled. "Thanks," he said. "Yes, I've never quite gotten over losing them. And even though I'm very anxious to see them after all this time, I have some anxiety that they ... well ... that they won't recognize me."

The men and woman in the group laughed nervously.

"Parents instinctively know their children—at any age," Marcy said softly. "Is there anything else you'd like to share with the group at this time?"

"Only that my arrival here was sudden and unexpected. I've left behind my wife Lynn, who's gravely ill, and my son Carson ..." John hesitated for a moment. "I wish they knew about this place. That it really exists, and that we'd all be meeting up with each other sometime in the future. Maybe then their grief would be more bearable," he concluded.

"Perhaps," Marcy replied. "What John is suggesting is a concept I'd like everyone here to give some thought to during your stay at Reunion Valley. Just try to imagine what life on Earth would be like if there were indisputable, verifiable evidence available of the existence of the afterworld. Do you really think people could handle that kind of truth?"

No one in the group volunteered to answer her question at that moment. They continued with introductions until everyone had a turn. Mickey and Lloyd admitted to their lengthy stay at Midway Manor, but said nothing about their improper use of the Data Room's sophisticated computer or their abrupt departure. They both suspected that Marcy Madeline Bates knew exactly what had taken place, and that she would probably be keeping a watchful eye on them.

Neither Mickey nor Lloyd was aware of the surprised look on John Holloway's face when they referred to their previous destination in the afterworld as Midway Manor. Nor were they aware of John's thoughts flashing back to his last moments with his wife, her natural belief in the novel that a Midway Manor had really existed, and his frustration that brought him directly to Reunion Valley.

With the introductions completed, Marcy held out her hand and pressed the clicker she had retrieved from her pocket earlier. The lights dimmed. She clicked it again and the dark blue drapes behind her opened to reveal a large movie screen.

"I know you're all anxious to visit with your family and friends, but first we'd like you to watch a short film we've prepared. It will give you a broad idea about the facilities here. Your individual rooms. The optional meeting areas. And some of the guidelines you'll be required to abide by during your stay. Does anyone have any questions before I run the film?"

There was a hushed murmur from the audience, but no one in the room spoke up. Marcy pressed the clicker once again and the short film began. All eyes were glued to the screen as their new world unfolded....

Chapter Thirty
Manhattan Melodrama

"Whaddya mean you're going to New York?"

Kathleen's question was loaded with attitude. In essence, it was a statement rather than a question. The implication was all too obvious to Carson. She didn't want him going anywhere.

"I *have* to go," Carson declared. "It's compulsive. I know I'm basically a skeptic, but I'm also an editor and there seems to be a sense of truth running through this *Midway Manor*, this so-called work of fiction. And Mother was never the delusional type. She was a realist, a pragmatist. She called 'em the way she saw 'em."

"You're nuts!"

"I'm not nuts. Anyway, worst case scenario, I'll get a good interview for the paper."

"How're we going to afford this little jaunt of yours? The airfare, the hotel, meals … how? Last month we had to sell stuff at the flea market to eat. Or did you selectively forget about that?"

"I didn't forget," said Carson, his voice trailing off as he thought about his mom, and then his dad. The loss of both parents so close together was more than he could bear. He knew the shock of what happened had not hit him fully, that the delayed reaction was yet to come. "We should be getting a check for the back-page ad tomorrow—"

"You can't use that!" Kathleen cut him short. "That's going toward next month's print bill. Besides, you can't use the paper's money as if it came out of your wallet. You know that. Remember what the lawyer said when we signed the incorporation papers?"

"Fine," Carson snapped. "Then I'll use the goddamn credit card."

"That's just great! Let's get deeper in debt. No use in being small potatoes."

"Kathleen," Carson said, trying to soften his tone of voice. He put his arms around her and held her tightly. "Please understand that this is something I just have to do. I'm grieving for my mom and dad and this is the way I'm dealing with it. I need you to support me right now, not fight me."

Kathleen pushed Carson away, disentangling herself from his arms.

"I really am sorry about your loss. It's my loss, too. But I just can't see how your going to New York is going to bring your parents back. If you wanna go off on some wild dog chase, you'll have to do it without my blessings."

"That's wild *goose* chase. But I'm not after geese. I'm after some answers. And finding those answers may somehow bring them back into my life." Carson suddenly realized he was breathing heavily. He tried to shake off the knot of fear he felt in his chest. *Fucking anxiety attack. Just what I needed …*

The plane landed at LaGuardia Airport without incident. Carson hated flying, but he did appreciate getting from one point to another in an economy of time. He also hated buses, which took forever. And he despised driving long distances as well. He loved trains, which he remembered fondly from childhood. But now there were only a few select train routes scattered around the country, and these pretty much limited to scenic nostalgic excursions. So flying was basically his only option when he needed to get somewhere fast.

The Armenian cab driver never stopped talking all the way into Manhattan, speaking with a heavy accent and a something-less-than-vague idea of the English language. Carson nodded politely and kept saying "Yeah, yeah, right" during the entire ride, never understanding a word the cabbie was saying.

Traffic in the city was heavy as the taxi weaved in and out, dodging limos, cars, trucks, buses, cabs … and people. In other towns and cities across the country, people wouldn't think of crossing the street anywhere but at an intersection when the light had turned green. In New York City, jaywalking was expected. The incessant honking reminded Carson of how hard it was to drive in Manhattan without hitting the horn at least once every thirty or forty seconds.

The Winslow was a small but well-appointed uptown hotel recommended by Allison Wallace. Getting the Wallaces' unlisted phone number hadn't been easy. Luckily, an old college buddy of Carson's worked for the phone company, and he owed Carson a favor. And when Carson had made the initial call, Danny Wallace himself answered and promptly hung up, thinking Carson was a salesman. However, several calls later and a brief conversation with Allison, explaining who he was and what he wanted, finally produced an agreement from both Danny and Allison on an interview. The interview would take place during dinner at the restaurant of their choice.

"It's fiction," said Danny Wallace as he gnawed away beaver-like on an ear of corn. "It's just fiction. A made-up story."

Carson liked Danny the moment they had shaken hands. His brown hair and neatly trimmed beard were obviously being slowly subjugated by gray, betraying his otherwise youthful appearance. His manner was friendly, and he smiled as if he knew this great joke and was about to share it with you.

"Listen, Danny," said Carson, "I'm an editor and writer just like you and your wife. But I read your book very carefully and there's something about your story ... something that rings true."

"We'll take that as a compliment, Carson," said Allison, raising her wine glass as if in a toast. "I guess we write pretty well, eh?"

"You do," said Carson. "But how did you come up with the idea for *Midway Manor*? I mean, the name, the details, it's ... well ... it's extraordinary, to say the least."

"It's a gift, I guess," said Danny, suppressing a smile as he thought about how it really was a gift from Allison's dad and his father.

Carson downed his third Scotch but he was still sharp enough to catch the look Allison gave Danny.

Allison, like Danny, retained a youthful presence, although Carson knew she was about fifty, his age. Her long, flowing dark hair, flashing brown eyes and full lips complemented her trim, full-breasted figure. Her smile, however, was what won Carson over immediately.

After dinner, the three returned to Carson's hotel and sat in the plush lobby lounge. Allison and Carson sipped Remy Martin cognac, while Danny, of course, in keeping with his long sobriety, nursed a diet cola. Danny insisted on picking up the tab.

After taking two sips of his second brandy, Carson began sharing his own life's story. How he had been born on Long Island and had grown up in Queens, then moved to Manhattan for not more than a year before meeting Kathleen, marrying, and finally moving back to Queens.

Carson explained how he had gone to work right after college, learning his craft as a cub reporter for a small newspaper in upstate Buffalo.

"I was doing fine for the first few months," said Carson, laughing, "learning to get the spelling of all those Polish names right. Then one day in the fall, the managing editor called me into his office and handed me a pair of boots that came all the way up to my hips. When I asked what they were for, he said I'd need them when it started snowing.

"That was enough for me. I took the first train back to Manhattan and got a job with a crafts magazine. That's where I met Kathleen."

Carson told Danny and Allison about the death of his father and later his mother, and then broke down and wept softly, the liquor smoothing the way for his emotional outburst.

Allison leaned forward and clutched Carson's forearm in an effort to comfort him. "I'm sure they're in a better place."

"Like Midway Manor?" said Carson, looking up and straight into her eyes. It was almost imperceptible, a fleeting nanosecond of recognition. And that was when Carson knew he had not been chasing geese. That was when he was almost positive that there really was a Midway Manor. Allison and Danny still denied the book was anything other than fiction, but Carson knew in his heart and mind that his mother was not hallucinating. And he was determined to get Danny and Allison to eventually level with him.

The next day, Carson went through the phone book, checking the listings for psychics. Indeed, he had always felt that most of them were frauds and charlatans, preying on people for an easy buck. But he also felt there were probably a few of them who were legitimate, who actually had some true psychic abilities.

Carson tried to be psychic himself in selecting one from the eight-plus columns of ads listed in the phone book. One of them caught his attention. It was a boxed ad with a pair of eyes under a small headline that read: "psychic sessions. Professional and accurate psychic readings. Please call for an appointment. Lorraine Williams."

Carson punched the number into the hotel room phone. It rang three times and then a click. The voice was live. "Psychic readings. This is Lorraine. How may I help you?"

Carson told her his name and asked to make an appointment.

"Two this afternoon is available. Is that good for you, Carson?"

"Yes," he replied, trying to keep the nervousness out of his voice. He felt like a twelve-year-old asking for his first date.

Later, Carson stood in front of the storefront, looking up at the small sign. He rang the doorbell and waited until Lorraine Williams appeared, peering at him through the glass door. She opened the door then and smiled up at him.

Lorraine was not what Carson had expected. She was a diminutive woman with rather plain features, though not unattractive. She wore a simple house dress and virtually no jewelry except for a wristwatch and a ruby birthstone ring.

She brought Carson to a medium-sized room in the rear. There were some colorful beads hanging in the doorway that Carson had to push aside as he entered. *At least there's one Hollywood touch*, he thought. They sat down at a small table, pointedly barren of the traditional crystal ball.

"No crystal ball?" Carson blurted, puzzled by his own disappointment.

Lorraine smiled. "I am sorry about that. It is just not something I need. Here," she said, stretching her arms across the table. "Hold my hands."

Carson complied. He detected the faintest trace of an accent but he couldn't place it. Her English was quite fluent, though devoid of the usual slang and contractions of most Americans. The woman remained silent for several minutes. Carson closed his eyes and heard the traffic outside, the screeching of tires, the ubiquitous honking of horns, and a siren off in the distance.

"I am sorry about your loss," Lorraine finally said softly. "I know how painful it is to lose your parents."

Carson was caught off guard. The tears streamed from his eyes. "I'm sorry," he said. "I didn't ..."

"That is okay, Carson. I feel your pain." She paused, closing her eyes briefly. "But please know that your father is in a safe place. He is with two men ... they are good people."

"What about my mom? Is she there with Dad?"

"No, she is in another place ... a really nice place. She is aware of what you are doing."

"How? How does she know?"

"I cannot say ... I ... I am not sure. But she will be joining your father soon."

Carson was overwhelmed. He had only half-believed in psychic ability, but this woman appeared to be truly gifted.

"Is there such a place as Midway Manor and Reunion Valley?"

"I am not familiar with those names. I am sorry."

"What about this place my mom is in. What's the name of that place?"

"Carson, I see visions," she said, chuckling softly. "It is not like I get a spiritual newspaper with names, dates and the weather."

As Carson apologized and prepared to leave, the psychic reached out and touched his arm. "I do need to caution you, Carson," Lorraine said with just a hint of foreboding in her voice. "I see a tall, red-headed man. There is danger associated with this man ... you should be careful."

"What is he—?"

"I cannot tell you anything more. Just be careful with this man."

Carson paid the woman for her services. He knew in his own mind that while this woman's uncanny ability to know about his parents was certainly convincing, it did not prove unequivocally that Midway Manor and Reunion Valley existed. The proof obviously lay with Danny and Allison, and Carson knew he had to get them to tell him their story, the real story. He wondered for a moment who the red-headed man was, then dismissed it as probably nothing.

When Carson got back to his hotel room, the first thing he knew he had to do was call Kathleen and explain why he would probably have to stay in New York another couple of days.

"Damn it, Carson!" Kathleen's voice screeched into his ear. "Staying there longer is gonna cost us even more money that we don't have!"

"I told you, honey, I need to talk with the Wallaces again. The psychic—"

"I don't give a shit about the psychic! I'm all by myself here, keeping these bastard creditors at bay." Kathleen softened her tone then. "I'm also lonely. Do you know how long it's been since we've had sex? I need you, in the office and in bed. Please, baby, come home now."

"Sweetheart, I'll get back as soon as I can. I have to meet with Danny and Allison and—"

Carson flinched when he heard the click and then the dial tone. He hated it when anyone hung up on him, especially his own wife. He took a deep breath and dialed Danny and Allison's number. It was Allison who answered.

"Hi, Carson. How are you?" Her voice sounded sincere, almost as if she were happy to hear from him. Carson couldn't block the image in his brain. He was in bed with Allison and she was on top of him, moving up and down with him inside her. Carson shook his head furiously, like a dog that had just gone through a sprinkler. He focused on the reason for his call.

"I need to meet with you and Danny one more time," Carson said, trying to sound as casual as he could. "There are a few more loose ends, things I'd like to ask you. I'll bring my tape recorder, if that's okay. Dinner's on me again."

"It's fine by me, Carson, but I'll have to check with Danny, of course. He'll be home any minute. I'll call you back."

Half an hour later, Allison called with Danny's approval. They were free that night, which meant Carson probably could get back to Kathleen by tomorrow evening.

Dinner was an Italian restaurant, with succulent veal, delicious marinara sauce, superb pasta, and lots of Chianti. With the tape recorder running, Carson asked them a number of questions regarding their family history, eventually leading up to the biggie—Did Midway Manor really exist?

Again, Carson studied their body language when he hit them with the question. Despite the wine, Carson again picked up on the way they looked at each other, how their bodies stiffened in their response.

And again, Danny and Allison denied that the book was anything but fiction.

Carson returned to his hotel room later, disappointed that he had been unable to get Danny and Allison to admit what he felt strongly was the truth. The book, the psychic, the fleeting but telling responses of the couple, and his mother's repeated ramblings about Midway Manor all combined to convince Carson that there was such a place.

But Carson needed an etched-in-stone affirmation of Midway Manor's existence, and he was determined to get it.

Chapter Thirty-one
The seventh floor

Mickey followed directly behind Lloyd as he crossed over the threshold into the small room. The ornate, squared area looked quite similar to a typical New York hotel elevator. In fact, if Lloyd hadn't known any better, he would have sworn he was standing in an elevator at The Plaza.

Both men knew, however, that this small room was called a SegWay. The odd name was mentioned twice. Once during the presentation of the short film shown by Marcy Madeline Bates to her new arrivals. And again when she gave everyone a room number and a gracious but straightforward order to go directly to an available SegWay, which would take them to the neighboring location of their newly assigned room.

Inside the boxed area, just to the right of the door, was a gray glass panel devoid of any button option to choose from. Mickey recognized the background music he had heard earlier, though it seemed louder inside the SegWay.

"It's not a radio or Muzak," said Lloyd, "so where the hell is it coming from?"

"I dunno, but I like it."

The SegWay door slid noiselessly closed, squeezing out their view of the ground floor. In unison, their eyes moved back to the smooth, button-free panel where a bright white number seven had now mysteriously appeared and began to flash on and off.

"I would guess that's us," Lloyd said, baffled by how the inanimate panel knew that the seventh floor was the site of their assigned private rooms.

The door through which they had just entered silently opened again, with barely any time passing at all. And there was no indication that any movement, in any direction, had ever taken place. But through the opened doorway the men could see standing against the opposite wall in the hallway a tall, whitewood-grained table with spirally turned legs. Sitting on the marbled-top piece of furniture was a statue of an elegant bird. And next to this exquisitely carved spread-winged figure was a white linen card disclosing the number seven.

"We're here," Mickey said in a singsong cadence, bravely covering up his uneasiness with the day's unfamiliar surroundings and events.

The duo stepped out onto the soft light blue carpet. Lloyd looked down the lengthy hall and declared, "This way."

"How do you know these things?" Mickey asked as he began to obediently tag along.

Lloyd laughed. "I can feel it. Can't you?"

Mickey didn't answer. He had no idea what his friend meant.

They ventured only a short distance down the hallway when the two stopped by a lounge where a small group of residents had gathered. John Holloway was among them. He immediately recognized Mickey and Lloyd as the men who had announced their stay at the destination named Midway Manor.

"Hello again. Come on in and join us." John said cheerfully, waving his hand. "That was an interesting film we just saw."

"John. John Holloway." Lloyd said, remembering his name easily thanks to his earthbound public relations skills. "Lloyd Wallace. And this is Mickey Parks."

John extended his hand first to Mickey who shyly accepted the handshake.

"Yeah, I know," John said. "You're the guys who were at Midway Manor for twenty-something years. Yeah, I bet you've got a helluva lotta stories to tell. Yessir ... I bet you do."

John pointed to an unoccupied, antique-white upholstered sofa puckered with soft, material-covered white buttons and a matching high-back chair nearby. "I know you probably haven't been to your new rooms yet, but please give me a minute of your time." He laughed then. "We've all got plenty of that!"

Mickey and Lloyd accepted John's invitation without hesitation. There was something curiously compelling about John that drew them to him.

"So," John began, "what's your take on this place … compared to Midway Manor?"

Mickey lingered over John's question, feeling a gut-wrenching twinge of loss. A loss for not having the option to sit at Midway Manor's computer anymore to retrieve information regarding the daily activities of his daughter Allison. A loss for not knowing what had happened to her or Danny after their brief contact by e-mail. A loss when remembering the disheartening words from Marcy Bates that it was the year 1998 back on Earth. When for Mickey, just hours ago, it had been 1996. *Two years … how could this be?*

Mickey was deep in thought when Lloyd's voice startled him. "You ask a pretty tough question," Lloyd said to John. "Perhaps the word 'compared' is what's throwing me off. I'd have to say I really doubt there's any place in the afterworld that doesn't overwhelm me … astonish me … the wonder of it all … and there's always the feeling of an ever-constant conviviality, to say the least.

"In just a matter of time I'll be meeting with family and friends whom I haven't seen in more than twenty years. Now that's a phenomenon in itself. But Midway … well, Midway Manor was and will always be in my heart … my home away from home."

John's eyes moistened. "You have a way with words. Any chance you were a professional writer?"

"Ah … but that was a long time ago. Back when I was on Earth. Yes, a very long time ago."

"I figured you were. My son Carson and his wife publish a little newspaper back in Tennessee. He's a damn fine writer himself. But I could never figure out why he and his wife Kathleen wasted their time putting out a paper that never brought them anything but grief. The two spend most of their time struggling to make ends meet. And with all his talent. It's a damn shame, I say."

"My daughter Allison's in publishing, too," Mickey interjected, his pride apparent by the tone of his voice and the glimmer in his eyes. "Lloyd's son Danny is, too. And our kids are married to each other," he added innocently, knowing full well it was his and Lloyd's unauthorized writing into their blank journals back at Midway that brought their adult children together in the first place.

"You don't say," John said with a straight face, not wanting either of them to know that Mickey had just revealed exactly what he sought in his not-so-obvious approach. John then tried to quickly unscramble the facts so far, thinking first of his wife whose terminal illness had her obsessed with a novel called *Midway Manor*, and there actually being a destination in the afterworld with the same name. And the two men who were sitting across from him had adult children named Danny and Allison. And there was no way it was just a coincidence that Lloyd's last name of Wallace was that of the authors of *Midway Manor*.

John wondered how Danny and Allison could have obtained information about Midway Manor, but his instincts told him this was not the time or the place to go any further. "And you, Mick?" he asked, "What did you do back in those good ol' days?"

"I bought and sold antiques ... and that sofa you're sittin' on, if it's the genuine article, would have sold for a small fortune back then."

The three men laughed, continuing to chat for a while until they agreed it was time to check out their rooms. The three left the lounge together, walking a short distance down the hall until John found himself in front of the doorway to his new room. He started to reach for the doorknob when he heard a noise. Startled, he stepped back.

"Did you hear that?"

"Yeah, I heard it," Mickey answered as he first stepped forward, then back, not sure whether he should move closer to the sound coming from behind the door or farther away from it.

"I heard it, too," Lloyd said. "And it definitely came from inside your room."

"Shssh. There it is again. Listen," Mickey whispered.

"What should I do?" John asked. "Seven fifty-five's my room number. That's definitely what was assigned to me. I'm positive. Here ... look ... here's my name on the card, too," he said, pulling the paper card out of its plastic sleeve affixed right next to the room number.

"I'd say go ahead and check it out," Lloyd answered with a chuckle. "I mean, nothing can kill you now. Besides, Mickey and I are right behind you. Right, Mick?"

Mickey was getting ready to give Lloyd one of his exasperated looks, but quickly decided to go along with Lloyd's advice to deal directly with the matter. The men remembered the short film they had viewed earlier and the part that explained how keys were not needed because the door to everyone's room was automatically locked when closed. The film explained how once a room was assigned by the administrator, mere contact with the doorknob by the occupant's hand would open the door. And only by the occupant to whom the room was assigned.

Mickey had wondered out loud why locks were needed at all in the hereafter, and it was Lloyd who had offered his own theory, that it was simply a matter of privacy, of making sure a stranger didn't open the wrong door and just barge in on somebody by accident.

"Okay, then," John said as he neared the door and reached out to place his hand on the brass knob.

"Wait!" Mickey yelled. "Maybe you should go back downstairs and check this out with that nice Bates lady. And ... Lloyd and I could even go with you."

John looked at Mickey and considered the option. "Not a bad idea." He glanced at Lloyd, whose self-assured demeanor showed no interest in Mickey's suggestion.

"Thanks, Mickey, but I'm gonna try the knob," John said. "After all, if it's not my room, the door just won't open."

John grabbed the knob and turned it to the right. *Click*. The door unlocked. He looked back over his shoulder to reassure himself that Mickey and Lloyd were still standing nearby. Their presence encouraged him to make the next move. He turned back to face the door and took a deep breath. Very slowly he pushed the door open just about an inch. John couldn't see anything at eye level through the crack. But he could sense that someone or something was nearby.

"What the—" John stopped when he realized a small black nose was pressed up against the crack in the door. "No, it can't be!"

"John, what's going on?" Lloyd asked, moving closer to the opening. But before John could answer, he had pushed the door open all the way.

John fell to his knees and stretched out his hand. "Yes ... yes, it's me, old fella. Come on, boy. It's Daddy." The miniature collie leaped up and rested his paws on John's chest, licked his face and then jumped down. The dog started yapping, his tail wagging rapidly back and forth. Seconds later, he scampered in a small circle and then leaped over and up into John's arms.

"Looks like these two know each other," Lloyd said to Mickey as they stood in the doorway witnessing the happy reunion.

John managed to stand up with the little collie still in his arms. His face was flushed from fighting back tears. "I'd like you guys to meet an old friend of mine. Sparky, say hello to Mickey and Lloyd." Sparky yelped, as though he understood.

Mickey leaned over and patted Sparky's head. "Nice to meet you, fella. I never had a dog myself, but I've never met one I didn't take a likin' to. And you sure are a handsome fellow … yes, you are."

"All right, Mick. Let me say hello to the little guy," Lloyd said teasingly. "Do you know how long it's been since we've had any encounters with a four-legged friend? Too long, I'd say."

Lloyd remembered the little calico his son Danny had for about ten years, how much his son had loved that little critter. And how upset he and Allison were when Bratly had taken ill. There wasn't anything the vet could do for her. *Wouldn't the kids just love to know that one day they'll be able to cuddle her in their arms again.* The thought made Lloyd warm and fuzzy all over.

For a brief moment Lloyd's heart ached, knowing there wouldn't be any more days of reading journals about his son or ever knowing how he was doing. He wondered how Danny had reacted to his not receiving the last e-mail—the one that had been cut off in mid-sentence.

And then Lloyd's thoughts turned to the vision of Marcy Madeline Bates' office, recalling the wall-to-wall computers and monitors she had all to herself. He had caught only a glimpse of her office when they had been standing just outside the doorway. That's when she had given him his room number. But Lloyd had seen enough to set his cerebral gears in motion.

Mickey watched as John headed over toward a beautiful, well-designed sofa and sat down with Sparky still in his arms. In fact, this was the first time that Mickey took notice of John's private quarters. "This room is really very nice," he said after taking a moment to actually feel the comfortable mood and restful tone of the décor. "Why, it's more than twice the size of the rooms we had back at Midway."

Lloyd nodded in agreement. "You're right, Mick. This room's actually set up with a living room to entertain visitors. Yes, it's very cozy."

"Have a seat," John offered the men, hoping to find out more about Danny and Allison and how they knew about Midway Manor. But Mickey and Lloyd declined, feeling even more anxious now to see their own rooms. Both of them quietly wondered if there might be any surprises waiting for them. And of course there would be—beyond their wildest imagination....

Chapter Thirty-two
Betrayal

Carson suspected something was wrong as soon as he opened the back door and stepped into his office. The building was strangely quiet. He hadn't seen his son Brian's car when he drove up, so he knew the kids were probably out. *But where were the cats?*

"Kathleen," he yelled as he turned back into the hallway and started to climb the narrow rear stairway. "Honey, I'm home." He chuckled at the familiar line.

He reached the second floor and checked Kathleen's office. Nobody. The two rooms where the ad sales people made their calls were also empty, as they should be at this time of the evening. The front office's door was closed and Carson opened it, freeing the four cats inside.

Carson climbed the stairs to the third floor. He walked through the kitchen and noticed that the door to their bedroom was also closed. *Ah, Kathleen's probably taking a nap.*

Carson was not at all ready for the scene that confronted him. Kathleen was there, all right. She was stark naked in their bed, and so was the man on top of her. They were oblivious to Carson's presence. Carson stared at the hirsute male buttocks as they rose and fell with deliberate cadence. Kathleen moaned and cried out as the man continued to thrust his manhood into her, and he knew his wife had reached orgasm. A moment later, the man yelled out, his seed obviously spurting deep inside Carson's wife.

Carson stood still, transfixed, unable to speak or move. At first, momentarily, he felt excited by the pornographic scene in front of him. And then a rush of other emotions overwhelmed him. Disappointment. Sadness. Anger. Fear.

"Omigod, it's my husband."

The man, obviously only in his twenties, pushed himself up off the bed and looked around for his pants. Kathleen slipped out of bed and reached for a robe.

"Honey, I ..."

Carson didn't wait for the rest of Kathleen's explanation. He turned and went downstairs and closed the door to his office behind him, locking it. The event was too much for him to deal with. He cried then, for a long time.

The days that followed were better than the nights. Carson concentrated on the paper's February issue, keystroking manuscript copy into his computer, proofing the galleys, cutting the long columns of type and pasting them down onto the mechanical boards.

He fought hard to block the images of Kathleen in bed with a stranger, concentrating instead on selecting photos and using the vertical camera in the darkroom to produce halftones.

But at night, lying alone on the living-room sofa, Carson found it difficult to fall asleep. He would stay awake for hours, playing the adulterous scene over and over again in his head.

Kathleen would come down to his office several times a day, pleading for forgiveness.

"Please, sweetheart, listen to me," she would say. "It didn't mean anything. It was purely physical. I barely know the guy."

And Carson would remain silent, refusing to speak to her.

The ache he felt in the pit of his stomach was much like the ache he had at age six when he wandered away from his mother at the state fair and got lost. There was fear, of course. But it was much more than that. The betrayal he felt was worse, like when he was fourteen years old and Sue Crutchfield told him she liked Timmy Grogan better, and gave him back the dime-store ring he had given her as a symbol of his eternal love for her.

Carson's reaction to Kathleen's infidelity was the same way he reacted to anything that displeased him. He would sulk. Not that he didn't harbor Walter Mitty-like fantasies of violent revenge. After his initial sadness and heartbreak, he conjured up images of tracking down his wife's illicit lover and shooting him dead.

But Carson was not a violent man. He had a temper, of course, but his frequent flare-ups would quickly subside. Once, while living in New York, he got into a shoving match with another commuter and actually exchanged several punches with the stranger. Neither man was seriously injured, but when Carson arrived at his office, he immediately went into the men's room and threw up. Not from any bodily injury, but from the trauma of actual violence.

Sulking was the way Carson usually handled life's insults and emotional injuries. Since he was a small child, he would withdraw from others as a way to protect himself from the slings and arrows of mental injustice.

Kathleen was an emotional wreck. *What've I done to Carson? How could I have hurt him so deeply? What a selfish bitch I am.* At first, she tried to rationalize her behavior, justify her sexual indiscretion by mentally blaming Carson for physically neglecting her. It was how she had allowed herself to seduce the young man who had come to read the electric meter.

But Kathleen knew in her heart she had been grievously wrong. Carson had just lost both of his parents. Between his loss and the pressures of the paper, it was no wonder that his libido had waned.

Every day, Kathleen would say a little prayer, asking God to forgive her and to let Carson also forgive her. And then she would go down to Carson's office and try to reason with him. She knew he would sulk, would withdraw from her. She was all too familiar with the way he handled emotional injury.

But in a few weeks, Carson softened. He began to respond to Kathleen. At first it was strictly business, answering questions regarding the paper that required his input. And then Kathleen told a joke and Carson could not suppress a chuckle. The barriers he had put up began to fall after that, and soon Carson was once again sleeping in their bed, and he and Kathleen were back to the way they were.

Not that Carson had entirely forgotten the hurtful episode. He hadn't. But in his heart he had forgiven Kathleen, and he somehow knew she would never stray again.

The first time they resumed having sex, they both had trouble reaching a climax. But subsequent sessions resulted in the "Johnstown flood," as Kathleen had so eloquently put it.

Carson finished the February issue of the *Tennessee Senior Citizen*, including the interview with Danny and Allison Wallace. When the mailing went out to subscribers, Carson made sure Kathleen put Danny and Allison down for several copies.

It was Allison who called, thanking Carson for the excellent article he had written about them. They chatted for a while, and Allison made Carson promise to call the next time he was in the city so they could get together for a drink.

Sam Roberts showed up two days after Carson started work on the March issue. He had answered an ad Kathleen had insisted Carson include in the February issue soliciting advertising salespeople.

"What's your experience, Sam?" Carson asked him.

"Well, I sold advertising for the *Mountain Record* for nearly two years."

"Why'd you leave?"

"I don't know. I just couldn't put up with their chicken shit anymore," he said, squirming around in the chair.

"What kind of chicken shit?"

"Well, you know, they didn't want me wearin' shorts, and a lot of times they bitched about me takin' my teeth out." He laughed then and Carson saw Sam wasn't wearing his upper denture.

"Look, man, I can sell advertising like nobody else. They say I can sweet-talk anybody, male or female, that I can just about charm the bark off the trees if I had to. That's why they call me Sudden Sam."

"How's that?"

"Well, one minute you got twelve pages with no ads, and then bam! The next thing you know, you got twelve pages filled with ads and business people beggin' to let them buy an ad on other pages in that issue."

"You talk a pretty good game, Sam." Carson paused, knowing he would hire Sam for a trial run. "But actions speak louder than words. When can you start?"

"I'll get on the phone right now."

"Well, Kathleen will go over procedure with you, familiarize you with the paper, the sizes we offer and the rates, and so on. Okay with you?"

"Just one question," Sam shot back. "You got a problem with shorts? And can I take my teeth out when I need to?"

"That's two questions, and the answer to both is yes. You can wear a dress and put your hair in braids for all I care. All I want is for you to stay on that phone and sell ads."

"Well, about the dress … never mind, I'll tell you about that later."

Carson smiled. He knew he had a real character on his hands, but somehow he knew this guy would indeed sell advertising for the paper, and they needed revenue desperately. *Maybe he would inspire the others, too,* Carson thought. *God knows, Rhonda and Vince could sure use some inspiration.*

Rhonda Wilkes was the very first telemarketer Carson and Kathleen had hired. She was a blond, buxom girl, with soft hazel eyes and an ever-present smile that disarmed anyone who might want to chastise her.

Her breasts were quite large and seemed to strain against the fabric of most any blouse or sweater she chose to wear. But looking at them for more than a fleeting second was a challenge. Rhonda would lock eyes with any man who approached her and seemingly defy him to peek downward toward her chest.

Vince Whitman was the second and third telemarketer Carson and Kathleen had hired. The tall, lanky twenty-six-year-old had answered Carson's classified ad, offering little experience but lots of enthusiasm. Boyishly good-looking in a Huck Finn kind of way, his tousled, uncombed hair matched the slept-in look of his clothes. But Kathleen liked him instantly and felt they should take a chance.

Vince did indeed sell a few ads that first week. He also called someone back in a corporate office long distance to curse at them for turning him down so rudely, as Vince put it. Of course, Carson had to fire him, but Kathleen was not happy with his decision. She pleaded with Carson on Vince's behalf, and of course they eventually hired him back.

As the days went by, Sam, Rhonda and Vince stayed on the phones and sold advertising space in the *Tennessee Senior Citizen*, with Sam turning out to be an inspiration to the others.

While Kathleen and Traci dealt with the paperwork and other office duties, Carson continued with his editorial chores. One afternoon, as Carson labored over the lead article for the next issue, there was a knock on his door.

"Yeah? Come in."

"Hi, Dad." When Carson looked up, he was surprised to see his son Brian standing in the doorway.

"Hey, Brian. What're you doin' here? Car trouble?"

"No. The car's fucking fine. I just … never mind."

Carson pushed away from the computer, swung around in his swivel chair and faced his son. He immediately sensed the familiar attitude in Brian's voice, a ring of disappointment and disapproval.

"What's the matter, Bri?" Carson's voice softened in an attempt to diffuse his obviously angry son. "C'mon in and close the door. Let's talk."

Brian swung the door shut and stepped down into the large room, walking past his father to the layout tables with mostly empty boards set up for the March issue.

"I just wanted to tell you I read your article about the couple you saw in New York." Brian continued to speak without looking directly at his father.

"I didn't think you cared about anything I wrote."

Brian started to leave and Carson grabbed his arm. "Hey, I'm sorry. I'm just surprised. Don't run off."

Brian moved away, dabbing a tear at the corner of his eye. "I miss Grandma, and Granddad, too. That book … that article you wrote. Ahh, never mind. This is so dumb. Forget it."

"What? Damn it, Brian, talk to me."

"I just wish there really was a Midway Manor … and that Grandma and Granddad could be there."

"Maybe there is, and they're there now."

"Yeah, right."

"I'm serious."

"I gotta go." Brian moved toward the door.

"Wait. I still don't understand the attitude."

"It's you ... and Mom. I mean, you're always fighting, and then you didn't speak to her for so long. Why've you been so mean to her?"

Carson wasn't about to tell his son the truth about Kathleen's indiscretion. It was between them, and it would remain their secret until the day he died. He knew he was probably more ashamed of it than she was, but he certainly admired Brian's loyalty and protective nature toward his mother.

"We've had some issues, but things are better now. I promise."

Brian let out a sigh of relief, as if a great weight had been removed from his shoulders. Carson stood up and pulled Brian into his arms, hugging him tightly. "I love you, Brian."

Brian smiled and hugged his father back. "I still wish there was a Midway Manor."

"I think there's a ring of truth to the Wallaces' book."

"You don't really believe that?"

"I do, and I'm gonna find a way to get them to tell me all about it."

Chapter Thirty-three
The scent of surprise

Mickey and Lloyd headed off in search of their own private quarters. They were confident there would be ample opportunity to meet with John Holloway at a later hour, remaining completely unaware of the significant news that John would reveal about Danny and Allison being the authors of a novel called *Midway Manor*.

After walking only a short distance down the hall, Mickey spotted his room number. "This is it," he said, immediately moving closer to the door and pressing his ear up against the white-wood panel.

"What're you doing, Mick? I thought you didn't have a pet when you were back on Earth."

"Just checking," he laughed. "Hey look, your room is right across from mine. I can check out yours, too, if you want."

"To tell you the truth," Lloyd answered, ignoring Mickey's good-humored offer, "I wouldn't mind if Danny and Allison's cat paid me a visit. As I recall, that calico was quite a beauty. I caught a quick glimpse of her one time at Danny's apartment. And I remember him telling me how he'd picked her from a litter of kittens. Apparently she'd climbed up the thin metal wires of her cage at the pet shop, slipped her paw between the rungs and snagged his jacket. She got his attention all right and she, of course, was the one he'd adopted."

"Hah ... the way I see it, I'd say that little calico picked him!"

Lloyd smiled. "You're right. She did. I should really make an arrangement to get her here. Yes, I think I'm gonna do that," he said, nodding, pleased with the idea. "But for now, let's get back to our business at hand. Whose room do you want to check out first? Yours or mine?"

Mickey didn't hesitate. "Mine. Okay?"

"Sure. Go ahead."

Mickey playfully pressed his ear up against the door a second time before he stepped back and turned the knob. Sunlight stretched across the hallway as he pushed the door open toward the living room area. "What the hell?" he said, instantly noticing a large arrangement of fresh flowers on the coffee table that faced an attractive, overstuffed sofa.

Mickey mumbled something about his allergies as he walked over to the bouquet. "There's a card here," he said, removing it from the clear-forked holder to read.

Mickey instinctively recognized the handwriting. The note was from his mother.

"Who's it from?" Lloyd asked as he watched Mickey maneuver his way backward and gradually take a seat on the sofa. "Mick ... the card? What's it say?"

"My mother's here," he answered, raising the card in the air and then using the same hand to unobtrusively brush away a tear. She has a room on the eighth floor and she's waiting for me."

"Wow!" Lloyd said.

Mickey set the card down on the coffee table and then leaned over to smell the bouquet of flowers. The scent flooded his head with childhood memories—of home-baked bread, cinnamon apples and a fresh turkey roasting in the oven.

Lloyd looked on as his longtime allergy-sensitive friend hovered over the arrangement with his face nestled in the middle of the delicate flowers. "Well, I never thought I'd witness a sight like this," Lloyd said.

"Come here and take a sniff. And tell me what you smell," Mickey urged his friend.

Lloyd obliged. "Mm-m-m, very nice," he answered.

"Did you smell the cinnamon apples? And the turkey?"

"What?"

"Or how 'bout my mom's home-baked bread? Now that's to die for ... excuse the pun."

"Have you lost your mind?" Lloyd asked rhetorically. I didn't smell anything but the mix of flowers. What in the ... wait one minute. If you think you smell what you say you smell ... that might be why your allergies aren't acting up."

Mickey straightened up, becoming fully conscious of what Lloyd was suggesting. "I'll be damned."

It was a fact that the physical spirit of Mickey's mother, whom he hadn't seen since he was fifty-two, was now miraculously a guest at Reunion Valley. But how was it possible that her gift of flowers could conjure up the favored scents of Mickey's childhood and ignore his allergy? Was it another phenomenon in the afterworld? Would Mickey ever learn the real story behind his sneezing binges? Would he ever realize that his fits of uproarious sneezing had everything to do with his passive nature and his self-imposed feelings of inadequacy? Even in the afterworld, he remained outwardly unassertive. He continued to respond to any emotional stress by sneezing. It was a subconsciously safe way to discharge his grief, his frustration, his hostility, or any other emotion. But the proximity of his mother made him feel safe, thus short-circuiting the sneeze syndrome.

As he sat back on the sofa, only a modest distance from the bouquet, he began to wonder whether his father might also be nearby. Mickey was not surprised that the thought made him feel somewhat frightened. *I do want to see my father,* he reassured himself, trying to overcome the anxiety growing in his gut from the negative memories that were beginning to surface. Memories that he had so prudently repressed for years. *He's my father. And I love him. And if Dad is here, maybe my three brothers are, too.*

"I need to see my mother right away," Mickey said, deciding that his mother might have news about the other members of his family.

"Sure, buddy," Lloyd answered. "Go ahead. I understand. Just give me a holler when you get back to let me know how it went. And wait for me, if for some reason or another I'm not in my room when you do get back."

Lloyd watched as Mickey hurried down the hall to take a SegWay to the eighth floor. "Yessir, go for it, Mick," he said to himself as he stood in front of the door to his room, more than ready to explore whatever might be on the other side.

Mickey stepped inside the SegWay and the door began to close behind him. He looked straight into the blank gray glass panel and shouted, "I'm going to see my mother on the eighth floor." The SegWay door closed and then immediately opened to the eighth floor.

After stepping out and looking up and down the long carpeted hall, Mickey squeezed his eyes shut, trying to get a gut feeling as to which way to head. But nothing came to mind. "Eight twenty-five," he said aloud, "are you this way?"

After walking several doors down, it was obvious he had made the wrong choice. "Damn it all!" He turned around and headed off in the opposite direction until he found himself facing the room number he sought. Mickey straightened his shoulders, sighed, smiled and then knocked gently on the door.

"It's Mickey," he heard a male's voice say from inside the room. Anthony Parks, the oldest of the four brothers, opened the door. "Well, don't just stand there, you old sonofagun. Mom's waiting," Tony cried, grabbing Mickey's hand and pulling him into the room.

Tony Parks' younger brothers were all taller than him by two to five inches. Dominick, the second-born, and Ralph, the youngest, jumped from their seats to greet Mickey. Their mother, Lillian, remained seated on the sofa as she tearfully looked on while her boys hugged and playfully pushed each other out of the way to get their turns with Mickey. A few minutes passed when Mickey, who was still surrounded by his brothers, stood facing his mother, eye-to-eye from across the room.

"Mom," he cried softly, moving toward the sofa, away from his brothers. Lillian remained seated and looked on intently as Mickey approached her. "I can't believe all this is happening. Never in my life did I think I would ever see you again."

Lillian took Mickey's hands as he helped her to a standing position, her eighty-seven-year-old body characterized by nothing but a frail skeleton and an earthbound life of hard times. She wore a pleasing and graceful white dress with a blue flowered print. Her silver hair was pulled back in a small tight bun, just the way she used to keep it. Mickey gently kissed her cheek. "I love you, Mama. I've never stopped loving you."

Lillian slid her hands from Mickey's gentle hold in order to touch his face. "Yes, you were a good boy, Mickey. A good boy," she said. "Come. Everybody sit down."

Mickey sat down next to his mother, taking her hand. Tony took his seat on the opposite side of her. Dominick and Ralph had each already claimed the two high-back chairs.

Dominick leaned forward and slapped Mickey's knee. "Look at those gray hairs. I don't remember you having them when I left."

Mickey laughed. "There aren't that many gray ones. And if you'd stuck around longer, you would've grown a few gray hairs yourself."

"This is so crazy," Dominick said, laughing. "Look, Ma, Mickey looks older than me now."

Lillian squeezed Mickey's hand. "It's all right, Mickey, your brother is teasing ... just teasing," she answered, taking on her familiar, over-protective mothering role.

Tony then cradled his mother's other free hand. "Ma, do you want to tell Mickey about Dad?" Lillian nodded her approval but remained silent.

Ralph exercised no patience with his mother's delayed response to Tony's question. "Dad's here at Reunion Valley," Ralph blurted out. "Miss Bates's got him down in her office right now. Yep, Dad's here," he repeated nervously. "We were talking about it just before you got here, Mick. And we were wondering how different he is now. Well ... you know what I mean."

Mickey knew exactly what Ralph meant. He also reasoned that their father would be different now. After all, there was no whiskey at Reunion Valley. No mood-altering liquor that could bring about the raging side of Gregory Parks. And there was no smoking cigarettes or cigars or pipes in the afterworld, their Dad favoring the latter.

No one in the poor, working-class Parks family would ever forget the time their father had fallen asleep with a lighted pipe. Etched in their collective memories forever was their miraculous escape during the night, the fleeing from the roaring flames while their home burned to the ground, the vivid images of their scant few possessions going up in smoke as they stood by helplessly.

But it was assumed that Gregory Parks had earned the right to drink his whiskey after the sun went down. He was the breadwinner of the family who worked long hard hours on the farm—seven days a week—trying to provide for his wife, his daughter and their four sons. And this hard-labored lifestyle had justified his being both domineering and threatening. No one, including Lillian, questioned Gregory Parks' authority or actions. Not before, during or after the tragic event of the fire.

Tony, Ralph, Mickey and Dominick knew the consequences of speaking up to their father. One time, Tony had been dared by his younger brothers to climb to the top of the apple tree out in the field.

Unfortunately, a dead branch snapped off and Tony fell to the ground, breaking his arm. "It was an accident," Tony had cried to his dad, speaking out and defending himself. But Gregory Parks had grabbed Tony's good arm in a fitful rage and dislocated his shoulder as well.

What the boys didn't know was that their characteristically protruding Parker chin was not inborn. It had slowly developed over the years. There was an ongoing unconscious clamping of their jaw muscles that coincided with their conscious decision to not speak out of turn with their father. The constant pressure had actually stimulated the growth of the jaw muscles that were anchored to the jaw bone, thus causing their pointed chins.

"Mickey, did you hear me?" Ralph asked, noticing he was unresponsive to his statement that their dad was downstairs in Marcy Bates' office.

"Huh … yes I did." Mickey answered. "I'm looking forward to seeing him," he said unconvincingly.

Dominick slapped Mickey on his knee again. "See, Ma, we told you."

Lillian smiled. "Everything's different now," she said. "I know this. Your father is not the same." She spoke softly and with an air of heartfelt awareness.

Her sons did not know that their mother had elected to be by her husband's side when he was first taken before The Council because of his actions back on Earth. Gregory Parks had been advised that only limited opportunities of the afterworld would be available to him unless he would agree to take a bold look back on his life. Lillian Parks was present when The Council spoke openly and freely about the many choices he'd made and how they had so negatively affected others.

Lillian and her sons were momentarily startled by the sudden knocking on the door to her private room. They all expected it to be Gregory Parks …

Chapter Thirty-four
Dark clouds

Allison looked up as Danny entered the room. "I just hung up with Carson Holloway. I thanked him for the nice write-up on us in his paper."

"I know. I heard you on the phone with him. I'm glad *that's* over with."

"Meaning what?" Allison asked, giving Danny a puzzled look.

"I'm still getting these vibes about him ... like he isn't finished with us yet."

Allison moved closer to Danny and cupped his face. "Ex-cuuse me, my sweet love, but I'm the psychic in this family," she said, leaning over to kiss the tip of his nose before lowering her hands to her hips. "And if we heard from him again ... that's a problem?"

Danny walked over to the old Victorian sofa and sat down. "It's not a *psychic* thing. It's ... it's a guy thing."

"Yeah, okay ... but you didn't answer my question. So what if we did hear from Carson again? What's the problem with that?" she asked, curling up in the oversized high-back chair directly across from Danny. "Are you jealous?"

"Hell no," Danny lied. "Carson's after a lot more than an interview."

"You mean he expects to do a follow-up on us?"

"Well, he might use that as an excuse, but it's not what he's after."

"So what *is* he after?"

"Let me put it this way ... we've had more than three hundred interviews over the past two years, but something went wrong when we met with Carson."

Allison couldn't imagine what Danny was talking about. She recalled their meetings with Carson. "Nothing went wrong. The only difference between our interview with Carson and all those other reporters was that Carson … how can I say it? Carson was emotional because he'd recently lost both his parents."

"I know the guy's grieving. I've been there, too. But you're overlooking the fact that he's picked up on things with us."

"What things?"

"I can't answer that."

"You can't … or you won't?"

"I can't. I can't say that we did or said anything different. But my gut tells me Carson saw right through us. He knows we're lying, that our book isn't fiction. And he'll be back to haunt us until he gets the truth."

Allison thought about what Danny said. "Maybe you're right. But so what if we tell him the truth, show him copies of the e-mails from our dads? Even if he wrote it up in his paper, how many would buy into it? Most people would figure it was a publicity stunt to sell more copies of the book."

"I don't know. If somebody in the government, somebody with clout, did believe it and examined the e-mails …"

"What?"

"Well, the country … the world … most people would never be able to handle it. I mean, what would it mean in the religious community? It'd be a mess … shake people up."

"I think telling Carson the truth wouldn't be a big deal. He probably wants to know because of his parents. I doubt he would publicize it."

"I think you're sweet on him, Allison. That's what I think."

"For crissakes, Danny." Allison could feel her face reddening, but before she could respond to Danny further, she became aware of the music on the radio. That homesick feeling in her gut, that ache for her father, was back as she listened to Willie Nelson singing "Stardust."

"Listen, Danny. It's a sign from Dad."

Carson was used to getting visitors at the office. Vendors, advertisers, people trying to sell them something, and occasionally readers. It was all in the course of a typical business day. But Carson could never have prepared for the visitor who knocked on his back door that morning.

"Just a second," yelled Carson, trying to compete with the loud banging on his rear door.

"I'm sorry to disturb you," the red-headed man said when Carson swung the door open. Tall, at least six-two, probably in his late thirties, the man introduced himself as Caleb, deliberately not offering a last name. "I need to speak with you."

"What about?"

"Your article about the people who wrote that book." He paused, and Carson noticed more than just a hint of wildness in his eyes. "You know, that Midnight Manor place."

"That's Midway."

"What?"

"I said Midway. *Midway Manor*. The book you're talking about. You got the name wrong."

"What?"

"It's not Midnight. It's Midway." Carson was getting irritated. "Anyway, what about it? I'm very busy right now."

"Do you realize how evil that book is?" The man stood annoyingly close to Carson as he spoke, displaying an obvious lack of social graces.

"Evil? How so?" Carson said, stepping backward as he suddenly remembered the psychic's warning. He became aware of the knot of fear developing in his gut.

"This Midnight Manor. Nothing about God or angels or anything religious. It's the Devil's work!"

Carson found himself on the defensive. "I read the book. There's nothing in there that could be construed as anti-God or against any religion. Besides, it's fiction, damn it." Carson couldn't help but realize the irony of his last statement. Even he believed there was some truth to the book, yet he felt a need to defend it as fiction.

"Something's got to be done to stop these people from writing any more of the Devil's work. And you're not helping matters with your articles!"

Carson restrained from pointing out that he had written only one article on the Wallaces.

"Do you have an address for these people?" The wildness in the man's eyes was more obvious than before.

"They live somewhere up north."

"Where up north?"

Carson became aware of Caleb's repulsively bad breath and tried to move farther away from him. "I'm not sure. Maybe Chicago," he lied. "Why do you need their address?"

"To stop them, of course."

"Stop them how?"

"They must be eliminated."

Carson was getting nervous. The man, Caleb, was now behaving erratically, flailing his arms and gesturing wildly. And Carson noticed the rather prominent bulge in the left breast area of the man's sports jacket. *Wallet or gun?*

"I'm afraid you'll have to leave," Carson finally said as calmly as he could. "I have a lot of work to do."

"What about the address?"

"I don't have it, sir." He gently nudged Caleb out through the door, silently praying the man wasn't armed. As soon as he closed and locked the door, Carson dialed Danny and Allison's number.

"It's Carson Dolan Holloway," Allison called out to Danny, who was in the kitchen pouring himself another cup of coffee. She deliberately enunciated his full name as a sort of protest to Danny's earlier, mildly jealous tirade.

Danny came back into the living room smiling broadly, aware of Allison's playful little game.

"And what does Carson Dolan Holloway want, pray tell?"

Allison's grin was quickly replaced with serious furrows in her brow. Her dismay was readily apparent to Danny as she listened to Carson's account of his ominous visitor that morning.

"What the hell's going on?" Danny asked after Allison hung up.

Allison described Carson's encounter with Caleb, his threat and the possible revolver hidden by the man's jacket. "Carson said he tried to throw him off by telling the man he thought we lived in Chicago or somewhere up north, but he says the guy's not stupid and will probably figure it out. He believes the man may try coming here to the city and tracking us down."

"I'll call the police."

"And tell them what? It's all hearsay. The cops won't do anything until the man actually threatens us."

"And who made you an expert on crime and police procedure?"

"C'mon, Danny. You know I was an editor on a detective magazine for more than a year." Allison laughed then. "Besides, I never missed an episode of *NYPD Blue*."

"So what do we do about it? Wait for the asshole to come up here and ventilate our bodies? This isn't comical. When it comes to religious fanatics, well, you remember what happened to *Hustler*'s Larry Flynt when he made fun of religion?"

"They shot the miserable bastard."

"I rest my case."

"We didn't make fun of religion."

"Look, honey, just make sure you keep the door locked and don't open it for anyone you don't know."

"I do that anyway."

"That's my girl."

"Oh, by the way. Carson said he was available to come back to New York if we wanted him to. He's worried about us and this Caleb guy."

"He's worried about *us*? Or *you*? And what's Carson Dolan James Bond Holloway gonna do, for crissakes?"

"Stop it, Danny. He's a very nice guy and he cares."

"Oh, he cares, all right."

Chapter Thirty-five
Unexpected reunions

As soon as Mickey had disappeared down the hall, hurrying off to meet with his mother on the eighth floor, Lloyd didn't hesitate to independently explore his own private quarters. A warm, welcoming ambiance was noted as soon as he surveyed the living room area from where he stood just inside the door. But Lloyd's visual search ended suddenly when a small figure appeared from around the corner at the far end of the sofa.

The petite, tri-colored cat with expressive, walnut-shaped eyes readily approached and gave out a melodious cry.

"Bratly?" Lloyd called, recognizing his son Danny's dearly loved cat. "Well, I'll be damned ... of course it's you. Hello, little lady," he said, knowing her not only by the smooth and brilliant multicolored coat, but by her unique melodic chant.

As soon as Lloyd spoke, however, the calico turned away and scurried back to the far side of the sofa. Just as quickly, she reappeared again carrying a small package in her mouth. She approached Lloyd and then dropped the parcel a few feet away from him, where he still remained standing as though frozen in place.

Lloyd finally moved forward, bent down and stretched out his hand. "Is this for me, girl?" he asked.

Bratly deliberately touched Lloyd's hand with her nose when he attempted to retrieve the small package. Her social gesture prompted him to first run his hand over her head, across her back and up along her smooth-haired, raccoon-like banded tail.

"Let's see what we have here," he said, picking up the parcel and then walking over to the sofa to take a seat. Bratly followed, jumped up next to him and gave out another breath-holding cry. Lloyd stroked her back again.

The wrapping was torn. It was obvious that Bratly had also been curious about its contents. Lloyd turned the package over as though the opposite side would reveal what was inside.

"Do you remember the old saying that good things come in small packages?" he asked the calico, shaking the container, still trying to make an educated guess as to its contents. "All right, then … let's find out," he said, still unable to come up with an answer and deciding to just tear away the tattered wrapping.

The small box was about five inches long and a mere one-inch wide. Bratly gave out another cry and Lloyd let her sniff the closed container. "I'm guessing that whatever's in here, girl, is a little something for me. But what can it be?" He lifted the cover then and broke into a fit of laughter. Bratly leaped off the couch, momentarily startled by the outburst.

"Look, Bratly," he said, barely able to contain his lighthearted mood. Lloyd carefully moved the opened box before her. "It's a cigar. See … it's only a cigar," he laughed, removing it from the small carton. "And it's a fake one at that!"

The unusual gift had a message that delivered overwhelming joy to Lloyd's heart. Yet it was much more than an unconventional but welcomed message that announced the imminent get-together he would soon have with his brother Edward. It was a heartfelt reminder of how the cigar-smoking Edward and the little joke he'd played on his brother had been the key that had convinced Danny that Lloyd's initial e-mail from the afterworld was legitimate.

What the message did not reveal to Lloyd, however, was all the others who were also waiting to reunite with him. All the others who were already gathered on the third floor with his brother Edward, anxiously anticipating Lloyd's grand entrance.

Up on the eighth floor, it was Mickey's older brother Tony who had responded to the sudden knocking on the door of his mother's private room. The caller was a twelve-year-old boy. His hair was straight-cut, dark and shoulder-length. He wore a flat-brimmed cap and trousers that extended just below the knees. Knee-breeches, as they were called, held up by suspenders.

"May I help you?" Tony asked, not recognizing the young man, yet sensing a strange familiarity about him.

The youngster laughed and playfully hit Tony's arm. "Get outta my way," he said. "It's me!" The lad then pushed his way past Tony and sauntered over to the others in the room.

Lillian covered her mouth. "Oh my Lord, dear God," she cried, immediately recognizing the young man, but too shocked and surprised to verbalize his identity.

The boy leaned over and kissed Lillian on the cheek, hoping to soften her astonishment. "Good to see ya again," he said, smiling, and then closing one eye to send her a playful wink.

Mickey, who was still seated on the sofa next to his mother, stared at the young boy as though he was a costumed trick-or-treater. Mickey believed the young man had to be someone he knew from his past.

Ralph and Dominick gawked at the lad's back as they watched him first kiss their mother and then shake hands with Mickey. The lad then twisted around. He was bearing a mischievous yet warm smile as he offered his hand to them, expecting nothing more than the same receptive greeting.

Tony, observing the salutations, yelled, "Ma, you know this boy?"

"Yes. Yes, Tony. We *all* know who he is," she answered. But again, Lillian refrained from identifying him.

The youthful stranger turned and extended his hand to Tony who did not raise his hand in return. "So who the hell are you anyway, kid?" Tony demanded, not wanting to play the game.

"It's me, Tony," the lad answered. "Don't you recognize me? Come on, take a good look."

Tony leaned into the boy's face, studied his green eyes, the unshorn dark brows and narrow lips. "It can't be. Son of a bitch, it can't be," he cried.

"It's good to see you, too," his father replied.

Yes, indeed, it was Gregory Parks' spirit appearing before his family in the body of a twelve-year-old. But Tony's brothers were still bewildered by the whole thing, each of them speaking at the same time, questioning who the stranger was.

"It's Dad, you guys," Tony yelled. "This is our goddamn father!"

"Tony!" Lillian cried.

"Okay, okay everyone. Take it easy," Gregory Parks shouted. Yeah, it's me. Would everyone just calm down now. I've got something to show you boys. Please," he implored, "please … everyone sit down."

Tony ignored the request and remained standing, staring at the twelve-year-old boy.

"You, too, Tony," Gregory said softly, reaching for his arm to guide him.

"Yeah, all right," Tony answered, quickly moving away to avoid being touched. "I said all right."

Gregory Parks quietly thanked Tony after he'd taken a seat back on the sofa. He then looked at each of his sons as he said their names. "I love you. I love all of you."

"This is ridiculous!" Tony exclaimed, staring at the twelve-year-old child who claimed to be his father. "Why come back as a kid?"

"Because I've got something to show you," Gregory Parks answered, pulling down his suspender straps as he spoke. He then proceeded to undo the cuffs of his white, long-sleeved shirt.

Tears streamed down Lillian's face. She knew what was coming. Mickey squeezed her hand. "Ma … are you all right?"

"It's okay, Mickey," she sobbed. "Just look."

They all stood transfixed, staring at Gregory Parks as he began unbuttoning the front of his shirt. "Now, when you see this," Gregory began, "I don't expect anyone's pity. I just would like you to take a quick look at what I'm about to show you and then please … please listen to what I have to say."

Their dad's words were cut off for a moment as he'd flinched from the pain while removing his shirt and tossing it on the floor. The uncovering revealed unsightly black-and-blue bruises and multiple bloody lacerations that ran down his arms, around his chest and across his back.

The Parks boys remained silent. They were all shocked, confused and distressed by the horrifying sight before them.

"My own father was a bastard!" the lad cried. "I never spoke of him to any of you before, except to tell you that he'd died when I was a young man."

Gregory Parks reached for his shirt then and began to carefully cover up. "My father was a mean, hateful man," he continued, "and I can't remember a single day in my childhood that he didn't beat me. Sometimes he'd beat me with his fists. Sometimes with his belt."

"Dad!" Ralph cried.

"Please, Ralph, let me finish what I have to say," Gregory interrupted. "I swore to God Almighty that I would never grow up to be anything like my father. I was twelve years old when I made that promise. And ... I was twelve years old when my father died. What you see here was the last beating he'd given me. The very last beating ..."

The twelve-year-old lad ignored the tears that streamed down his face. "I broke the promise that I made back then. I broke that promise," he repeated over and over again, bowing his head in shame. It was immediately apparent to Mickey and his brothers that their father was overcome with remorse for the years of abuse he had inflicted upon them.

"What's happening?" Mickey cried out. Mickey and the rest of his family looked on and watched as the young boy miraculously transformed before their eyes, his physical spirit visibly taking the form of a man in his seventies.

In mere seconds, the husband and father they all knew as Gregory Parks stood before them. He faced his family and quietly spoke about his alcoholic, all-too-often brutal behavior as a husband and a father. He spoke openly and freely, as though he had been given a double-dose of sodium Pentothal. And then Gregory Parks begged for absolution. Not absolution for any wrongdoings that had taken place back on Earth. But absolution here and now in the afterworld because he was no longer the man he used to be.

There was no hesitation in the minds of Mickey and his brothers. They were all in agreement ... giving their father the forgiveness he sought.

"I'll be back," Lloyd said to the little calico, anxious to get down to the third floor to meet with his brother Edward. Bratly was curled up in a half-circle on the sofa. Her bright, wide eyes stared steadily at him as he spoke, as though she understood. Lloyd looked down. He wondered whether he should change into a suit and tie, and then realized he hadn't even checked out his bedroom. Perhaps there wasn't a walk-in closet filled with tailored suits and silk ties available to him like there had been at Midway Manor.

"I look okay?" he asked rhetorically. Bratly lifted her head, still staring straight at him and then slowly lowered it back to a resting position. "Okay, then," he answered, taking the cat's motion as an act of approval.

Lloyd hurried off to take a SegWay to the third floor, fully expecting room three-fourteen to be that of his brother's personal quarters. On the way he bumped into John Holloway, who was also rushing to meet with his parents.

"I need to talk to you and Mickey about something really important," John said.

"First chance I get, John."

Room three-fourteen turned out to be one of the Banquet Rooms, available to Reunion Valley visitors for large group get-togethers. There were more than two hundred people gathered in the room. A banner with the words "Welcome, Lloyd" hovered over him as he entered. Balloons and streamers inexplicably floated about in mid-air with no strings attached. An empowering energy of joy filled the room. There was lively music playing, but again not a single sign of how or where it was coming from.

Lloyd's parents and his brother Edward were the first to welcome him. As the foursome moved through the crowd to a table designated in Lloyd's honor, some guests shook hands with him as he passed by. Others shouted his name and cheered. In the delight of the moment, Lloyd spontaneously greeted Dorothy Wallace, his ex-wife, with a lover's kiss.

"You haven't lost your touch, Lloyd," Dorothy said, feeling somewhat lightheaded. "How's Danny doing? Did you connect with him?"

"We did, but it was cut short by Mr. Patrick, uh, The Authority," Lloyd explained. "We never got the answers to unexplained mysteries to them."

"Oh dear, that's too bad."

"Well, at least we made contact. How about your sister, Naomi?"

"She's downstairs with Jennings."

"Jennings?"

"Jennings ... Naomi's husband. C'mon, Lloyd, you met him at least twice."

"Oh, that's right. I remember. The college professor. Tall, thin. Nice guy, but awfully quiet." Lloyd looked around the room at the animated gathering. "Well, what's the plan? I mean, are you gonna be around for a while? Maybe we could hang out later."

"I'm sorry, Lloyd. Naomi, Jennings and I were planning on leaving here first thing in the morning."

"Where the hell're you going?"

"Certainly not to Hell. We're going to check out the City of Lights."

"City of Lights?"

"Yes, and I don't mean Vegas. It's supposed to be a fabulous place. Better than Las Vegas."

"Okay. Maybe Mick and I can join you all when we're finished here."

"That'd be great," she said, and smiled when Lloyd squeezed her hand.

After they were seated, every family member, coworker and friend took a turn at the podium welcoming Lloyd. They each gave a brief account of their earthbound relationship with Lloyd, often sharing a tale that would humorously dispute his hail-fellow-well-met reputation.

During the reunion festivities, Lloyd was surprised at how many times his thoughts flashed back to his son Danny. At how much his heart ached to make a connection with him again. His brother Edward sensed something was bothering him. "Thinking of Danny?" he asked.

"Yeah. How'd you know?" Lloyd really wasn't surprised at Edward's intuitiveness. It had come in handy for his brother so many times during his career disseminating intelligence for the CIA.

"Have no care ... Edward's here!" he whispered half-jokingly.

Chapter Thirty-six
All in a day's journal

"Damn it, Carson, why in heaven's name are you going to New York?"

Lynn Holloway sat inside the small computer room at Midway Manor, her words exploding with frustration as she read her son's daily journal boldly displayed on the screen in front of her. She assumed Carson would be distraught. After all, he had just lost both parents within a week's time. But reading about his plan to take off to New York was completely unexpected, and it provoked much more than anger in her.

"Don't go," Lynn begged, as though he could actually hear her plea. "Please, Carson, stay at home with your wife. Kathleen can help you through this. She can. And what about my grandson? You know how upset Brian's been over my illness. You need to be there for him."

Lynn put her hands over her face, trying hard to fight back the tears and her own feelings of loss and separation.

"Oh, John," she cried softly, switching her thoughts to her husband and wishing he hadn't gone directly to Reunion Valley. "I need you."

Lynn had initially met with the director, Joseph Patrick, as soon as she had arrived at Midway Manor. She expressed her eagerness to join her husband at Reunion Valley, and emphasized how her visit at the Manor would be for no more than two days.

"Everything okay?" Mr. Patrick had asked, detecting a hint of sadness on Lynn's face when she had stopped by his office on the second day, informing him of her need to spend some additional time at the Manor.

"Why, yes, everything's just fine," she had lied. "I'm sorry, I've changed my mind. I hope it isn't too much trouble for you to postpone my departure."

"Why, not at all, Mrs. Holloway. You're welcome to stay at the Manor for as long as you'd like. Just give me a few hours' notice whenever you decide to leave."

When Mr. Patrick asked if there was anything else he could help her with, Lynn had shaken her head, remaining cautiously silent. She believed the director to be the last person she should confide in. After all, her son Carson was intent on learning the truth about Midway Manor and maybe telling the world all about it through his newspaper.

During the next few days Lynn continued to read Carson's daily journals, finding out that he had indeed made the trip to New York. And when her son hadn't satisfied his need for the truth about the afterworld—in the course of his so-called interview with Danny and Allison Wallace—he'd even gone off and tried to get some facts from a psychic.

What next, Carson? Why do you need any kind of proof about the afterworld? Why not just believe in it?

And another day passed.

Lynn closed the door behind her and turned on the computer.

"Damn it, Carson, leave that lovely couple alone," she said aloud when she began to read about Carson's second visit with Danny and Allison Wallace.

Lynn's mind wandered. She had known relatively little about the authors of *Midway Manor* until now. She remembered how she was drawn to their novel in the bookstore, the cover art beckoning to her with a welcoming mystical appeal. She understood intellectually that it was just a made-up story. But before she had gotten the chance to read the book herself, she had landed back in the hospital. And after John read it in its entirety to her, she still felt in her heart that the story had an enchanting sense of reality about the afterworld. And she wondered if others who had read it felt the same way.

Lynn had not given much thought about the afterworld until she had come across the novel in the bookstore. At first, she had questioned her terminal illness, her medication and even her sanity as she fought with the idea that believing in life after life and a place called Midway Manor was nothing more than her way of coping with the little time she had left on Earth. But believing in the afterworld so wholeheartedly enabled her to cope with her illness and her pain, and to peacefully accept the inevitable.

Now ... here she was. Midway Manor really existed. She sighed and continued to finish reading Carson's journal. Lynn felt surprisingly pleased and approving when she had read that the authors of *Midway Manor* had, once again, not revealed a lick of information about the afterworld.

And this same journal revealed Carson's escapade in New York had finally come to an end. "That's right, Carson ... go home. Go home to your wife ... and your son," she said, trying to shake the uneasy feeling still stirring inside her. Knowing her son so well, she figured this meant the matter wasn't really over.

The next day, when Lynn called up her son's daily journal, she almost fell out of her chair. The journal's description of the scene that confronted her son when he opened the bedroom door was just as hurtful to Lynn if she had been standing right there alongside Carson in the doorway. She recoiled in horror as she read about her daughter-in-law's indiscretion. Lynn really loved Kathleen, adored her actually. She had always felt that Kathleen was the best thing that ever happened to her son. So there was no anger; just sadness for Carson. Lynn felt his pain and she agonized over this. She turned off the computer, unable to read further, and left the room.

Lynn roamed the halls of Midway for hours, trying to sort things out in her head. She later returned to her room and began reading about the various destinations in the afterworld. Lynn also listened to the musical cassette tapes of Mickey Parks and Lloyd Wallace, coming out only for an occasional meal. Not that she needed to eat in her new non-earthly condition, but it was hard to discard a lifetime of routine sustenance.

Three Earth-weeks later, Lynn was in for an even greater shock when she returned to Carson's journals. She shuddered when she read Caleb's words, "They must be eliminated." She read on about how her son called Danny and Allison and warned them about Caleb. For a moment, Lynn considered calling up a journal on Danny and Allison, but decided to join her husband John in Reunion Valley. She hurried off to find Joseph Patrick and begin her next journey. She didn't know if the authors of *Midway Manor* were in any real danger, but if they were, John might know a way to help.

As soon as Lynn concluded her welcoming session with Marcy Madeline Bates at Reunion Valley, she found her husband John waiting for her just outside the door. Their eyes locked for a few moments before Lynn fell into his outstretched arms. And then she wept, feeling safe in the warmth and familiarity of his lingering hug. A few moments passed when John sensed something else may have been behind her tears. He pulled away without letting go.

"You look fabulous," he said, the words tumbling off his tongue, forgetting to ask her if something was wrong, remembering only how lifeless and pale she had been the last time he had seen her.

Lynn blushed. "Oh, John, don't embarrass me," she said, smiling. Until now, she hadn't really given much thought about the dramatic change that had taken place in her.

John tilted his head. This time he sensed something behind her smile. "What's wrong? Is Carson okay?"

"Carson's fine," she answered with an indignant tone in her voice. Lynn cleared her throat, trying to distract her husband from pursuing the issue.

"Well, that's hard to believe. That kid's *never* been fine. How's he handling all this?" John asked, figuring his son had to be out of his mind having lost the two of them.

"Did you know I just came from Midway Manor?" she asked, still avoiding his question.

"Yes, I did. So tell me about Carson. How is he?"

Lynn placed a hand lovingly on the side of her husband's face. "I don't think it's Carson we have to worry about. But I could be wrong. I've got so much to tell you, I don't know where to begin. Can you take me to my room so we can have some privacy?"

John could hardly wait to find out what Lynn had to share with him. And he was anxious to tell her all about his visit with his parents, and this unfinished business he had with Mickey Parks and Lloyd Wallace. "Let's go," he answered, escorting her to a SegWay. "What room did they give you?"

"Seven fifty-five."

"I know the place. Yeah ... that's *my* room!" he announced, seductively pulling her closer to his side.

John hesitated before opening the door to their room. "Oh, by the way, we've got company inside."

"What company? Your mom and dad? Who?"

"Nope," John teased, flinging the door open.

"Oh, my God ... it's Sparky!" Lynn scooped up the little collie. And there was an exchange of licks and kisses before Lynn sank into the sofa next to John.

"Tell me about Carson. Tell me everything," John insisted.

Lynn didn't gloss over Carson's trip to New York. She wanted her husband to know how determined their son had been, trying to yank the truth from Danny and Allison about the afterworld.

"As though the truth would be the only way to end his anguish," she argued. "Carson took that trip to New York and *abandoned* his wife and our grandson. That's what he did. He *abandoned* them." Lynn deliberately pointed this out before she told John about Kathleen's one-night stand. "Of course she messed up," Lynn admitted. "And shame on her for doing what she did. But where was Carson when they needed to be there for each other?"

John listened attentively as Lynn went on. But so far he wasn't shaken by any of the news that his wife had imparted. Carson was being Carson and that was no surprise. He squeezed Lynn's hand, feeling a pang of guilt. "Ah-h, sweetheart," he said, "I'm so sorry. I hate that you had to find all this out on your own."

Lynn knew John was sincere. "Well, even in the afterworld, my dear, I do understand that we can't be in two places at the same time," she answered. "But after I read about that crazy man who'd barged his way into Carson's office, I couldn't stay at Midway Manor another minute." Lynn elaborated on the intruder's visit, the phone call to Allison to warn her about a man who called himself Caleb, and how he had threatened to eliminate them.

"They're here!" John finally interrupted, quite upset by the news.

"Oh, dear God! The authors are here? He killed them?" Lynn cried.

"No … no. Not Danny and Allison. Their dads, Mickey Parks and Lloyd Wallace."

"I know those names," she said, remembering the label on the cassette tapes she'd listen to at Midway Manor.

Lynn and John Holloway hurried down the hall to Lloyd Wallace's room. "Well, hello, John," Lloyd said when he answered the door to the sound of urgent knocking. He looked over at the woman who stood by his side.

"This is my wife, Lynn. She's just arrived from Midway Manor. Please … may we come in? It's really urgent that we talk to you. And could we get Mickey Parks to join us?"

Lloyd raised his brow, baffled by their unexpected visit, completely unprepared for what the Holloway's were about to disclose. "Well … sure. Come on in and make yourself comfortable. I'll get Mick. He's just across the hall." Lloyd quickly introduced John and Lynn to his brother Edward who was sitting in the living room, and then he left to get Mickey.

Edward remained seated during the introductions. He had overheard the brief conversation at the front door, and now, with the senior couple sitting directly across from him, he easily noted the tension they were both trying to hide. "You don't mind if I stay?" he asked politely, not expecting to move from his spot even if they did.

"You would be Danny Wallace's uncle … yes?"

Edward smiled and nodded, figuring John was either making small talk or had something to say about his nephew. *Odd*, he thought. *How does he know Danny?* They all waited in silence for a few minutes until Mickey and Lloyd returned and joined them in the living room.

When Lynn made a glowing reference to Danny and Allison's novel, *Midway Manor*, the two dads looked at each other with Cheshire-like grins. It was immediately evident to them that even though they hadn't succeeded in e-mailing the answers to Earth's unsolved mysteries to their kids, Danny and Allison had been resourceful enough to use the e-mailed details about Midway to write a novel instead. What was not readily apparent to Lloyd and Mickey was why they had lost two years in their overnight spiritual transport from Midway to Reunion Valley. And now their e-mails may cost Danny and Allison their lives.

"Our son Carson knows Danny and Allison. He traveled to New York last month and interviewed them," Lynn said, an emotional catch in her voice. "He wrote about their novel in his tabloid. And there was this red-headed man who visited my son and he was angry ... he told Carson he was going to ... what was it? ... get rid of Danny and Allison. John, could you please tell them the rest?"

John leaned over and squeezed Lynn's hand. "We really don't know if there's a problem or not. But you guys might want to go back to Midway Manor and use their computer to check on what's going on with your son Danny and his wife. Just to make sure they're all right."

"We can't go back," Lloyd said, getting to his feet.

"We broke the rules," Mickey explained.

"I wish there were some way I could contact Carson," said John.

"There are computers in Marcy Madeline Bates's office," Lloyd said as he began to pace, "but I don't know how we could get to them."

"I can get to them." Edward spoke up.

"How?" Lloyd asked. He knew his brother was very talented in the area of espionage and he often envied the cloak-and-dagger life he had led back on Earth. He also knew if anyone could get to Bates's computers, it was Edward.

"When?" Mickey asked, accepting Edward's claim without any doubts.

"Right now. John, you and your wife stay here. Lloyd, Mickey, come with me." At first a silent observer, Edward had quickly assumed a leadership role, a role with which he had always been comfortable.

"No way I'm staying here," John said, standing up. "Lynn will be okay here, but I want to be part of this. If there's any chance of contact with my son ..."

"That all right with you, Lynn?" asked Edward.

"No. You gentlemen act like we're back in the real world. What could happen to me, or any of us? We're already ... well ... dead!" Lynn paused, not at all comfortable with her own words. "I'm going too."

They all laughed then, realizing the truth of Lynn's little speech.

"She's right," said Edward. "What was I thinking?"

Chapter Thirty-seven
Breakthrough

The weather in New York was typical for February: bitter cold, with a wind chill that ripped right through the skin. Allison hurried along the sidewalk, being careful not to slip on the icy remnants of last week's snowstorm. She pulled the fur collar of her coat tighter around her neck as she finally reached the front door of Gristede's, her favorite grocery store. The force of the wind slammed the door shut behind her, almost hitting her in the back.

All this for a goddamn can of soup. I oughtta have my head examined. Allison's mind raced as she went down the aisle, eventually finding her favorite brand of soup. She placed several cans into her basket, then headed over to the bread section. She couldn't shake the scared feeling she had, wondering if this nut job Carson called about would actually track them down and try to hurt them.

Allison waited somewhat impatiently in the checkout line, silently regretting how she had tried to stop Danny from going into the office on a Saturday. She hated quarrelling with Danny, but she hadn't wanted him to leave her alone. When he did return, she knew they'd probably have a few more words about it before they eventually patched it up.

After paying the checker, Allison left the store, defiantly braving the unfriendly coldness of the day. Again, she made her way along the treacherous sidewalk, now facing into the wind. Her cheeks felt numb as she finally reached their apartment building and lurched into the foyer, clutching the bag of groceries tightly.

Allison made a mental note that Al the doorman was nowhere around. *Probably in the basement catching a smoke. Bastard. Anybody could walk in.* Still clutching the bag of groceries, she leaned against the wall and managed to poke the elevator button with her little finger.

A minute later she emerged from the elevator and trudged down the hallway to their apartment. She wondered if Danny was already there as she fumbled with the key and pushed the door open with the grocery bag.

Allison never saw the red-headed man coming. Caleb's hand covered her mouth and stifled her scream as they both careened through the doorway and into the apartment. The bag tore open and sent the cans of soup and other groceries slamming across the floor. Allison wrenched free as Caleb used one hand to close and lock the door. He turned and grabbed for her, regaining hold of her arm. She gasped when he pulled out a large switchblade knife and waved it back and forth in front of her face.

"If you scream, I'll cut you!"

"W-What do you want?" Allison's tone was half scared, half angry.

"Sit over there, Mrs. Wallace!" Caleb ordered, pointing the knife toward the Victorian sofa. He reached for the light switch on the wall behind him. The steely glint of the blade flashed in Allison's eyes.

"Who are you?" Allison asked, already guessing the answer. "How do you know my name?" Her eyes darted from the knife to the stranger's face and back to the knife again.

"I'll answer all your questions in a minute. Just sit down." He backed up and eased himself down into the well-upholstered chair facing the couch, still holding the knife menacingly in front of him.

"Your husband ... Mr. Wallace ... he should be home soon. We'll wait for him."

Allison gave a little jump when the phone rang, startling her. Caleb gestured with the knife. "Go ahead. Answer it. But don't say anything that'll make me use this."

Allison recognized Carson's voice but responded by using Carson's father's name. "Oh, hi, John."

"Allison, what's wrong?" Carson could detect the fear in Allison's voice.

"Danny isn't here right now, but I'm expecting him home soon."

"Is Caleb there? Did he find you?"

"I'm sorry, John, but I can't talk right now. I've got something on the stove I have to get back to ..."

"Jesus, he *is* there. Am I right?"

"Yes … yes, okay then. I'll have Danny get back to you." Caleb jumped up out of the chair and moved in close to Allison, holding the knife to her throat.

"I have to go—" Caleb grabbed the phone from Allison's hand and plopped it back down in its cradle. Seconds later, they both heard Danny's key turning in the lock. Caleb pressed the blade tight against Allison's throat as the door swung open and Danny stepped into the apartment.

"What the hell …"

"Take a seat, Mr. Wallace. We're gonna have a nice chat first, you hear."

"What do you mean *first*? First before what?" Danny asked as he sat down.

"Before I make the world safe from y'all's evil words."

Danny started to get back up and Caleb pressed the knife tighter to Allison's throat until a droplet of blood appeared. Allison flinched and tried to pull back.

"You sonofabitch!" Danny yelled. "You fucking bastard! I'll—"

"You'll what?" Caleb said as Allison started crying.

"Why are you doing this?" Danny asked, sitting back down and trying to keep calm. The adrenalin rush of fear gripped his body. Fear for Allison, fear for himself. He pictured both of them lying there in a pool of blood, the life oozing from them.

"The book you wrote. All those lies. That crap about a Midway Manor. No mention of Jesus Christ, our savior, or God himself! I can't let y'all write any more of this."

"It's a novel! Fiction!"

"It sounds real, hear, and people will believe y'all."

"Okay, it's true! All of it!" Danny leveled with the man, feeling desperate.

"Listen to you! You're pathetic!"

"It *is* true!" Allison cut in. "All of it is really true. I know it sounds crazy but our dads contacted us through the computer."

"Through the computer?"

"Yes … by e-mail."

"E-mail? Oh, yeah, and my daddy's a possum!"

"It's true! I swear it!" Allison cried.

"And there is no God, no Jesus?"

"We never wrote that." Danny chimed in. He didn't think Caleb believed them. He certainly wouldn't if he were Caleb. But he figured it was worth a shot.

"There's The Authority." Allison kept talking, looking directly into Caleb's eyes, which were darting back and forth. She tried to ignore his offensive bad breath. "We don't know who The Authority is."

"So y'all're trying to tell me The Authority's God?"

"We can't say one way or another. We don't know." Danny spoke quickly, his eyes fixed on Caleb's ever-present knife.

There was a long silence as Caleb obviously considered what they were saying, mulling it over in his distorted mind that carried painful childhood memories.

"Bullshit!" He walked around to the back of the sofa and took hold of Allison from behind. He held the knife in such a way that left no doubt in Danny's mind that Caleb was preparing to slit his wife's throat.

Danny stiffened, ready to lunge forward and try to take Caleb out before he could harm Allison. All three waited, listening to the sounds of silence, the hum of the computer, the ticking of the kitchen clock …

The break-in was no big deal. Edward fiddled with the locked door and suddenly they were in Marcy Madeline Bates's office, staring at her elaborate computer setup. No alarms. No bells and whistles. Edward quietly surveyed the room.

"Over here," he said, motioning to Lloyd to sit at one of the computers. Lloyd sat down and within minutes found himself in an e-mail situation. He typed in Danny and Allison's e-mail address from memory. A simple message followed:

Hi, Danny and Allison, we're in Reunion Valley and found a way to contact you again. Allison, your dad is with us; and Danny, so are your Uncle Edward and Carson Holloway's mom and dad. The first thing we need to know is that you're safe and sound. Love, Dad

Lloyd hit the Send key and waited. In seconds, a message came back that the e-mail was undeliverable and may be due to a block.

"Damn it!" Mickey said. "I knew it was going too smoothly. Nothing's that easy."

"Okay," said Edward. "John, do you know your son's e-mail address?"

"Yes."

"Good. Sit here and type a brief message to Carson."

"I'm not much of a typist."

"Nobody's perfect," Mickey quipped.

"Do your best, John."

John slowly pecked out a message to his son:

Dear Carson, this is your dad. Your mom and I are in a place called Reunion Valley. We know all about your meeting with a red-headed man and his threat to the authors Danny and Allison. We are here with Lloyd Wallace, Danny's father, Mickey Parks, Allison's dad, and Danny's Uncle Edward. They've tried to contact Danny and Allison but there was a block. Do you know if they're okay?

Edward reached around John's arm and hit the Send key. The minutes passed, seeming like hours, while they waited for a response. Lloyd continued to pace while Lynn clung tightly to John's arm. Mickey got up and paced along with Lloyd. Edward moved over and sat in front of another computer.

Suddenly, John's computer sprang to life. A loud beep made all of them jump.

Dad, my God! Dear Dad. I'm here and I got your message. I'm stunned. I hardly know what to say. I'm thrilled to know you somehow live on. How are you ... and Mom? Tell her I love her and miss her so much. Kathleen's here with me and she sends her love, too.

I called and spoke to Allison a little while ago and I think this nutcase Caleb is there in their apartment with them, threatening them. I was just getting ready to call the police in New York.

John looked at Edward, who told him to tell Carson to definitely go ahead and alert the New York police, that they'd get back to him in a little while. John complied and sent the second message to Carson.

"Edward," said Lloyd, "how the hell are we going to get this block lifted? Any ideas?"

"I'm running a scan right now, but it'll take a few minutes before I can get you through." Edward got up then and moved over to a second computer and typed in some codes. "I know how to get into the newspapers back in New York. I'm calling up tomorrow's *Daily News* ..."

Lloyd's heart started to race as he watched his brother scan the newspaper pages on the screen one by one. Mickey also felt a panic, an impending doom as Edward skimmed through the next day's newspaper stories. *What if he finds a headline, "*WRITERS MURDERED!*"? What if—*

Suddenly, the first computer Edward had been scanning to break the block began to beep. Edward moved over and keystroked several codes. "There, the block's lifted."

Lloyd resumed his position at the keyboard, retyped the letter to Danny and Allison, and hit Send ...

"You've got mail!" erupted from the computer in the corner of the living room.

Danny and Allison looked at Caleb, their eyes pleading for permission. They both knew they had to use whatever excuse they could to stall the man from going through with his threat, to buy some time.

"Go ahead, look at your mail," Caleb said finally. "Hah! Maybe it's a message from beyond." He released Allison and she got up shakily, staggering over to the computer. Caleb followed her, half turning to keep Danny in sight. Allison sat down and clicked the mouse. As she read, she felt an enormous rush, as if all the blood had suddenly gone to her head.

"Danny! It's your dad! My dad!" She began to sob uncontrollably as she continued reading the rest of the e-mail. Caleb looked over her shoulder at the computer screen, digesting Lloyd's words carefully.

"It's some kind of trick! Y'all got someone to e-mail you this drivel."

"It's no trick, Caleb!" Danny got up and moved slowly toward them. *Got to get his knife. Got to keep him from hurting Allison.*

"Stay back!" Caleb grabbed Allison around the neck and held the knife close to her throat again.

Danny froze. *Gotta get the knife. Gotta—*

The pounding on the door distracted them all. "Police! Open the door!"

Danny lunged at Caleb, realizing this would be his only chance. He threw his whole body into the man, knocking him backward. Allison broke free and ran to the door as Danny grappled with Caleb.

Allison tried to keep her hands from shaking as she fumbled with the lock, finally pulling open the door and letting the police rush in, guns drawn.

Danny yelled as Caleb managed to slice open a deep gash on the side of his hand. Despite the sight of his own blood, which made him swoon, Danny swung his left fist, hitting Caleb on the side of his head. Caleb raised the knife again, preparing to plunge it into Danny's chest.

The cop's bullet thudded into his shoulder and spun him half around. Caleb dropped the knife and slumped to the floor.

"Danny!" Allison yelled, rushing over to him. She made a useless attempt to stop the bleeding with her handkerchief.

"An ambulance is on the way," one of the cops said, guiding Danny to the sofa. He grabbed a doily from a nearby table and wrapped it around Danny's hand.

"Is he?" Allison nodded toward Caleb's inert form lying on the floor.

"Nah," the cop said. "Just a shoulder wound. But he's gonna be a bit sore for a while. What's his problem, anyway?"

"He didn't like anyone who didn't have red hair," Danny said, grinning with relief.

"Look at their computer!" Caleb had regained consciousness and was sitting up, holding his arm. "They're communicating with dead people!"

"What's he babbling about?"

"I don't know," said Danny, shrugging his shoulders. "The psycho ward at Bellevue might be a good place for him."

Several more cops had shown up by then. "We'll need statements from both of you," said an overweight sergeant as he started writing on a clipboard. Despite the winter weather, he was visibly perspiring.

Later, after paramedics treated Danny's injury and left with the police, Allison got back on the computer and responded to Lloyd's e-mail. With Danny at her side, she briefly recounted the day's events. She avowed their love for them both and assured them they were safe. They waited for a response from the dads …

"They're okay!" Mickey cried, as he leaned over Lloyd's shoulder while reading the e-mail from Allison. But the rejoicing came to a halt as the door suddenly swung open and Marcy Madeline Bates stood rigidly in the doorway, her once perpetual smile replaced with a severe frown.

"Well, my goodness, folks. I believe there's been an infraction of the rules. This room is off limits to all of you."

Lloyd spoke up first, using his best public relations voice. "Now, Miss Bates, I apologize for the intrusion, but we've had—if you'll pardon the expression—a life-or-death situation."

"Go on."

"If I may," said Edward, gently nudging his brother behind him. He spoke softly, in a tone usually reserved only for those in the highest echelon of government. It was a respectful yet authoritative voice, and Miss Bates instantly softened. And for some mystifying, cosmic reason, she agreed to let Mickey and Lloyd and the Holloways send a last e-mail to their families.

"But try to keep your communication brief. Even I have to answer to The Authority. I could get into a bit of trouble for this, so let's get it over with as quickly as possible."

"What're they gonna do, shoot you?" Mickey cracked.

"No, Mister Parks. But there are some, shall we say, less-than-pleasant things that could happen. Banishment, for one. I enjoy my position here at Reunion Valley and would prefer staying here a while longer. You should know about penalties. You and Lloyd lost two years for what you did at Midway Manor."

"Sorry," Mickey said. "It was just a joke."

"Apology accepted. And now, lady and gentlemen, if you would …"

The five nodded their silent agreement and Lloyd resumed his position at the keyboard, with John Holloway doing the same at a nearby computer.

"Let's go for a walk," said Carson, buttoning up his wool jacket.

"Are you nuts?" Kathleen asked rhetorically. "It's colder'n an axe murderer's heart."

"That's a pleasant simile."

"What's with the walking?"

"I just want to get some air and talk. It's not every day you exchange e-mails with your deceased mom and dad."

"All right, I'll get my coat."

Later, as Carson and Kathleen strolled through the cold Tennessee night, they reflected on the momentous events that had taken place earlier. Neither of them now had any doubt that death is only a brief pause in the journey of life. And both rejoiced in the knowledge that one's departed parents will still exist at some level. They wondered what great adventures awaited them in the years—centuries—ahead.

"I'm sure you're not in any hurry to leave here," said Kathleen, "but it has to be comforting to know that sometime in the future you'll be reunited with your mother and father." She stopped then and tugged at Carson's sleeve to turn him around to face her. She cupped his face in her gloved hands. "Honey, when my folks pass on, even though I'll miss them terribly, the knowledge that I'll be with them again someday will make the grieving so much easier."

"I know, sweetheart. I'm so much at peace with myself because of all this."

"All I can say is I'm glad you insisted on going to New York."

"You can also be glad Caleb showed up on our doorstep."

"Yeah. Um, is that like giving the Devil his due?"

At the same time in New York, Allison and Danny sat in the living room of their cozy apartment, wondering about basically the same things.

"How do you feel about what happened today?" Allison asked Danny as she sipped her cognac.

"Which event? Caleb or the dads?" Danny swirled the liquid around in his brandy snifter, noticing how Diet Coke was a lot darker than Allison's alcoholic version.

"Both."

"As far as Caleb's concerned, well, there are probably a lot more just like him out there."

"Meaning?"

"Meaning I don't think I'm gonna do any more writing about the afterworld, fiction or nonfiction."

"And your mom, our dads, darling Bratly?"

"It was great to hear from them one more time, and to know we'll see them again someday, for sure." He paused. "Of course, I don't know where they'll be. They said they were probably gonna move on from Reunion Valley. And I have no idea where Bratly will go. What about you? How do you feel about all this?"

"Well, I hope I never run into anyone like Caleb again. But I'm not in a hurry to meet up with our dads just yet. I kinda like my life here."

"Me, too."

And somewhere, at some unknown destination in the universe, perhaps in a place called The City of Lights, two dads once again shared their music together, playing the haunting, unmistakable refrains of a "Stardust" melody.